PENGUIN BOOKS

Miral

RULA JEBREAL is an award-winning journalist who specializes in foreign affairs and immigration rights issues. She was born in Haifa, studied and worked in Italy as an anchorwoman for many years, and now makes her home in New York.

JOHN CULLEN is the translator of more than fifteen books from French, Italian, German, and Spanish.

Miral

· RULA JEBREAL ·

Translated by
JOHN CULLEN

PENGUIN BOOKS

PENGUIN BOOKS
Published by the Penguin Group
Penguin Group (USA) Inc.,
375 Hudson Street, New York, New York 10014, U.S.A.
Penguin Group (Canada), 90 Eglinton Avenue East, Suite 700, Toronto,
Ontario, Canada M4P 2Y3 (a division of Pearson Penguin Canada Inc.)
Penguin Books Ltd, 80 Strand, London WC2R 0RL, England
Penguin Ireland, 25 St Stephen's Green, Dublin 2,
Ireland (a division of Penguin Books Ltd)
Penguin Group (Australia), 250 Camberwell Road, Camberwell,
Victoria 3124, Australia (a division of Pearson Australia Group Pty Ltd)
Penguin Books India Pvt Ltd, 11 Community Centre,
Panchsheel Park, New Delhi – 110 017, India
Penguin Group (NZ), 67 Apollo Drive, Rosedale, North Shore 0632,
New Zealand (a division of Pearson New Zealand Ltd)
Penguin Books (South Africa) (Pty) Ltd, 24 Sturdee Avenue,
Rosebank, Johannesburg 2196, South Africa

Penguin Books Ltd, Registered Offices:
80 Strand, London WC2R 0RL, England

First published in Penguin Books 2010
1   3   5   7   9   10   8   6   4   2

Translation copyright © John Cullen, 2010
All rights reserved

Originally published as *La strada dei fiori di Miral* by Rizzoli,
RCS Libri, Milan. © 2004 RCS Libri S.p.A., Milano.

PUBLISHER'S NOTE
This is a work of fiction. Names, characters, places, and incidents either are the product
of the author's imagination or are used fictitiously, and any resemblance to actual
persons, living or dead, businesses, companies, events, or locales is entirely coincidental.

LIBRARY OF CONGRESS CATALOGING-IN-PUBLICATION DATA
Jebreal, Rula.
[Strada dei fiori di Miral. English]
Miral / Rula Jebreal ; translated [from the Italian] by John Cullen.
p.   cm.
ISBN 978-0-14-311619-6
1. Orphanages—Jerusalem—Fiction.   2. Orphans—Jerusalem—Fiction.   3. Palestinian Arabs—
Jerusalem—Fiction.   4. Arab-Israeli conflict—Fiction.   I. Cullen, John, 1942–   II. Title.
PQ4910.E37S8713 2010
849'.936—dc22   2010015828

Printed in the United States of America
Set in Minion with Canterbury Display
Designed by Elke Sigal

For Julian

•

And to all the Israelis and Palestinians
who still believe peace is possible

ACKNOWLEDGMENTS

Thanks to my family for giving me the confidence to face the dark side of our memory. Thanks to Julian for going back there with me and helping me to connect my past with my future. I'd also like to thank Sophie and Jerome Seydoux for caring so much and nurturing each step of this journey. Thanks to Bianca Turetsky for her keen ear and kind manner. Thanks to Thomas and Elaine Colchie, my agents and my friends. A special thanks to Hind Husseini and my father, Othman Jebreal, whose humanity and love of education saved my life and put me on the road.

Miral

PART ONE

Hind

1

At dawn on September 13, 1994, a chill ran through the Arab Quarter of East Jerusalem, as word of Hind Husseini's death spread from house to house even before Radio Jerusalem broadcast the news. That morning, the rattling sounds that usually accompanied preparations in the souk moved from the narrow lanes and alleyways of the Old City to the edge of Saladin Street, along which the funeral procession would pass. Many shopkeepers kept their rolling shutters down and stood with folded arms in front of their places of business. The haggling and bargaining over goods had stopped as soon as word spread that the coffin was leaving Dar El-Tifel orphanage, the place, nestled at the foot of the Mount of Olives and facing the Old City, to which Hind had dedicated her life and that, ever since its founding in 1948, had become a symbol of hope for Palestine's present and future.

In the Arab Quarter, Palestinian flags hung from the windows of the houses, and those residents who had not gone down into the street stood on balconies, throwing handfuls of salt, rice, or flowers onto the coffin as it passed by. Everyone came out to honor a woman who had lived with courage and humility. Men had tears in their eyes. A feeling of deep dismay settled over Jerusalem, a great sense of loss, as if one of its gates had suddenly been shut forever.

Hind Husseini was born in the Holy City of Jerusalem in 1916, when it was still part of the Ottoman Empire. She spent the first two years of her life in Istanbul, where her father was a judge. Her father died a few months before the fall of the empire, on the tail end of its defeat in World War I. Her mother brought the family back to Jerusalem. At the time, Palestine was making the transition from Turkish rule to its new status under the British Mandate, which lasted until the birth of the State of Israel in 1948.

Hind, her mother, and her five brothers moved into a house in the Armenian Quarter that had been in the possession of the Husseini family for centuries. Her mother and father had lived in the spacious five-bedroom dwelling after they were married, and its living room was still furnished with the same colored rugs and pillows that Hind's mother had embroidered in her neighboring village. In the center of the room, a hookah sat on a typical Arab table, a wide silver tray mounted on dark wooden legs.

Upon their return to Jerusalem, Hind's mother took charge of the farmlands and livestock she had inherited from her husband and his family, in the outlying district of Sheikh Jarrah. Early each morning, she would make her way to the farms to oversee the various workers. Her companion on those daily excursions was her oldest son, Kemal, whom she wished to teach the family businesses so she could turn them over to him one day. Early in the afternoon, mother and son would return to the Old City, stopping along the way at the family's principal residence, Hind's grandfather's house, located a short distance outside the city walls. Hind would be playing there with her brothers and cousins, and they would all remain there until dusk, when they would return home. When relatives asked Hind's mother why they made this daily migration, she would unhesitatingly reply, "My husband knew that if anything were to happen to him, we would go back to our house in Jerusalem, so his spirit would know where to find us."

Hind's mother loved that man for most of her life, having married him at the age of fourteen, in accordance with a matrimonial agreement arranged by their families. Since she was of noble birth and her future husband belonged to a clan whose members occupied the most prominent civil and religious posts in the city—from governor to mayor to mufti—the wedding ceremony turned out to be quite a spectacle. The bride arrived on a white horse, a purebred Arabian, followed by her entire family. She brought as dowry three tracts of land and two houses, while the groom, in keeping with an ancient Arab custom, gave her a copper chest lined with red velvet overflowing with gold jewelry especially fashioned for the occasion: bracelets, necklaces, earrings, and rings. Despite their beauty, Hind's mother rarely wore her gold ornaments, for she considered displays of wealth vulgar. The celebration took place in the house of the groom's family, where the women had prepared grilled lamb spiced with cardamom and cinnamon; basmati rice with pine nuts and raisins; squash, carrots, and leeks sautéed with onions and nutmeg; yogurt; and various trays filled with mixed fruits. The dancing began toward evening and didn't end until long past midnight, when the parents of the bride and groom accompanied them to their new home in the Armenian Quarter. The young couple's relatives waited outside the house until the hills of Jerusalem turned pale pink with the first light of dawn. Only then did the groom reappear to present proof that his marriage had been consummated and his bride was truely a virgin.

A certain tranquility still reigned in the Jerusalem in which Hind took her first steps. Even though she was a Muslim, as a child she spent every Christmas Eve at the American Colony Hotel, which was once the palace of a Turkish pasha. Every year its owner, Bertha Spafford, a rich and eccentric American, threw a Christmas party in the hotel for the children of the quarter, who were served a turkey dinner with bread and raisin stuffing, followed by dessert and the distribution of presents. In a corner of the main lobby stood a Christmas tree, a gift from Hind's mother, who with the help of her sons had dug it up from her property. At the end of the festivities, the children would follow Bertha outside to witness the transplanting of the tree to the hotel grounds, "because," as Bertha would tell her young guests, "if we let the tree die, then the Christmas party will have served no useful purpose." Following dinner it was customary to sing Christmas carols in Arabic, after which the Christians would attend midnight Mass in the Church of the Holy Sepulchre.

Bertha and Hind's mother eventually established a small infirmary for the farmers who worked the Husseini lands. One day when a newborn was abandoned at the infirmary door, the two women, helped by a volunteer physician, immediately took the baby in and cared for it until they found a farmer and his family who were willing to adopt it.

Hind and her brothers received an excellent education. Their mother expected them to spend at least a couple of hours each day reading. Their books of choice included some novels in English, acquired with Bertha's help. Hind's mother was particularly insistent on her daughter's instruction, because, as she said, education elevated a woman's social status. Hind was sent to Women's College in Jerusalem, while her brothers, like young men from other important Palestinian families—Husseinis, Nashashibis, Dijanis—completed their studies at prestigious universities in Damascus or Cairo.

Hind was privileged to spend her adolescence in one of the most fascinating cities in the world. Although some signs of the disasters to come were already evident, in those days Jerusalem was still a place where children could grow up in peace. Hind's mother would have liked to marry her off in grand style to one of her cousins, but Hind was intent on continuing her studies in Damascus. The Arab revolt against the British Mandate in 1936 interrupted both the mother's projects and the daughter's dreams.

To the two women who washed the body before it was wrapped in a shroud—so that the deceased would stand before God perfectly pure, as prescribed in the Koran—the features of Hind's face seemed as serene as when she was alive, unblemished by the excruciating agony that had afflicted her in her final hours.

Hind had awakened the previous morning drenched in sweat, and although she tried to hide the pain her illness was causing her, her daughter Miriam decided she should go to the Hadassah Hospital, where the physicians who had her in their care were based. In the end, Hind allowed herself to be persuaded, but she asked first to pass by Dar El-Tifel. She wanted a last look at the grounds of her beloved school.

At that time of year, the garden was no longer graced by the marvelous blossoms that spread their strong perfume to the surrounding lanes and courtyards at the beginning of summer. That fragrance accompanied Hind's happiest memories, evoking the flowering season, when sunlight pours down on the hills of Jerusalem so intensely that the houses blend with the sky.

Hind remembered how bare the spot had been before the school was established, without the rose garden, the olive trees, the lemon trees, the palms, the jasmine, the pomegranates, the grapefruit, the magnolia, the fig trees, the little grapevine, the cinnamon and henna trees, without the mint, the sage, and the wild rosemary. And without the little fountain she had built in the center of the courtyard, exactly like the one her family had when they lived in the Armenian Quarter. Her thoughts dwelled on the memory of that place as it once was—before the fragrances, the bright colors, and the laughter of little girls as they chased a ball on the playground, safe from the tragedies that were taking place outside its walls.

Miriam, the school's vice-principal, a robust woman of imposing stature—broad shouldered and nearly six feet tall—raised Hind to a sitting position in the backseat of the car. Consumed by her disease, Hind had grown extremely thin, and her voice was faint. "When you came to Dar El-Tifel, I was the one who took you in my arms," Hind said, her eyes smiling as they always did. At the age of one and a half, Miriam had lost both her parents: her father, a fedayee, had fallen in battle, while her mother had been killed in an ambush. The imam of the mosque in the child's village had brought her to the school. She was undernourished and had pneumonia. Hind received her and put her in the care of the school physician, her cousin Amir. Miriam grew up inside the walls of Dar El-Tifel and decided to remain there even after she graduated. Her affection for Hind was that of a daughter for her mother, and during the long months of Hind's illness Miriam looked after Hind with loving care, pushing her in her wheelchair around the school grounds for several hours each day and, when needed, lifting her up in her own strong arms. She washed her, too.

As the automobile passed the school gate, Miriam watched Hind turn to cast a final glance at the Mount of Olives, which was vibrant with silvery reflections as its trees shook in the first fall breezes.

Hind saw her Jerusalem with different eyes now, saw it rooted in soil drenched with innocent blood, and under that soil were its tunnels dug under synagogues, crypts, and secret passages. Simultaneously, however, Jerusalem reached upward, its minarets and steeples jutting into the sky. She thought that contradiction mirrored the history of this vexed land, of the tragic destiny that had made it at once the kingdom of heaven and the kingdom of hell. As the car left the Old City behind, she was dazzled for an instant by the light reflecting off the houses built of gleaming white stone, as if to signify hope and peace, despite everything, despite everybody.

Hind thought back to the most difficult moments of her life, which were associated with those that were most tragic for her people: the massacre at Deir Yassin, Black September in Jordan, and then the outbreak of the war in Lebanon. She thought of the Sabra and Shatila massacres. Each of those moments had signaled another defeat, the reenactment of an unchanging script in which the Palestinian people invariably ended up losing.

Gazing out the car window, Hind landed on a thought that was never very far from her mind: the Palestinians of Jerusalem were obliged to fight on two fronts, one internal and one external—mostly against themselves, first, to avoid falling into an absurd spiral of violence that would surely lead to their defeat; and then against unscrupulous political forces ready to serve up their land on a silver platter, like an exchangeable commodity.

She thought about the First Intifada, about all her efforts to keep Dar El-Tifel's schoolgirls away from the demonstrations, and about how she had succeeded in saving a few lives. Many well-to-do Palestinians had left the country, hoping to make new lives somewhere else; Hind, on the other hand, had decided to stay and to do something for her people. More than a conscious decision, it had been her destiny, which she fulfilled without wavering. In her vocabulary, the word *privilege* had a unique significance: it meant the condition of being able to help others. Although she never married, she was, as she often laughingly told her girls, "the woman with the most daughters in all Jerusalem." Indeed in 1948, not long after her thirtieth birthday, when Hind was an elegant open-minded young woman, a poet had compared her to Jerusalem, "the bride of the world." As the car pulled up in front of the hospital, she wondered, "How will they manage without me?"

After completing her studies, Hind taught in the Muslim Girls' School in Jerusalem. Later she founded, with several colleagues, an organization dedicated to combating illiteracy in her country. As one of the group's most active members, she had traveled the length and breadth of Palestine, promoting the opening of new schools in even the most remote villages. She would drive to refugee camps in a large school bus and come back with children whose mothers, poor women unable to provide their offspring with an education, were more than happy to entrust them to her. At the time, Hind was convinced that the salvation of the Palestinian people would depend on the cultural liberation of its youth. The organization she helped to establish put out a magazine whose goal was to make people aware of the conditions facing the most disadvantaged children.

After the end of World War II, just when the world seemed to have found peace again, Palestine began its descent into a nightmare. It was as if questions unresolved elsewhere had suddenly exploded in its midst, like a fatal firestorm. This time the walls of the Old City, an ancient symbol of security, were unable to defend its inhabitants, because the war was already inside.

All her life, Hind had nourished the conviction that religion was not the sole or even the main cause of the Israeli-Palestinian conflict, which was mostly based, as she saw it, on politics. But her voice was like a whisper compared to the incessant din of weapons spreading death and pain in its name.

The Arab bourgeoisie left the city en masse. Many families planned to come back when the fighting was over, and Hind's colleagues assured her that they would resume working together very soon. But most of them would never return to Jerusalem; they would go on with their lives in Amman, Damascus, or Cairo. At the same time, as the Israeli army proceeded with its conquest, the Old City gradually filled up with evacuees from the villages, who were left with no recourse but to flock to the city and try somehow to survive there.

Hind was the only member of her organization who decided to remain in Jerusalem. As her sole precaution, she abandoned her house in the Armenian Quarter for a few months because the southwestern part of the Old City was too exposed to Israeli fire.

Meanwhile, all the men went to the war, and the women to work. Without schools to attend or adults to watch over them, children roamed the streets. This was when Hind decided to open a small kindergarten in the heart of the Old City. It consisted of two simply furnished rooms, one with a dozen beds and the other with several chairs and little tables. Not long afterward, when the fighting spread to the city center and prevented the children from reaching Hind's school, she was forced to close it down.

2

On April 9, 1948, as soon as a lull in the fighting allowed her to do so, Hind Husseini returned to Jerusalem, where the governor had invited her to a meeting about the refugee emergency. The young woman entered the Old City through Herod's Gate and walked the narrow streets, observing the sparsely scattered stalls that were all that was left of the lively confusion of the souk, which once teemed with vegetables and where the intense fragrances of mint, cumin, and cardamom had mingled with extravagant displays of fruit.

A month before the establishment of the State of Israel, an atmosphere of gloom permeated the Old City. In the Jewish neighborhoods, greetings were muted, and passersbys avoided one another's gaze. Uneasiness was even more palpable in the Arab Quarter, where the muezzin's call sounded more like a protracted lament than the usual joyous invitation to prayer.

Approaching the Church of the Holy Sepulchre, Hind came across a ragtag group of children. There were about fifty of them: some sitting on the edge of the sidewalk, leaning against one another, while others stood motionless on the side of the street, as if waiting for somebody. As Hind drew near, she noticed that the smallest children were barefoot. Many of them were weeping and almost all had mud-spattered cheeks and dusty, matted hair. She immediately sought an explanation from the oldest girl, who looked to be about twelve and was wearing torn trousers and a shirt with ripped sleeves.

"Where are your parents?" Hind asked. "And what are you all doing out here in the middle of the street?"

"This is where they left us," replied the girl, barely holding back her tears.

Hind sat down beside her. "What's your name?"

"Zeina," the child replied between sobs.

Zeina told Hind that she had heard gunfire all night long in her village, Deir Yassin, and that she had seen houses, including her own, catch fire. She had looked for her parents, crying out to them, but since all she heard was gunfire, she hid herself. When morning came, some armed men suddenly snatched her from her hiding place and brought her to the village square. There she found other children, but nobody from her class at school. She and the other children were herded into a truck, and then the armed men dumped them, without a word, near the gate to the Old City.

"Wait for me here, Zeina," Hind said reassuringly, stroking the girl's hair where it was stuck to her forehead. "I have to speak to someone, and then I'll come right back."

$\mathcal{A}$nwar al-Khatib, the governor of Jerusalem, had never met Hind Husseini, but he was well aware of her commitment to helping the country's disadvantaged children. As soon as he saw her enter the meeting room, he recognized the characteristic determination of the Husseinis.

Hind immediately asked to speak. "Excuse me, but before you call the assembly to order, I wanted to tell you about a group of children, fifty or so, that I met just a few meters from here. They're survivors of a massacre."

"At Deir Yassin," the mutasarrif replied, having learned of the incident just an hour before.

"They're dirty, hungry, and scared," Hind said. "There's no time to waste. We must help them immediately." She repeated the story she had heard from Zeina.

Seated behind a heavy wooden desk cluttered with yellowing papers, the governor stroked his beard as he listened to Hind. His eyes remained fixed on an engraving that portrayed Jerusalem at the end of the nineteenth century, as if to fathom just when and where it had begun, the conflict that was now bringing to light all the rottenness that once lay dormant in the belly of the city.

When Hind finished speaking, he explained to her that he had to consider the problem in its entirety, and that for the moment he would be unable to address the needs of those particular children. "We have so many refugees that we don't know how to help them all."

Hind rose to her feet and headed for the door. Turning to the governor, she sought out his eyes and said in a calm but firm voice, "I understand. Go on with your meeting. For my part, I'm going to see what I can do for them."

Anwar al-Khatib couldn't help but be impressed by the young woman's intransigence. She was determined to help those orphans at any cost.

4

When Hind returned to the children, they were still in the street, right where she had left them, despite evidence that meanwhile a gunfight had riddled the plaster of a nearby house. They stood there frozen, petrified by the incident. Hind took the smallest child by the hand and said to the others: "Come with me, children, all of you. I'm going to take you home."

To reach Hind's house, the odd procession had to cross from one end of the Old City to the other. Anyone who saw them pass was struck by the contrast between that little army of barefoot, disheveled children and the elegant young woman who led them. In the meantime, news of the massacre at Deir Yassin—carried out by the Irgun militia with the hidden consent of the Haganah, the regular Israeli army—had made the rounds of the city, rebounding from shop to shop, from one vendor's stall to the next, before the newspapers had time to print it.

It didn't take long for people to make the connection between the news of the massacre and the fifty-five traumatized children, the older ones holding the younger ones by the hand, that odd parade marching through the streets of Jerusalem behind Hind Husseini.

. . .

Hind's house was a big villa of white stone, shaded by a large, lux-urious garden. Her mother and two housemaids sadly watched as the group of children arrived and were momentarily rendered speechless when Hind asked them to help wash and feed her new charges.

When her mother and the maids started asking questions, Hind—who at that moment had only the children on her mind—replied curtly that they were the survivors of Deir Yassin. "I'll put them up in the kindergarten for the time being," she added, before proceeding to escort the smallest children to the bathroom.

Dramatic situations tend to generate conflicting emotions. On the one hand, there's an increased sense of solidarity and mutual support, but at the same time an insidious, almost instinctive feel-ing of envy is directed toward those who appear more fortunate. In the days to come, people with wicked tongues would accuse Hind of stinginess, of not spending enough of her money to help others. She responded to such taunts by declaring that her entire cash re-serve amounted to 128 Palestinian dinars, and that she intended to use it all to help the surviving children.

Others, however, instantly saw the importance of what she was doing. Among them was Basima Faris, the principal of a nearby school, who came one day of her own accord to offer help in car-ing for the children. Basima was a no-nonsense, upright woman unafraid to look men in the eye and ask for what the children needed. With this ally at her side, Hind went every day to the city's merchants and shopkeepers, who were almost always happy to do-nate food, clothing, and blankets. Even so, Hind knew that eventu-ally the money she had set aside would not guarantee her orphans even a single meal a day. She decided to visit the governor's palace again, this time with Basima.

Anwar al-Khatib was in the meeting room with some local merchants. The two women stood just inside the door and waited for the gathering to finish. The governor had not noticed them and was speaking to his guests. "If you want me to grant you a business permit," he said, "you must all promise to send a sack of potatoes, a sack of rice, and a sack of sugar to Hind Husseini's school."

The oldest of the merchants answered without hesitation: "I've heard about this courageous woman. I'll send the items you've named to the orphanage today. And I'll throw in some fruits and vegetables, too." The other businessmen nodded in agreement.

At this point, the governor rose and noticed the two women. Hind's face clearly showed surprise, for up until that moment she had considered the governor an obstacle. Her eyes revealed that she was intensely moved. Al-Khatib came over, smiling affably, and inquired as to what he could do for them.

"I have nothing to ask for," Hind replied, returning his smile. "We've already obtained what we wanted. You fulfilled our request even before you heard it. We thank you from the bottom of our hearts, you and all the merchants."

In the succeeding weeks, the fighting in Jerusalem intensified. The Israelis made repeated efforts to penetrate the Arab Quarter of the Old City, but its imposing sixteenth-century walls, with their massive gates, served to defend it for a while. Jerusalem was to become a city divided in two: East Jerusalem under the control of the Arabs and West Jerusalem under the control of the Israelis.

One morning Hind arrived at the kindergarten to find all the children in the courtyard, huddled in a circle, the littlest ones weeping desperately. "What's the matter?" she asked. "Why are you crying?"

Zeina stepped forward and reported that they had been woken up by gunfire during the night, and since it went on and on, they assumed the soldiers were going to destroy everything, as had happened in their village. They decided the best thing to do was to assemble in the courtyard, ready for the soldiers to come and take them.

That day Hind decided that she would always sleep under the same roof as the children. She also realized that the place was too dangerous, and when the ceasefire finally came, she made preparations to transfer the orphanage to her grandfather's house in Sheikh Jarrah. Explosions had damaged the house, but it had to be repaired in any case, and now a second building would be constructed, surrounding the main residence. The old residence would become the dormitory, while the new building would house the school.

Hind applied once again to the magnanimous governor, this time during a meeting at which he was hosting some of the most prominent members of the city's upper middle class. Wasting no time in beating around the bush, the young woman declared to the assembly, "I know that many of you have been financing the resistance." The governor rolled his eyes and started to reply, but Hind stopped him with a gesture and continued: "I'm only asking that you also finance the project of establishing a home where orphaned children can be brought up. That's a form of resistance, too; in fact, it's the best resistance. As you well know, they are the future generation, but for now, they need us. We cannot abandon them. When they become adults, we shall need them, but not if they're weak and hungry. We'll need tenacious, strong, educated people. They will be the ones to build our future Palestine."

Once again, the governor complied with her wishes. As it turned out, the funds he allocated were insufficient, but Hind found that she could count on the financial support of many Palestinians, including those from families that were less well off.

5

In September 1948, Dar El-Tifel, the "Children's Home," was born. In the turbulent months following its birth, this institution—a combination of school and orphanage—grew indispensable, a fact noticed by many, including the governor. If he had first viewed Hind's project with a bit of skepticism, he was now receiving, day by day, a growing number of requests from all over the country to help children who had been orphaned or inadvertently abandoned by their parents during the precipitous flights from the villages.

One afternoon, Hind received a visit from al-Khatib. Sipping mint tea on the patio of the school, he confided that the situation in the rest of the country was more serious than anyone in the city could imagine. As he wearily passed a hand over his white head, Hind saw that this elderly man, who in the course of his life had witnessed a long series of tragedies, seemed to be buckling under the weight of the terrible recent months. "I fear the worst is yet to come," he confessed.

Strolling with Hind in the unkempt garden that would become the school's flourishing park, the governor spoke with absolute frankness about the confidential information he had received that very morning concerning Deir Yassin. In evident anguish, making long pauses, he described the account written by the envoy from the International Committee of the Red Cross. Although the children's story had given some idea of the brutality of the attack, nothing had prepared him for what he read in that report. In a quivering voice, without looking Hind in the eye, al-Khatib told her that his shock had turned into a suffocating mixture of anger and sorrow as he read how ruthlessly and systematically the slaughter had been carried out.

"The report," he said, his voice choked with tears, "speaks of 254 people massacred in cold blood. Not only young men, but old men, and women and children who were shot in the back as they tried to run away. Houses were burned and women raped. Forty men were seized, stripped naked, and brought to West Jerusalem. They paraded them through the streets, and then executed them in front of a crowd. How will those fifty-five children forget what they saw?"

Hind remembered the children's eyes when she found them near the souk. She recalled their terrified looks, their dirty hands, their shaky legs. Now she watched some of them playing outside the tents that served as a makeshift home until the dormitory was finished. She saw others sitting alone, here and there, and knew decisively that she must do something to give them a chance. They would never forget—she was sure of that—but she would do all she could to give them a better future.

Meanwhile, the governor had resumed talking, walking slowly as he did so, gazing from time to time toward the Old City: "But what worries me most of all is that the Haganah didn't participate directly in the massacre. They left it to extremist groups like the Irgun and the Stern Gang. I'm afraid they may be using Deir Yassin as a threat to persuade us to abandon our villages. Whole areas of Galilee are being depopulated. Ancient communities are breaking up under the blows of the Haganah's propaganda. So it's entirely in their interest to publicize the brutality of what happened." Al-Khatib paused and turned to look Hind in the eyes before continuing: "Our people are scattering. We're risking a diaspora. I fear that cruel acts of revenge will mark the beginning of a fatal spiral, like what happened with the Mount Scopus attack." The governor pronounced the last words almost in a whisper, as if he himself were frightened to hear them.

The Mount Scopus attack to which the governor referred was the Palestinian retaliation for Deir Yassin. It took place on April 13, 1948, four days after the massacre, when a convoy of two buses and two Israeli military vehicles was ambushed on the road to Jerusalem. The buses, containing many civilians, were set on fire. The British eventually arrived on the scene, after a six-hour gunfight that left more than seventy Jews dead.

Hind, who had remained silent during his speech, sank exhausted onto an old wooden bench.

Over the course of the following years, the governor's words proved prophetic. News of the slaughter at Deir Yassin did indeed rebound from village to village, generating a mass exodus of Palestinians to the neighboring Arab states, particularly Lebanon and Jordan. When the eastern part of Jerusalem was ceded to Jordanian control, Hind considered the move a mistake, believing a regime of Palestinian self-government to be a far more advisable solution. However, she decided to involve herself as little as possible in political matters.

Having recently completed the rebuilding of the old white-stone villa, Hind decided to accompany her mother on the hajj, the sacred pilgrimage to Mecca.

When she reached her journey's goal, she knelt before the black stone, the holiest spot for every Muslim, touched her forehead to the earth, and thanked God for all the progress she had made in her work and for all the support she had received. "Help me, help me, help me," she said, repeating the prayer three times in accordance with Arab custom. "Help me build a home for these children." At that moment, she decided she would never marry.

6

A few days after returning from Mecca, Hind was seated at her desk when she received an unexpected visitor, an officer in the American army. He was a man of about forty, with ash blond hair and intense blue eyes that reminded her of the Mediterranean.

"Hello, I'm Colonel Edward Smith," he said to her with a smile she considered overly friendly.

"Pleased to meet you, Colonel." Hind held out her hand to shake his.

He lifted it gently and grazed it with his lips.

Withdrawing her hand, Hind attempted to overcome her embarrassment. "Please have a seat, Colonel, and tell me what I can do for you."

The colonel seated himself on the chair opposite Hind's desk and began at once to explain the purpose of his visit. "Miss Husseini, some years ago, I was the president of the American University in Cairo. Your uncle and older brother were students of mine. In fact, you and I go back a long way. We knew each other when we were children, in the days when everybody called me Eddie. But a few years' difference seems like much more of a gap at that age, so maybe that's why you don't remember me."

Hind was taken aback by her visitor's sudden switch to familiarity, but she supposed it was called for if he really was a childhood friend. However, she didn't recognize his face, nor could she recall where she might have seen him. Seeing her confusion, he added, "We spent several Christmas Eves together at the American Colony Hotel."

Hind began digging in her memory, where she glimpsed a faded image of a tall, thin boy who had a knack for repairing the toys that the younger children invariably broke shortly after receiving them. She remembered those blue eyes smiling at her while she sat on the rug in front of the fireplace, weeping over her new rag doll's torn dress. He didn't know how to sew, he told her, but he would do his best to have it mended. A few days later, he returned the doll to her, its dress in almost perfect condition.

"Eddie, of course," she said suddenly, trying to hide her emotion. "Now I remember." It was the first time in years that she had seen one of her childhood friends. "Can I offer you some mint tea?"

As he sipped tea from a green glass with a golden rim, Eddie told her of his plans. "I'm going to stay in Jerusalem for a few months before I return to the United States. I have a room at the American Colony. This morning I looked out my window and saw all these children, playing in the midst of ruins and tottering walls. When I inquired about what was on the other side of the gate, they said it was you and told me about the work you're doing. I wanted to meet you, and . . . now I just want to ask if there's anything I can do for you."

Hind felt almost embarrassed by this unexpected offer of aid. "I'm touched," she told her guest sincerely. "I see you haven't changed."

"Oh yes, I have, unfortunately—I've changed a lot. Life leaves you no choice. But I don't forget to lend a hand to someone who I think deserves it. And people like you are really hard to find, believe me."

Hind, who had spent all her money and had even resorted to selling her mother's wedding jewelry, asked her old friend if he could assist her in securing financing to complete work on the school. He told her that he would use all his influence to help.

Eddie kept his word. Within a few weeks, he found a Saudi petroleum company, Aramco, which was prepared to finance the building of the walls enclosing the grounds as well as the construction of the school. From then on, after tea almost every afternoon, he and Hind took a walk around the property to see how the work was proceeding. They talked to each other about their lives, their dreams, their disappointments, and their successes. Theirs was not a romantic relationship, but during those months they formed a deep friendship that would continue by correspondence for many years to come.

On a chilly December morning that just barely mitigated the sun's lukewarm rays, Eddie left Jerusalem for the United States, for good. He and Hind promised they would keep in touch. They never saw each other again.

In the meantime, Hind did not wait idly for new donations to arrive. Eddie's offer of help had shown her the path she must follow to obtain financial support.

To guarantee her school greater autonomy in its educational choices, she decided to concentrate upon international agencies and organizations rather than on local government entities. She wrote to a Kuwaiti sheikh, Muhammad bin Jassim Sabah, who a few weeks earlier had publicly declared his desire to improve the quality of childhood education in the Arab countries, including his own. Hind described to him the activity of her boarding school and the program she intended to carry out, and before long the sheikh replied by sending her a considerable amount of money.

Not long afterward, she happened by chance to read a magazine article about the directors of an Anglo-Kuwaiti corporation, among them the sheikh Muhammad bin Jassim Sabah himself, who were currently in Jerusalem. While they had also come to visit al-Aqsa Mosque, the chief purpose of their trip was to recruit Palestinian teachers, engineers, architects, and physicians who were prepared to move to Kuwait. Hind quickly changed her clothes, putting on her best dress and a necklace of handworked silver. Without giving the matter a second thought, she headed for the Jerusalem Hotel, where, according to what she had read, the foreign visitors were staying.

Arriving shortly after lunch, Hind found the directors on the point of retiring to their respective rooms for the traditional afternoon nap. Summoning her rhetorical abilities, she attempted to persuade them to follow her instead to Dar El-Tifel, where they would be able to visit her school and see the results that she proposed to offer them in return for their economic support.

After an initial moment of bewilderment, the gentlemen agreed to go with her. She tried to capture their interest by discussing her projects frankly and explaining that her principal aim was to provide the most disadvantaged children with a proper education. The sheikh observed the children, saw how much work remained to be done on the buildings, and listened to Hind with a religious silence. Then he took her aside and told her that he would speak of her school wherever he went and would do everything in his power to help her complete its construction. "Every two months, write me a letter and tell me what point the work has reached and how much money you need. And, as God is my witness, I will always support you." As he was leaving, the sheikh took Hind's right hand in his and said, "Miss Husseini, what you do honors not only your people but the whole Arab world."

The sheikh kept his promise, and in a short time checks began to arrive, not only in his name but also from the most unlikely corners of the Arab community, from persons she had never met or even seen. Hind used the new finances to complete the construction as well as for hiring qualified teachers.

A short time later, the sheikh invited her to visit his own country. She was stunned by Kuwait's riches and by the rapidness with which it was marching toward modernization; wealth and speed seemed to be the country's characteristic features. And yet she felt something lacking, even though she was incapable of identifying what it was.

After she returned to Jerusalem, Hind realized that Kuwait, for all its perfect schools, its clean, efficient hospitals, its new highways, and its artificial oases in the desert, could not possess the cultural breadth of a place like her own city, whose history stretched back over millennia, and whose luminous white stones continued to gleam despite having been spattered with blood countless times over the centuries. Perhaps this was Jerusalem's secret: that it still appeared pure despite the horrific crimes that had been committed within its walls.

In this city of many faces, every affirmation seemed destined to produce irreconcilable contradictions. Perhaps its citizens appeared so adamant, so reluctant to compromise, precisely because they felt they were living on the edge of a precipice. For thousands of years, countless civilizations, tribes, religions, and armies had contended to control this city—besieging it, conquering it, losing it, and rendering it a crucible in which joy and suffering were fatally combined. Hind thought that was why the crusaders perceived the city simultaneously as paradise on earth and the entrance to hell. Jerusalem's inhabitants often found themselves forced, despite themselves, to choose sides; from one morning to the next, neighbors who had always greeted one another could find themselves pointing rifles at each other instead. Such irrational behavior had manifested itself so frequently over the course of the centuries that it had acquired an unwholesome logic of its own.

As the years went by, Hind and Eddie kept up a regular correspondence. During that time, he got married, had two children, and often reiterated his desire to return to Jerusalem to visit Hind and see how her school had evolved.

Despite some difficult periods during which provisions barely sufficed to guarantee the children one frugal meal a day, Hind never lost heart, continuing with her customary determination to champion her school. With time the number of orphans and refugees who were full-time residents and the number of day students increased considerably. Realizing that she would need to enlarge Dar El-Tifel, Hind wrote to her older brother Amin, who, with her four other brothers, owned the buildings and the plots of land around the school.

> Dear Amin,
>   After our father's early death, we too were orphans.
> But we were happy children; we lived in these beautiful
> houses and we could play on these lovely grounds
> overlooking the Old City. Why not make these orphans
> happy, too, as we were then?

Amin replied in kind: He spoke to the rest of her brothers and they decided they would gladly turn over to her the titles to the buildings and land for a token price.

> Dear Sister,
> You are quite right to say that we as children were in part orphans after our father died. And yes, we were happy children and lived in fine houses and were able to play in the fields facing the Old City. We gladly cede our real estate behind yours so that your institute can grow and you can continue making your children as happy as we once were. We hope life in Jerusalem under Jordanian authority has made life easier. Please send my love to mother.
> Amin

7

In 1967, after the Six Days' War, the rest of Palestine fell under the military occupation and the number of child refugees greatly increased, in particular the number of abandoned girls. Following an agreement with the city authorities, Dar El-Tifel, which had been a mixed orphanage for nearly twenty years, became primarily an orphanage and school for girls. Analogous institutions exclusively for boys already existed in Jerusalem. Dar El-Tifel would continue to accept boys, but only those younger than six. Hind was convinced that this was the right decision, because she knew that females were always the most vulnerable victims in cases of abandonment, and that without a decent education they would be marginalized. Later that year, the area of the city in which the orphanage was located passed from Jordanian to Israeli control. Hind was used to negotiating with the Jordanians for permits and authorizations, and especially to resolve the problem of identification papers, which many orphans lacked. Now she was required to deal with the Israeli military authorities. "I don't like soldiers," she told her mother. "Their hands are stained with blood. Whenever I meet them, I can't help wondering how many people they've killed with those hands."

With the passage of time, Dar El-Tifel became not only a renowned school but also a beacon for all the Arabs of Jerusalem. Its mere existence offered reassurance, and every little Palestinian girl who had survived the war or had been abandoned in front of a mosque, who had lost one parent or both, could find there a bit of serenity and a sound education.

As the school was enlarged and two new buildings erected, Hind developed its pedagogical system. After a few years, her intuitive measures coalesced into a distinct method that allowed the schoolgirls to play an active role in the classroom. Older pupils assisted the teachers in instructing the little ones, and the most gifted of these girls would, if they wished, be able to become teachers in time.

Strict discipline was the order of the day, particularly with regard to the schedule; the girls rose every morning at six, and lights were turned off every night at nine o'clock sharp. Physical activity was an integral part of the curriculum. When Hind observed the students complaining about the long hours of gymnastic exercises, she liked to repeat the Latin proverb *mens sana in corpore sano*, "a healthy mind in a healthy body."

Hind desired her girls to be cultured and multilingual. She also wanted them to stay aloof from politics, fearing that the Israeli authorities would close the school at the slightest suspicion that anti-Israeli propaganda was being disseminated inside.

For the good of her institution, Hind tirelessly continued to solicit funding wherever her oratorical abilities could have an effect: Saudi Arabia, Lebanon, Jordan, Kuwait, and Egypt. Along with providing generous annual donations, those countries committed themselves to adopting an increasing number of her pupils.

Girls who had attended the institution, some of whom would

later take up residence in the West, never forgot Dar El-Tifel, and a few of them acknowledged their fond memories in very concrete ways. Nual Said, for example, had arrived at the school in the late 1950s, orphaned by both her parents. She found a family there within its walls and, after graduating from Dar El-Tifel, won scholarships to study psychology, first in Jordan and then in the United States, in Chicago, where she married a pediatrician of Mexican descent and gave birth to two little girls. She never returned to Jerusalem, but one day she arranged a surprise for Hind's students. That morning a big truck turned onto the tree-lined drive leading to Dar El-Tifel. At first the custodian at the gate thought the driver had made an error, but he was forced to reconsider when an official-looking letter declared that Nual Said, an alumna of the school, hereby donated a truckload of shoes, dresses, and stationery to the schoolgirls currently enrolled. Apart from such conspicuous yet not altogether rare gestures, tokens of gratitude from former students allowed the school to carry out improvements every year.

Hind's energies were totally absorbed by the administration of the school, her activities ranging from soliciting funds to fine-tuning syllabi and even extending to counseling the girls about personal matters. Over the course of the years, she would have to make frequent use of her charisma and influence to protect the school and its students, retaining her calm composure even in the most dramatic situations.

During rare periods of free time, Hind tended the garden, seeking in the harmony of the various plants the serenity she was unable to find outside the walls of her school, and devoting herself to the cultivation of her flowers with the same exquisite attention she lavished on her girls. Convinced as she was that good fruit is above all the result of loving care, she left nothing to chance. In the month of March, when the rose garden was in full bloom, Hind spent the evening hours immersed in the fragrance of the freshly opened blossoms, mesmerized by their myriad forms and colors. When the girls saw her busily pruning the plants or pulling up weeds, some of them would join in and help. Such spontaneous demonstrations of affection were frequent, for the children of Dar El-Tifel respected her and followed her lead. In fact, they all called her Mama Hind.

8

*D*uring the autumn of her life, Hind lived through a second youth, mentally speaking. Her leukemia progressed, ravaging her body, but news of the birth of a Palestinian state gave her great joy. She was especially impressed by the multitude of celebrations throughout the Arab neighborhoods that had followed the Oslo Accords.

From the terrace of Dar El-Tifel, near the tall magnolia tree that had stood with Hind through the most dramatic moments of Palestinian history, she had a view of Saladin Street, East Jerusalem's main commercial thoroughfare, which was packed with joyous, dancing people making their way toward Herod's Gate to enter the Old City. Hind would have liked to take to the streets with her fellow citizens, and this surreal vision induced her to abandon her usual prudence and hang the Palestinian flag from the balustrade of the terrace facing the city, despite the fact that, at the time, doing so was strictly forbidden.

Showing the flag from the terrace was a liberating gesture whose deeper significance she would grasp only later. At Dar El-Tifel, she had raised and educated generations of young Palestinians, and now those little girls, those young and older women, would help to administer the infant state. Her work was complete, she thought; her journey had reached its end. Now others would have to roll up their sleeves and build Palestine.

Hind's adopted daughter Hidaya interrupted this train of thought, bringing in a silver teapot and three green glasses with golden rims.

Hidaya had been brought to the orphanage many years before, as a three-month-old infant with neither parents nor identifying documents. Later Hind would tell her that the first time she took her in her arms she felt a deep attachment to her, a special feeling that in years to come would constitute the basis of a true mother-daughter relationship as well as a deep professional bond. Hind had offered her a finger, which the baby immediately squeezed hard with her little hand. It was a sign of the affection that was to bind them forever; Hind immediately adopted her, giving Hidaya her own family name, and later began teaching her all aspects of running the school, so that one day she might take Hind's place.

As Hidaya Husseini grew up, she distinguished herself by the scrupulous precision with which she carried out the little duties assigned to her and, later, through her strong passion for teaching. As she saw her daughter approach with the tea, Hind experienced once again the strength of the bond she had felt when Hidaya was still in diapers; and now, having come to the final chapter of her own life, she felt certain that she, like any self-respecting leader, had prepared her successor.

The tea was hot and very sweet, just the way she liked it. The fragrance of mint penetrated her nostrils and filled her with a sense of profound serenity.

A short while later, Hind's cousin Faisal Husseini appeared at the door. He was a robust man with a kindly air and the proud dark green eyes he had inherited from his warrior ancestors. As the highest Palestinian civil authority in Jerusalem, Faisal Husseini had headed the Palestinian delegation during the negotiations that led to the Oslo Accords.

Faisal described what was happening in the Old City, the groups of people forming at every intersection, the automobiles honking their horns, the music resounding harmoniously in the narrow streets as all Arab Jerusalem reverberated with the joy of its citizens.

As he stood by the window, Faisal turned his gaze in the direction of the Jewish Quarter, tensing for an instant. This did not escape Hind, who asked him what he was worried about. Her cousin refilled his cup, and then confessed that the current celebrations put him in mind of a story told by his father, of the day when euphoria had spread throughout the other part of the city. It was November 29, 1947, the day that United Nations General Assembly Resolution 181 approved the division of Palestine into two states. And that was also the day of the *nakba*, the "catastrophe," the beginning of the Palestinian diaspora. "In that instance," he said, "there was a direct transition from firecrackers to bombs."

Faisal went over to his cousin and sat down beside her, taking her right hand in his. "The Palestinian governing class has been in exile for many years, Hind, and they don't know how things have changed in recent times. They've never lived together with the Israelis. Frankly, I don't trust this optimism. It seems false to me, superficial."

Hind tried to reassure her cousin—and, at the same time, herself—by saying that the worst was surely over. But Faisal went on, unconvinced. "Believe me," he said, "what I'm saying isn't defeatism, it's only an objective analysis of the situation. Those people haven't been here all this time, and now they're back to collect the fruit of the work of others. I make no accusation; I'm simply stating the facts. They don't know what it means to live under Israeli occupation, to coexist with a people that suffered in the past and whose actions are dominated by fear. The new Palestinian state exists only on paper. Now we have to build it, and to do that, it's necessary not to forget the mistakes of the past that the PLO made in Jordan and Lebanon." Faisal paused, poured himself more tea, and drank a long swallow. "Forgive me, Hind. On such a great day I should think only about rejoicing in our success."

"My dear Faisal, I understand. You've always fought so that the Palestinian state could be established on a solid basis, with consideration for tradition and history. But maybe the situation isn't as negative as you think. Maybe people who have lived abroad and have no experience of the suffering we've witnessed will find it easier to create a functioning country that respects both Arabs and Jews. Maybe the new Palestinian governing class will surprise us." Her words, however, were more an attempt to comfort her cousin than a faithful reflection of her feelings.

Hind asked Faisal to accompany her into the garden, where he was to listen to her verbal will.

"Remember," she said after reading the will aloud, "the school must remain in the hands of the students. They're the ones best suited to run it. Hidaya will supervise the place—she's prudent and conscientious—but it will be necessary for you to watch over them."

A short while later, Hind bade her cousin farewell. She knew he was a sensible man, and now that guns were finally being put back in their cabinets, there would be a need for men like him.

She returned to the terrace as the fading sunlight fell upon the Judean Hills. "Will I die in Palestine?" she wondered, while observing several of the older girls as they returned from the city. Among them she recognized Miral, one of her favorites, and beckoned to her.

Miral had finished her exams in May, and now, like every other orphan, she was continuing to live at the school while she planned for her life after Dar El-Tifel. Hind recognized many of the features of her own adolescence in Miral. She admired the girl's courage. Ever since she had become aware of Miral's political activity, Hind had counseled her to remember that what the new Palestinian state needed were not heroes prepared to sacrifice their lives for its sake but intelligent persons who would work for its good, because she was firmly convinced that prudence was the most precious virtue in politics. Hind considered Miral an authentic hope for the future of Palestine. She knew how attached the girl was to her people but also how much she wanted peace and how far removed she was from the fanaticism that was currently taking hold. Hind wanted her to have a chance.

Miral stood before Hind, her eyes shining and her face flushed with excitement. Her words were at first confused and her phrases heightened by emotion. Hind told her to calm down, to sit beside her, and to start again from the beginning. Miral confessed that she had often disobeyed Hind's orders about taking part in the intifada, and she described the demonstrations she'd participated in and the meetings she'd arranged to warn the girls of the methods used by the Israeli secret services to recruit informers. With a touch of pride, Miral revealed that she had helped many students become involved in the Palestinian uprising. But despite these revelations, Hind felt that Miral still hadn't disclosed the entirety of her involvement.

Hind had every reason to be concerned about the extent of

Miral's activism. For one thing, the girl had been caught not long before, and Hind's prohibitions had obviously been reiterated in vain. Although Hind felt like a worried mother whose daughter was about to embark on her first journey alone, she was touched by the girl's frankness.

Now that her time at the school was drawing to a close, Hind's favorite student had put aside the logic that once governed their respective roles and demonstrated that she trusted Hind—even if she left out a couple of details.

Hind couldn't get to sleep that night. She listened to the street noises, the shouting of her still-euphoric neighbors as they returned home from a day of celebrations. The following morning, Jerusalem would awaken as it did each day, wrapped in a veil of instability. Perhaps it was the city's position that made it at once so appealing and so fragile, situated between Europe and Africa, between the desert and the sea.

Hind died one year and two months after the Oslo Accords. At Hind's funeral, Miral was among the mourners, and her sister, Rania, was at her side. Miral had returned to Dar El-Tifel for the first time since she left school. The year before she had watched Hind get into a car and travel down the avenue leading to the city for the last time, and as she did, she remembered walking along that same avenue with her sister and their father when they first arrived at the school.

The funeral was not only attended by the principal civil and Palestinian authorities but also by many women. This reflected an issue to which Hind had devoted her life—women's rights. On this day they participated in a ritual whose chief roles were usually taken only by men.

Hind often told her schoolgirls that the true leader was the one who left heirs; as part of their upbringing, she had taught them to carry on her work so that the orphanage school would not die with her. She would have been happy, on that day of lament, to see how her teachings were realized.

As the coffin was carried from the mosque, the women, whose heads were covered with white veils as a sign of purity, bore traditional gifts—rice, flour, salt, meat, fruit, clothes, and money—for the family of the deceased, which included the girls of the school. When the funeral procession arrived at the cemetery, a large group of women, defying the precepts of the Koran and the authority of the mufti, refused to abandon Hind's body at the burial place.

A heated argument ensued between the mufti and one of the women, an older teacher at Dar El-Tifel who was well known to the mufti; she had been a student at the school in her youth and had spent almost all her life at Hind's side. "Zeina," the mufti said, "please don't make me use force. Go now." But with the same proud look she'd had in her eyes when Hind spoke to her for the first time—after she and the other fifty-four children from Deir Yassin had been abandoned at the wall of the Old City—Zeina stood her ground, whereupon the mufti tried to induce her to leave by means of a gentle nudge. The crowd was struck dumb when Zeina responded by giving the city's highest Muslim religious authority a slap in the face.

When all was said and done, Zeina and the other women got their way and remained by Hind's side until the end, demonstrating how that extraordinary woman had, through her example, taught them not only patience but also tenacity.

The Arab community of Jerusalem felt such grief at Hind's passing that the period of mourning lasted ten days instead of the usual three. Every evening a muezzin went to Hind's resting place to pray. For several weeks, articles and poems dedicated to her appeared in the daily newspapers, and many ordinary citizens paid homage at her grave, which was always adorned with flowers. People brought her roses, carnations, and olive branches—the plants she had loved most.

Among the last things she had whispered to her girls before dying—words that would remain etched in their memory long after the failure of the treaty—was that peace was not only possible, it was vital. For both sides.

PART TWO

Nadia

1

fter helping her younger sister, Tamam, finish her homework and her mother mend the fishing nets, Nadia remained seated for the remainder of the afternoon on the steps leading down from the little hill in front of her house in the middle of nowhere, an area known as Halisa. From that spot, she had a view of the entire city of Haifa and could glimpse the sea amid all the white houses and new buildings that were springing up haphazardly around the harbor. Nadia's father was a fisherman who had drowned, a few months before, during a storm. At the funeral, Salwa, Nadia's mother, stood beside the coffin and announced to her community that she was expecting a baby. Soon thereafter, Nadia, her pregnant mother, and her eight-year-old sister moved into a smaller house. With Nadia's help, her mother continued to repair fishing nets after the baby was born, and Nadia cleaned offices two afternoons a week, but their lives became more and more difficult. On weekends they would gather prickly pears and go to the beach to sell them to passersby and tourists. There were many days when Nadia and her family ate only a single meal consisting of a piece of homemade bread sprinkled with olive oil and *zatar*, a mixture of ground oregano and sesame seeds.

A sudden noise distracted Nadia from her daydream. She turned around to see a short man with extremely pale skin, an unkempt beard, and an incipient paunch that was pressing against his black leather belt. The man stared at her without moving or saying a word; his eyes were tiny, and Nadia didn't like the look they gave her. She was about to turn around and find the sea again, when the man called her by name.

Stepping closer, he asked if she recognized him, then embraced her, kissing her on the cheek with moist lips that made her shiver in disgust. As she later learned, the man's name was Nimer, and he worked in the port. Although he said he had attended her father's funeral, Nadia couldn't recall ever having seen him before.

According to Arab tradition, it was not good for a woman's reputation if she and her daughters lived alone, for the common belief held that a husband guaranteed social protection. Thus, eight months after the funeral, Nadia's mother got married again, this time to Nimer, the man who had stood in front of Nadia on the hill. He moved in with them in their neighborhood in Halisa.

Nimer was a shrewd businessman who dearly loved money and cultivated good relations with the fishermen of the city. He started managing the net-mending operation, keeping for himself all the proceeds from the work, which Nadia and her mother continued to perform by themselves. One of his strongest convictions was that his wife and stepdaughter were insufficiently productive, and so he had Nadia drop out of school when she was only twelve. "Work strengthens the mind and the body," he liked to say, as he watched his stepdaughter bustling about the nets from daybreak till dusk.

Nadia's little sister Tamam was only eight, but Nimer decided that the time was right for her to drop out of school as well. She was already rather skilled at knotting nets, and he saw no reason why she shouldn't do more of it.

His wife's efforts to dissuade him were in vain. "Another pair of hands is always needed," he said, justifying himself by declaring that he had taken on four more mouths to feed. He constantly reminded the girls that he had done his part; now it was up to them to demonstrate their gratitude.

Nadia wondered what she should be grateful for, since she and her mother and sister were earning money for him, while he did no work, spent his time gambling, and forbade them to buy anything except simple food and a few articles of secondhand clothing. However, observing that her mother made no objection, and knowing full well that her stepfather, when he wished to be particularly convincing, would use his belt, Nadia ended up giving in.

At those moments, when their backs were burning under the leather strap, the girls would look at their mother and wonder why she did nothing to defend them. She, in turn lowering her eyes and covering her ears to block out the screams, would run into the adjoining room. A woman of little education, who cowered before her husband's authority, she thought that putting a good face on a bad business was better than running the risk of finding herself and her girls alone again. The result was that she sided with her husband in every circumstance, remaining loyal and devoted to him and sacrificing her daughters.

Their first year together passed in a sad, recurring cycle of domestic violence—little instances in which Nimer bullied everyone while Nadia's mother became smaller and smaller, less and less present. The girls grew accustomed to the rage their stepfather systematically took out on them and could sense when it was about to arrive, like a wave that swells up before it crashes into the rocks. They recognized it from the expression on his face when he came home, from his narrowed eyes and clenched lips. At such times, the slightest wrong move or a single misjudged word would suffice to unleash all his fury.

One morning Nimer entered the bathroom by mistake while Nadia was taking a shower. Surprised, he stood motionless in the doorway and watched her for a length of time she found interminable. In her embarrassment, Nadia tried awkwardly to cover herself with her arms and hands. After a few seconds, her stepfather turned around and went away.

That same evening, he entered the girls' bedroom and slipped into bed with Nadia, who had recently turned thirteen. The bed creaked, and Nadia felt the man's whole weight bearing down on the mattress. A heavy odor enveloped the room, a mixture of tobacco and sweat that penetrated her nostrils. "Hi, Nadia," he whispered, kissing her on the cheek, and she was conscious of the same sensation of clamminess and filth that had disgusted her the first time he kissed her. Then he began to touch her, and Nadia felt his rough hands descending lower and lower. She remained still the entire episode—pervaded by a feeling of nausea and fear of something she didn't understand, breathing only at intervals, trying not to make the slightest noise and not to think about the odor that was robbing her of air. Finally, without a word, her stepfather went away, closing the door behind him.

Nadia couldn't fall asleep that night. She felt sick and somehow dirty, without knowing why. She lay stretched out, her legs stiff, her body trembling incessantly, until the first rays of the sun lit up the summit of Mount Carmel. She knew that her stepfather would leave soon and waited until she heard the door close. Then, slowly, she got up. Her muscles ached from the rigid position she had maintained all morning.

Nadia filled the tub with steaming hot water and immersed herself in it. Instantly she began to tremble again. She placed her arms around her drawn-up legs and burst into tears. Her mother, passing the bathroom on her way to the kitchen, saw her daughter but asked no questions. Nadia scrubbed herself with a sponge until her skin was red and irritated. Then her mother reappeared in the doorway and reminded her to bring the prickly pears to the beach and to pick up the nets from the fishermen.

While she combed her hair, Nadia looked out the bathroom window at the lower part of the city. The clear morning sky allowed her to see Haifa Bay shimmering in all possible shades of red and yellow. Some noises rose from the port, the sounds of a ship docking or putting out to sea, but the neighborhood was still relatively silent, despite the fact that the previous night her adolescence had been shattered.

At eight o'clock, she woke up her two sisters, then fixed breakfast for Tamam and gave the baby, Ruba, some milk. At that moment, she made a decision: she would find some way to get out of that house.

The years went by, and none of the changes Nadia had dreamed of took place.

She became one of the most beautiful girls in the city, and her stepfather continued to visit her at night. Nadia let herself be violated, silently harboring a hatred that was barely masked by her deep black eyes. There had been a time, a few years earlier, when she had tried to rebel, threatening her stepfather and swearing to tell her mother everything, but a beating with his belt was the only reply he gave her.

One day she noticed Nimer staring at her little sister Tamam. Nadia knew that gaze very well, and a blind rage came over her. Gathering her courage, she told her mother the whole story while they were mending nets together. She didn't expect her mother to do anything to protect her. Perhaps she only hoped to find some solace for what had become an intolerable suffering. What she certainly did not expect was that her mother would spring to the man's defense and declare that it was surely Nadia's fault for provoking and seducing him.

If there was one thing for which Nadia had developed a profound intolerance as she was growing up, it was weak women who submitted meekly to the injustices perpetrated by their husbands and to the rules of their community. When she heard her mother's reaction, Nadia decided that the time had come for her to leave home.

She went to bed feeling as she had felt so many years before, on the night when she had lost not only her innocence but also the possibility of ever being happy. She lay awake for hours, under the covers, and then she got out of bed, trying not to wake up her sisters. For a long time, she gazed at them as they slept peacefully. At least part of the reason why she had put up with all those terrible years had been her desire to remain at her sisters' side, but she couldn't take it anymore.

She waited for her stepfather to get up, and then she confronted him. "I've told Mama everything, and now I'm going away. But if you dare to lay so much as a finger on one of my sisters, I'll make sure you pay a heavy price."

The man stared at her for a moment, flabbergasted by her self-assurance, a quality he had not recognized in her. Then his eyes regained their usual cruelty, and he replied to her with a sneer: "What do you think, you little whore? A fruit tree grows in my garden and I can't taste the fruit?"

Nadia grabbed a gas lamp and threw it at him, but he dodged it. Then she went to her room, and while Nimer laughed scornfully on the other side of the door, she took a few articles of clothing from a drawer, caressed her still-sleeping sisters with her eyes, tucked a little bag under her arm, and headed for the door. Her mother ran after her. She caught Nadia's arm and pulled it, trying to embrace her, with tears in her eyes. "Please," she said, "don't tell anyone what happened. If you do, you'll ruin our reputation. Think of your sisters—their reputations will be ruined, too."

"You disgust me," Nadia said. Her eyes were also full of tears, but they were tears of anger. "You should have protected me, and you did nothing."

"I am doing something. I'm staying at my husband's side, because that's my proper place, and your sisters are too young to go away with you. Here, take this."

She handed her daughter some money, which Nadia snatched from her hand, judging the offering the least her mother could do for her. She considered her mother as guilty as her stepfather, and she hated her at the same time that she pitied her. The year was 1959, and Nadia knew that it wasn't at all easy for an Arab woman in Israel to rebel against her husband. But Nadia had no choice; she had to leave, because the alternative to leaving would have been death. Nothing on earth could have made her bear the rape, the violence, the tyranny one minute longer.

She raced down the hill and away from that house like a madwoman chased by ghosts. She didn't turn around.

2

When Nadia arrived in Jaffa, a sense of freedom rose up in her. She felt the bitterness of a difficult choice but was proud of herself for having had the strength to rebel against such cruelty. "From now on, I make the rules," she told herself as she walked along aimlessly. "Nobody's going to make me suffer anymore."

Jaffa was smaller and tidier than Haifa, which was, above all, a port, where everything revolved around the loading and unloading of goods and the activities of the underworld that flourished there. Jaffa, on the other hand, seemed to have developed harmoniously, filled with public amenities, restaurants, and hotels and surrounded by green parks. The streets were lined with lemon, mandarin, and grapefruit trees, and the rose-colored houses of Jaffa had a colonial style that, though outdated, was decidedly more charming than Haifa's modern buildings.

After wandering through the city all afternoon, she saw a sign: HOTEL SHALOM. She thought, "Maybe I'll find a little peace there," then crossed the street and entered the lobby. The middle-aged Russian matron at the reception desk was surprised when Nadia asked for a single room. The hotel's guests were usually tourists or businessmen away from their wives and looking for fun.

Nadia took a room with a terrace overlooking the sea and immediately fell asleep, finally able to release some of the tension that had accumulated in her during the past several hours and to feel relief at having escaped from a bad dream that had lasted for years. After her nap, she took a long bath and went down to the desk to ask if anyone on the staff knew of a restaurant that was hiring waitresses. The Russian lady replied that she knew a restaurant owner, one of her regular clients, who was indeed looking for help, and she gave Nadia the address.

The owner, a Moroccan Jew named Yossi, was immediately struck by the beauty of the girl, who displayed the self-confidence of a grown-up.

Nadia showed herself to be a hard worker, but she was melancholic, and at times her eyes were so sad that Yossi wondered what could have wounded her so deeply. Apart from that, she was perfect. Customers left her lavish tips, and she was always willing to help out her colleagues. One day she asked Yossi if he knew anyone who had an apartment to rent; the hotel was too expensive for her to consider living there permanently. He offered her his beach house, facing the sea, which he and his family used only in summer. At first Nadia was reluctant to accept, but in the end it seemed too good an opportunity to pass up.

Her friendship with Yossi grew from day to day. He saw her home each evening, and they talked at length about their respective lives. Actually, it was he who did most of the talking; he told her that he had been married for twenty years but that the love between him and his wife had vanished long ago. He loved his native country, and he was fond of repeating that there was nothing in the world better than wandering around the medina in Fez, lured in one direction or another by the smells and colors of the souk.

One evening Nadia asked him if he would like to come in for a drink. Taken by surprise, he wasn't sure how to respond. He decided to accept. Nadia, who knew very well what she was doing, intended to demonstrate to herself that her sensuality was intact and that she had overcome the trauma of the abuse she had suffered. Yossi and Nadia became lovers, and she asked him to teach her everything about that subject.

Sometime later, Nadia offered to put on an exhibition of belly dancing in the restaurant, and Yossi gladly accepted. The show was such a success that it was repeated the following day and the day after that. Soon it became the restaurant's main attraction. "I'll never be like my mother," Nadia thought as she danced, pretending not to notice the covetous eyes of the men sitting at the surrounding tables.

One day Yossi arrived at the restaurant in an obviously agitated state. Nadia saw that he remained restless for the entire evening. Once he had brought her home and they were lying between the soft linen sheets, he showed her a ring and said, "Nadia, I love you, and I want to marry you." Although her fellow waitresses would have given anything for such a proposal, Nadia was terrified by it.

The following day, she packed her things and, without any explanation, left for Tel Aviv.

Some years went by, and Nadia adjusted well to life in Tel Aviv, which to her was the capital of the world. Once in a while, she felt a bit of nostalgia for Yossi and his kind manner, but she quickly forgot about him. Since wages were higher than in Jaffa, she entertained hopes that someday she could save enough money to travel and visit distant places. She had no desire to see her mother again, but when she learned that her sister, Tamam, had also run away from home, only to be caught and shut up in a Christian religious school, Nadia decided to go and visit her.

It was a Saturday morning in March, and the sun's rays warmed the windows of the bus. After leaving Tel Aviv, the vehicle climbed the rocky hills of Judea and Samaria, eventually reaching Nazareth.

Tamam was elated to see her older sister. When she took Nadia back to her room, they gazed into each other's eyes for a long time without speaking; then Nadia broke the silence and began telling Tamam about the past few years, first in Jaffa and later in Tel Aviv, mentioning her work as a dancer, her economic independence, and—especially—her freedom. She told her sister that she felt reborn, far from their stepfather's tyranny and their mother's weakness. What she missed most of all, however, was having someone she could talk to, someone with whom she could share her experiences, someone she could trust completely. She missed her sister.

In turn, Tamam described her life in the school, the strict schedules, the hard-eyed nuns, and the attitudes of the other girls, who tended to avoid her because she was a Muslim, even though they were all Arabs. But despite its harshness, the place was basically tolerable, Tamam said, compared to the hell of home. She cast her eyes down for a moment, and then seemed to fix them on a part of the wall where the plaster had come loose. Only at that moment did Nadia notice how bare the room was, how lacking in anything that might express the individuality of the person living there.

Drawing near to her sister, looking down to meet her gaze, she realized that Tamam was hiding something. Nadia saw a sadness in her sister's eyes that reminded her of her own state of mind during the first heady days after she left home. Suddenly a shiver came over her, a question crossed her mind: maybe their stepfather had abused Tamam, too. When Nadia asked her, the younger girl wouldn't reply at first, but her resistance was weak and she needed to tell somebody. A few minutes later, clutching Nadia's hands tightly in her own, Tamam admitted that their stepfather had violated her for the first time on the very day that Nadia left home.

After visiting Tamam, Nadia walked back down the street leading to the bus station, with feelings of rage and guilt gnawing at her. Nimer had abused Tamam systematically, almost as if he were carrying out some kind of vendetta against the sister who had dared to revolt against him and go away. She walked rapidly, arms straight down at her sides, fists clenched, her whole body a contracted nerve. Her instinct urged her to run away again, even though it would be her sister she'd be running away from this time. Tamam was a reminder that neither of them would ever be free from the past they shared.

In response to her mother's weakness and the oppression she had submitted to, Nadia had developed an uncommon pride, becoming a beautiful, arrogant young woman who was too injured to share her sadness with anyone else. She would do that only once in her life, years later, when she would spend three months in prison for punching an Israeli woman who had insulted her because she was an Arab. It was there that she met Fatima.

PART THREE

Fatima

1

$\mathscr{F}$atima gazed up at the sky through the bars of her window. It was six-thirty in the morning, and the prison was still wrapped in a muffled, dreamlike atmosphere. There was no sound, not a single cloud, not a bird; everything seemed frozen in place.

In half an hour, the guards would open the doors, and everything would begin again, as it did every day: the din, the words, and the continual feeling of emptiness.

She stretched wearily on the bed, looking up at the metal mesh of the bunk above her, which had been unoccupied for several weeks. Five years had passed since her arrest, five long years in which time had become so distended that it no longer existed. For months she had been promised that she could work in a nearby hospital, but they still hadn't called her. Bureaucratic problems, she guessed.

She was sure they'd call sooner or later. They needed nurses, and she was well qualified.

The Six Days' War of 1967 worsened the Palestinian situation. At that time, Fatima was working at the hospital in Nablus. There she cared for wounded soldiers, civilians, and children, seeing in the process things she thought no one should see in this life.

The war had been quick but ferocious. Women and children reached the hospital in desperate condition, their faces often unrecognizable. Dying Arab soldiers were brought to the hospital as well, and in their eyes Fatima had read confusion and fear, the same emotions she had seen in the refugee camps where her aunt and her cousins lived.

She had never forgotten the expressions on their faces, just as she could still see her parents being humiliated by Israeli soldiers every time they passed a checkpoint. They would pretend that nothing was wrong, tell her everything was normal, but she would nevertheless manage to hear the unspoken words—words of terror and of indignation at having been punished for crimes they had not committed. Freedom is one of those things that you don't notice until you don't have it. Fatima knew that in 1948 the Israelis were experiencing the realization of a two-thousand-year-old dream. She was only a child at the time, yet she couldn't get rid of the feeling that it was at the expense of her people and her family.

And yet as time passed, she had tried to put aside those rancorous feelings and to concentrate on her own life. Whenever she was studying, she would make an effort to withdraw herself from the sounds of her house, which was too small for her large family, from the neighbor's constant screaming at his wife, from the stench of garbage left to rot in the sun. Fatima hated her neighborhood in Jerusalem. She hated the soldiers, with their smug looks and their fingers always on their triggers. She had studied diligently and worked long hours to become a nurse, and she had finally moved to Nablus, two hundred kilometers from Jerusalem.

She would make her way down the bright, coldly lit halls of the hospital in Nablus with an assured step, wearing military trousers, gym shoes, a white T-shirt, and white coat. It wasn't long before her dedication earned her a promotion to head nurse.

Every morning she walked to work through the Arab Quarter of Nablus, her kaffiyeh wrapped around her neck, nodding an occasional greeting before slipping into the labyrinth of narrow streets in the Old City. No one who saw her could have imagined that this inconspicuous woman, with such a reassuring, good-natured appearance, would soon become the first Palestinian woman to organize and attempt to carry out a terrorist attack.

She had already been dividing her time between her nursing and her political involvement. At the hospital, she had met Yasir Arafat, with whom she was to form a close friendship in the future.

During the Six Days' War, wounded women and children from the cities, along with a stream of young soldiers' mangled bodies, were brought to the hospital.

Many of them suffered without complaint; perhaps they unconsciously accepted theirs as a tragic destiny that kept repeating itself again and again, a game in which they were pawns moved about by more powerful forces. As she disinfected, treated, and stitched those lacerated bodies, she told herself that no reasons could ever justify so much anguish.

She felt as though it were 1948 all over again. Fatima could see her parents once more, recalling their efforts to protect her and to make her believe that their life under the Israeli occupation was an unchangeable fact. She had grown up convincing herself that children in other places played hide-and-seek amid rubble and piles of garbage. But she was nine when the great change came, too old not to remember the life before it, which had suddenly come to an end without anyone ever explaining why.

All the pain, hatred, and resentment she had tried so long to suppress boiled up in her during the war, and that was when she decided to do something. The staff at the hospital had been advised that all wounded soldiers were prisoners of war: upon their discharge they would go into the custody of the Israel Defense Forces.

It began with a soldier she was caring for, a young Jordanian of Palestinian origin. With eyes he could barely manage to keep open, he implored her to help him escape from the hospital. Fatima didn't have to think twice. Since the young man had returned to Palestine to fight for the Palestinian people, she felt that the least she could do was to help him get home. She gave him some clothes that belonged to a fellow hospital worker, and the young soldier quickly disappeared.

The next step was a natural consequence of the first. If she had helped him, she could help others, too.

And so she went to work, destroying medical records, burning uniforms, and obtaining civilian clothes for her patients. The military authority, perplexed, tried to figure out what had become of these soldiers. There was a great deal of confusion. Fatima's operation, however, was short-lived. The hospital administration had already begun to suspect her when some Arab soldiers were captured while attempting to escape from the hospital. Even though none of them gave Fatima's name, guilt nevertheless fell on her. The administration didn't have her arrested, but she was fired on the spot.

Fatima, however, felt neither worried nor guilty. On the contrary, the episode convinced her that she should move from collusion to action. Now that Jerusalem was completely under Israeli control, the resentment of the city's Arab inhabitants had grown exponentially. What Fatima felt was an almost physical need to do something concrete for the cause she believed in, something that would leave a mark. She considered words and speeches to be important, but she was convinced that alone they were insufficient to change reality.

A few days after she was fired from the hospital, Fatima returned to her family's house in East Jerusalem. It was there that she found the person she was looking for, a young man with a neatly trimmed beard and short, bristly hair. Continuing to pick out her vegetables, she gradually got closer to him, met his eye, and gave him an unequivocal smile. "Hello," she said. "My name's Fatima."

"Hi, Fatima. Pleased to meet you. I'm Maher," the youth replied, not in the least bit surprised at her boldness. He smiled as if they had known each other all their lives, but continued to dart glances in all directions. As the leader of a small resistance group answering to the PLO, Maher was aware of and responsible for any political activities in the neighborhood of East Jerusalem.

Before Fatima could explain the reason for her approach, the young man interrupted: "I've heard about what happened to you. You were fired because you tried to save some Arab fighters."

Fatima nodded.

With a knowing smile, he said, "You are very brave."

Fatima looked at him without a word. In a way, it was up to him to steer the course of their conversation. "At the moment," he said, stroking his beard and smiling, friendly but discreet, "we need people like you. This war is not over yet."

Fatima understood what he was proposing, and it was exactly

what she wanted to do. She felt that she had a mission to fulfill, a purpose whose accomplishment would make her life worthy of being lived. She no longer wanted to treat bodies wounded in battle; she wanted to prevent them from being wounded. She wanted to strike at the enemy's heart.

Fatima never asked herself, neither before nor after the attack, whether intentionally planning the deaths of the people, many of them Israeli soldiers crowded inside a movie theater, was an effective means of promoting the liberation of her people. The only thing that counted for her was avenging the profound injustice to which her people was subjected.

She spent a long time planning the attack with Maher and five other men, all between the ages of twenty and twenty-six. Safe inside the walls of the Old City, they had daily meetings over a period of several weeks, gathering on the roof of a different house each evening, with one of them acting as a lookout. At first their plan was to print and distribute flyers, but Fatima persuaded them that such a course of action was ineffectual and probably would just get them arrested. Without batting an eye, she told her comrades, "The only language they understand is violence. It's the only message we can send that is capable of making them see that we exist and that this struggle will continue."

"But, Fatima, what you're saying goes way beyond our usual activity. We—all of us here—we are not soldiers. We distribute flyers." The speaker was a young man whom Fatima, the only woman in the group, had intimidated with her confidence.

"Propaganda hasn't worked," she replied. "We've put out propaganda for years, and here we are, still licking our wounds. We need to create panic—there's no other way. We have to hit them in their daily activity, just as they do to us."

After a few weeks, Fatima became the leader of the group, and lengthy discussions of possible targets and technical matters began in earnest. She was certain that a military attack was the only appropriate response to the cycle of violence that was drenching their land with blood. She knew that the military supremacy of the Israeli army would doom any uprising or attack on it to failure, so in the end she chose a civilian target, the Zion movie theater in West Jerusalem, an establishment frequented almost exclusively by members of the Israeli armed forces, particularly in the evening. This decision set off another animated debate, and once again Fatima offered an unequivocal response.

"Look, boys, think of it this way: when the Israeli bombs fall on our heads, they strike civilians and soldiers indiscriminately, and the tanks in the refugee camps almost always run over our children."

It took more than a month for the bomb to arrive from Lebanon.

On October 8, 1967, Fatima, carrying a purse full of explosives, entered the Zion theater, mingling with the prostitutes who frequented it, and left after a quarter of an hour, so as not to arouse suspicion. At their last meeting she had told her comrades, "I know we're going to be asking ourselves for the rest of our lives whether or not this was a just thing to do. But the Israelis must understand that until the day we're free in our own country, they won't be free in theirs." The bomb didn't go off.

Fatima didn't flee to Jordan. One week after the failed attack, she and the rest of her group were detained as a result of testimony given by the cashier at the movie theater. The five young men refused to name Fatima as their leader, and she, too, rejected every accusation until the police finally arrested her entire family. Then she was compelled to confess in order to obtain her family's release. Her trial concluded with her being sentenced to imprisonment for two life terms plus eleven years for refusing to stand in court. She was the first Palestinian woman to be arrested for political reasons.

She was also the only Arab prisoner and the only political prisoner in a jail full of women. Prostitutes, murderers, thieves, and regular criminals—they assiduously avoided her at every turn. Fatima read a great deal, as she always had, realizing that even if a book couldn't change the world, at least it had the power to make prison walls disappear. Some nights she would read Samih al-Qasim in the moonlight:

> From the window of my small cell
> I can see trees smiling at me,
> Roofs filled with my people,
> Windows weeping and praying for me.
> From the window of my small cell
> I can see your large cell.

In her nocturnal moments of anguish, she sought refuge in memories of her childhood, when wishful dreams and fond illusions could still lull her to sleep.

2

The bus proceeds slowly, immersed in the blinding light of noon. It's filled with kids in various school uniforms and workers wearing stained overalls and worn-out shoes. Fatima is on her feet, holding on to one of the supports. Other people get on the bus at the next stop, and now it's really crowded. There's a noticeable odor, pungent and nauseating.

The girl sitting in front of her has fallen asleep; her mouth is half-open, and she's clutching a handbag to her chest. The bus brakes suddenly, making the passengers lurch forward and then back. The girl's bag opens and a book falls out. Fatima stoops to pick it up; it's a volume of art history. She gazes at one of the illustrations. It shows a beautiful woman, completely nude, standing on a large seashell. Her skin is milky, her head tilts toward one shoulder, and a winged figure exhales a wind that gently tousles her long blonde hair. On the woman's left, a nymph offers a cloak. Behind her, the ocean's horizon is lost in the blue of the sky. The girl wakes up. Fatima hands her the book and smiles. For an instant, the world seems to be in harmony with the image in the book, even inside that crowded bus, on the bumpy streets of Jerusalem, with its white houses piled one on top of another and the Mount of Olives in the background.

Then the cell door opens with the grating metallic sound that awakens her each morning.

Fatima eased into consciousness, her head still full of the painting she had dreamed about. After a moment, she raised her upper body a little to see which guard was on duty. But the door had closed again, and Fatima found herself looking at a tall, slender young woman with full lips, light brown eyes that almost seemed yellow, and long, straight black hair. "But there's no room for Venus in this tormented land," Fatima thought. "This is where beauty dies."

Without much enthusiasm, she said hello to her new cell mate, turning on her side and resting her head on her pillow.

Nadia gave a slight nod, her only response, and then quickly clambered up to the top bunk. After a few seconds, however, she came down again, walked over to the water basin, observed its contents with a certain disgust, and asked how often they changed the water.

"It depends," Fatima replied.

"Depends on what?"

"On the guards. Look, everything in here's like that, more or less. Your best course is to get used to it," Fatima concluded, sitting on the edge of her bed.

Nadia shrugged, but a brief smile crossed her lips. She felt an immediate sympathy for this short, compact woman with frizzy hair, green military trousers, and a flat nose that added an element of character to her face.

Their differences provided the glue that held them together, a friendship born in a prison where they were the only Arab women and where, moreover, one of them had been arrested for political reasons. By a sort of alchemy whose deeper workings remained a secret to both of them, unaccustomed as they were to sharing confidences with strangers, it took them only a few days to understand that they could trust each other. They quickly began to unburden themselves, and when they could find no words to explain their meaning, a look or gesture would suffice. And so they discovered that during the very period when Nadia had begun to work as a waitress at the restaurant in Jaffa, Fatima was gradually drawing closer to political activism. Their worlds were far apart, but they had both ended up inside the confined space of a prison cell, and in their months of forced cohabitation the wariness that had enveloped their two existences subsided. Both of the women, but particularly Nadia, found that it was possible to look at the past in a new light.

"Weren't you afraid?" Nadia asked one day, when Fatima was telling her about the attempted attack.

"No, not for a minute. It was like this, Nadia: Fear wasn't an emotion I could feel, because I basically didn't care about anything, including my own life. The only thing that counted was the success of our plan—I couldn't see past that."

Nadia stared at her new friend, amazed. It was the first time she had ever met anyone so involved in the Palestinian cause. Nadia had never considered herself either an Arab or an Israeli, and the vagaries of politics had made little or no impression on her. And here she was now, in the company of a woman who had given everything she had for something whose necessity Nadia couldn't even see. What most fascinated her about Fatima was her fearlessness, especially her indifference to her own fate. Nadia wasn't all that attached to her own life either, but the difference was that if she were to risk it, it certainly wouldn't be while fighting for a cause. Except, perhaps, for her own cause, which was her personal freedom.

"It was so hot, my hair was plastered to my forehead," Fatima said, continuing with her story.

Attracted by the discovery of a world she knew nothing about, Nadia again concentrated on Fatima's words.

"The air was heavy with the smell of sweat, tobacco, and stale perfume. Everything was shabby, and whiffs of filth and garlic kept cutting through the other smells. Before he handed me my ticket, the cashier gave me a quick glance, and then he said it would be a good evening for me, that the place was packed with guys eager to spend their money. I said I was glad to hear it, and that I didn't doubt they had money to spend. I saw him turn and look at me out of the corner of his eye. When I entered the theater, nobody inside noticed me—everyone's attention was fixed on the screen, where a young blonde was being molested in a bed in her dream. Those excited soldiers couldn't have imagined that in a few minutes they would be protagonists in another film altogether."

Fatima paused briefly and then began again: "After about fifteen minutes, I left my bag under my seat and walked out of the theater." She took a sip of water before describing what was to be one of the proudest moments of her life. "As I was walking away, I waited for a big boom. And I waited another fifteen minutes. People began to run out of the theater. I stayed where I was. I saw the police arrive, and then the cashier talking to them."

"The one who sold you the ticket," said Nadia.

"Yes, it turned out that he noticed me leaving and found the bomb under my seat. He called the police. He gave them my description, and it didn't take them long to identify me and arrest me."

Nadia couldn't believe that anyone could feel such blind hatred for someone they didn't know. It was different for her; she had felt the same hatred, had nourished the same thoughts of revenge, but her rage had been directed at a precise individual, one she knew well and who had robbed her of childhood.

"I didn't think of them as men anymore, Nadia," Fatima explained. "I saw them as soldiers. They symbolized the injustice that was being inflicted on us. You see, Nadia, military occupation is a fierce monster. It slowly extinguishes your dreams, your hopes, and even your future. And gradually it changes who you are."

Weak light filtered through the narrow window of the cell. The evening must have already turned to morning. Nadia had begun telling her story after lunch, sitting on the lower bunk next to Fatima, who listened with a frown on her face the whole time as Nadia told her about the abuse she had been subjected to, about her mother, about her later meeting with her sister, and then about her search for freedom and her refusal to have sustained relationships with men.

Fatima saw in Nadia a strong woman who was at the same time fragile and delicate. She was oppressed by her past, not only because of the physical violence she'd experienced, but also because of all the constraints that had been imposed on her. She had learned to react in the only kind of language that had been taught to her since her birth: instinct mixed with anger. Even in prison she took great risks, on many occasions, by demonstrating intolerance for authority, which didn't go over well with the guards.

Nadia fell asleep leaning against the peeling wall of the cell, her head inclined to one side. Fatima watched her for a moment in the semidarkness: Nadia's slimness and well-toned muscles made her look energetic. Her beauty made her radiant despite the brutal punishments life had dealt her.

The next day, she told Fatima the rest of her story, beginning with her journey to Tel Aviv.

3

A couple of months after she arrived in Tel Aviv, Nadia began to feel at ease. The city was very lively, filled with shops and new buildings. There were restaurants, bistros, and movie theaters everywhere, and the streets were alive with people, day and night, so much so that she felt as though she were in one of those Western cities she often heard about, places where carefree people enjoyed themselves in nightclubs and danced in discotheques. She had made many friends, and she was seeing several men. She felt free to do whatever she liked, and this, to her way of thinking, meant she had already scored a major victory. At the same time, however, she knew that this relatively serene phase of her life would not last long. Her moods were as unstable as the breezes on the city's waterfront, which in the morning blew from the sea to the land and in the afternoon from the land to the sea. Nadia had many men, but no serious relationship. "As far as I'm concerned, any stable bond is a potential source of prohibitions, frustration, and contempt," she explained to Fatima. She didn't want any man to have control over her life.

To earn as much money as before, Nadia had started giving

belly dancing lessons in her home. A friend of hers, an older Israeli woman named Yael, suggested that she perform in her husband's nightclub, which was one of the most fashionable spots in the city, frequented by rich businessmen on their travels and by some of the most high-profile people in the country.

It was a very welcoming, tastefully furnished place, softly illuminated by light filtering from valuable, chased lanterns, with an inlaid ceiling and red velvet sofas covered with silk pillows. Before long Nadia's beauty and rebellious nature; her deep, elusive eyes; and her sinuous, assured movements made her the chief fascination of the club. While she danced, moving among the tables, she liked to feel the customers' eyes on her, with their heavy burden of desire. Many of them left her generous tips, but if anyone touched her or even grazed her, or if someone made a proposal she judged improper, she would make a sign and the offender would be swiftly ejected from the nightclub. The owner let her have her way, even though his customers were the most influential men in the city. He didn't want to lose his main attraction.

While dancing one evening, Nadia noticed a young man whose eyes remained fixed on her the entire time. At the end of the show, he invited her to have a drink at his table, and contrary to her usual policy, Nadia accepted. Maybe the decisive factors had been his gentle manners and his eyes, which reminded her of a child's. Beni—short for Benyamin—told her he was a Catholic businessman from Nazareth. When the nightclub closed, they made a date for the next day.

In the following months, she became more relaxed, abandoning her wary attitude, and attempted to leave behind her long-standing distrust of men. She seemed finally to have found a little peace. After her show, she no longer remained holed up in her dressing room with the lights dimmed, listening to tragic songs and emptying bottles of arrack until the nightclub closed. Instead, she would change quickly and join Beni at his table, the same one where she had seen him for the first time. Together they wandered around the city's markets or traveled to cities and countries she had never seen. Beni showered her with jewelry, clothes, and gifts, while Nadia's body responded generously to his attentions.

One evening the owner of the nightclub, who had grown fond of Nadia as if she were his own daughter, noticed that she seemed glum. She denied it, claiming that she felt fine, that nothing was wrong. She danced even better than usual, and her looks were so darting and evasive that the customers sat in silence for a long time at the end of her performance, still intrigued by her movements, which seemed to belong to another world.

Without even changing into her normal clothes after the show, Nadia went over to Beni's table, where he was smoking a cigar, and sat down. The other customers watched them with curiosity and envy.

"I've been waiting all day to tell you, Beni. I'm pregnant. We didn't plan for this, but I'm so happy!"

Beni, who was inhaling a mouthful of smoke, started coughing. For a few moments he stared silently at Nadia, as though trying to decipher what she had just told him.

"And you? Are you happy, too?" she asked him, trying not to see the turmoil in his face.

"Of course, of course it's good news," he finally managed. "It's just that you've taken me by surprise, that's all. I wasn't expecting it."

Nadia's face lit up. "Then tomorrow we'll celebrate."

That same evening, Beni spoke to his family about his love for

Nadia. He told them everything: that she was a Muslim, that she was a dancer, and that she was pregnant. As far as Beni's family was concerned, the most troubling aspect of the affair was the young woman's profession. They could accept that she was a Muslim, and they could accept that she was expecting a baby, but a belly dancer would bring the family dishonor.

That night was an exceedingly long one for Beni. Torn between his love for Nadia and his love for his family, he made his decision and never went back on it.

Nadia waited a long time for him, but he did not return. Perhaps she felt more vexed by the cowardly way Beni had left than by the separation itself. Once again she had been shamed and sadly humiliated.

She didn't know if the deciding factor in Beni's flight was her being a dancer or her being a Muslim, but, in any case, for the first time in her life she felt discriminated against by her own people. Everyone thought she was an Israeli. She considered herself integrated, and she'd never given a thought to the possibility that she could be the object of such a strong prejudice. Until that moment, her beauty and her emancipated attitudes had served as her safe-conduct into Israeli society, but now, suddenly, all her certainties had been shaken. After having rejected the rules of her own community, she had never thought of herself as a Muslim. Now she was being abandoned, not because of the choices she had made, but either for a quality she had inherited or for belonging to the nightclub world that she herself looked upon as absolutely distant and strange.

When her daughter was born, she experienced great joy, but within a few months, Nadia realized that she couldn't reconcile the irregular life she led with the fixed hours her baby imposed on her or with the obligations the child's upbringing required. As soon as she left the stage, she would hurry to her dressing room, where she would invariably find her daughter crying from hunger or thirst, or in need of a change. Nadia loved the child very much, but she felt awkward, and she was afraid of making the mistakes that her own mother had made with her. When she looked at her baby, she couldn't help remembering the innocence that she herself had lost so early.

One day she received a visit from her sister Tamam, who in the meantime had left the religious school in Nazareth and married Abbas, a gentle and intelligent man who had an ice cream parlor in Haifa. Tamam told Nadia that their mother sincerely regretted having behaved so spinelessly in the past and would very much like to see Nadia again. Their meeting was possible only because her stepfather, Nimer, had been the victim of an accident at the port. A jammed winch had dropped three tons of cargo on him, flattening him like an inkblot.

The meeting with her mother was not the easiest of encounters, particularly for Nadia. No matter how hard she tried to remember a nice moment with her mother before Nimer came into their lives, she could not let go of her residual resentment. After all, her mother was the person responsible. Nadia spoke a little about her life in Tel Aviv and about the difficulties of raising her child. Tamam and Abbas offered to help her, but her mother declared that she would take on the care of the little one herself. "Please!" Salwa implored Nadia. She felt lonely now that her youngest daughter, Ruba, had also gotten married and moved to Nazareth, where her new husband had relatives.

Nadia was surprised to hear such an offer coming from the very woman who had abandoned her to her fate. She could read her mother's sincerity in her eyes, but how could she simply forget everything, just like that, and take an eraser to the past? Besides, many years before she had sworn to herself that she would make it on her own, and she had no intention of eating her words.

"Nadia, we're here—we'll be close to her," Abbas gently assured her. Until that moment, he hadn't said a word.

In the end, Nadia accepted. She knew she had no choice, and she was certain that Abbas and Tamam would watch over her daughter in Haifa.

Doubly humiliated by having been abandoned by Beni and by needing to ask for help, Nadia gradually began to take refuge in the oblivion that alcohol offered. She frequently ended her evenings completely drunk. Sitting before the mirror in the dressing room, she would look at her face, with its smeared makeup, at the heavy hair falling over her eyes, and regret that, all things considered, she had done nothing with her life, nothing more than rhythmically undulate her hips for the delectation of a few sweaty businessmen, smarmy industrialists, and smelly local officials.

She felt that the best part of her was not evident in the seductive movements of her body, and at times she thought that some customers could read the truth burning in her eyes. She thought they could see her story, which was not as beautiful as her lips, her breasts, her buttocks, but which was as deep as the sadness she drowned in bottles of arrack. At the end of every show, she called for a bottle of liquor and shut herself in her dressing room, where she drank steadily, mechanically, until her muscles relaxed and the objects that surrounded her faded into the background. She wondered what the rest of the world was like and what it was about Israel in particular that made it such a difficult place to live. Almost every night came to an end with her falling asleep like that, imagining herself strolling the streets of a distant city, one of the many she hoped to visit eventually—Paris, London, Tokyo. . . .

When she reached this point in her story, Nadia remarked to Fatima, "If you're born in Israel, that means you are born as an Arab or a Jew, and every day there will be someone who glares at you suspiciously. I pretend not to notice, I walk with my head high, but more and more I feel as though I'm being scrutinized and judged. I'm a minority within a minority because I don't belong to anyone or anything. I have olive skin, black hair, full lips; my entire physical appearance is a reminder that I'm a Palestinian. I associate with them, I go to their clubs, and their music is the same, just as their food is the same as the food I eat. And yet I have never felt that I was one of them."

Why did she necessarily have to be either Arab or Jewish? Couldn't she just be Nadia, Nadia the rebel, Nadia who was free?

Fatima had remained silent the whole time, listening to Nadia's story and observing her rapt eyes. She seemed to be in another world, and Fatima had refrained from interrupting her out of fear that Nadia might wake from her memories and realize that they were no dream, they were her real life. Fatima was baffled. She, who had loved, hated, and was ready to kill for her people, could not and would not understand Nadia's way of thinking. And yet Fatima perceived a common origin in their stories, as if the same sorrow had led them to make different choices.

Nadia took up her story again and told Fatima the last part, the part that had caused her to wind up where she was.

She was with some friends in a nightclub on the beach. The palms were swaying, stirred by a light breeze. Lamps shed a warm light on gaudily colored carpets that muffled the steps of those entering and leaving the club. Nadia was unaware of the young man seated at the next table, but he had been staring at her for some time. His companions, a broad-shouldered, middle-aged gentleman with a pleasant face, and a diminutive young woman, seemed to be deep in conversation. But the girl had discovered that her boyfriend's attention was fixed on Nadia, and every so often she cast a hostile look in Nadia's direction and then, with a false smile, quickly turned back to the man she was talking to. Nadia got up to say hello to an old friend, a woman who was seated at the bar. As she passed the next table, she finally noticed the young man, an Israeli with whom, not long before, she'd had a brief fling. She limited herself to greeting him with a crisp nod.

The lad sprang to his feet, and with the excuse of ordering another drink, he walked over to the bar and sat down on the stool next to Nadia.

A few minutes later, when Nadia was returning to her table, the girlfriend looked at her and sneered, "Arab whore." Nadia punched her with such force that it knocked the girl down. Nadia's temples were throbbing, while an expression somewhere between fear and surprise registered on the girl's face. Blood was streaming down from her right nostril, soaking the white collar of her blouse. Nadia was on her feet, her legs slightly spread, her arm bent at chest level, her hand still clenched into a fist. The young woman on the floor had acted out of jealousy, unable to stand the sight of her man, or perhaps only her friend, so obviously interested in Nadia. But what stung Nadia more than anything was that "Arab" had been thrown at her as if it were the most common insult anyone could utter. Whether she considered herself an Arab had no importance; it was what she was, period, and there were people willing to offend her solely because of that.

A heterogeneous crowd of onlookers had gathered, and for several moments nobody offered any assistance to the diminutive young woman who had challenged Nadia's pride. Then the older, pleasant-looking fellow helped the girl to her feet, as the clamor of the club's patrons was drowned out by approaching police sirens. Nadia was loaded into a squad car, which then made its way along the seafront through the Saturday-night throngs. She looked out the window and saw a palm tree bent by the wind, leaning toward the sea. Nadia bit her tongue and the sweet taste of anise mingled with the salty bitterness of blood.

On the day after she heard Nadia's account of the incident, Fatima was hanging the prisoners' laundry out to dry in a little courtyard. She could see a slice of sky framed by the gray walls and thought at length about what she would do if she were in the same situation as Nadia: able to leave prison in a few months and come to terms with freedom.

When she finished her work, she went back to the cell and stretched out on her bed, waiting for Nadia to return. Her eyes stared at the ceiling, at the pieces of plaster that were about to fall down and the damp stains that highlighted its perimeter.

When Nadia reentered the cell, she smiled at Fatima, who smiled in return. When was the last time she'd done that?

Fatima's influence on Nadia grew daily. Fatima especially tried to persuade her not to resume the life she'd had before, not to go back to dancing in Tel Aviv, but to go to Jerusalem, to Fatima's family; her relatives would surely help Nadia. During the last month of Nadia's detention, when Fatima's relatives came to visit, they asked to speak to Nadia as well. They were cheerful, good-natured people, and Nadia started thinking that maybe her friend was right.

And so, much sooner than either of them wished, the moment of separation arrived. For Fatima, life in prison would resume its monotonous course; she would go back to enduring the hostility of the other prisoners alone. But Nadia was leaving her with something more. Her many questions had made Fatima reflect for the first time on what she had done and on many beliefs that she had never called into question.

The night before her release, Nadia pondered various experiences she'd had during the past six months. Sharing her story with Fatima had made Nadia realize that she had never thought of herself in terms of membership in a group, not until she was called an "Arab whore." Nadia thought, "Maybe Fatima is right when she says that no one can be free if her own people are not. No Arab is free in this country." She hadn't thought about that before. And if she hadn't thought about it, maybe it was because she hadn't been thinking, and that made Nadia feel empty. It was a dangerous line of reasoning, though, because it contained the possibility of living as a prisoner in your own land even if you weren't in jail, and of backfiring against anyone who might look for different ways to survive, who might choose to engage in something other than the struggle for her country.

As dawn was breaking on that final morning, Nadia reflected that prison had granted her the luxury of being able to think in the abstract for the first time in her life.

Later that morning, before giving Nadia one last embrace, Fatima told her, "You're going to regain your freedom, but that won't automatically make you happy. Whatever you do, do it in such a way that all the things we said to each other continue to mean something. Don't forget; do it for me."

4

Nadia soon felt comfortable with Fatima's relatives and with life in Jerusalem. Fatima had led her family to think that Nadia also had been incarcerated for political reasons. From the very first day, she was on friendly terms with them, and she soon familiarized herself with the narrow streets and lanes of the Old City. She quickly decided to become engaged to Jamal, Fatima's brother, who had fallen in love with her the first time he saw her in the prison. A few weeks after her arrival, Jamal asked her to marry him, and she accepted. She never mentioned to him that she had a child in Haifa.

Jamal Shaheen was a considerate, quiet man, and Nadia envied his serenity, which was accompanied by a rationality she knew was lacking in herself. She was happy to slip into the tranquil life of a future bride, which was made up of preparations, parties, and other weddings for her to participate in. While Jamal worked as an imam in al-Aqsa Mosque, leading the morning prayer, he also worked a second job as a night guard to put aside money for their wedding. Nadia was endearing herself to all and fitting seamlessly into the city's social fabric.

It amazed her to think that prison, against all expectations, had given her the chance to make a new life for herself. Her disquiet seemed to have dissipated without her noticing. The news that she had been in prison with Fatima spread rapidly through the neighborhood and brought her boundless respect from its inhabitants, who forgave her Western clothes, her boldness, and her smoking. They were convinced that she had been arrested for political reasons, and she herself was convinced that her reaction to being insulted as an "Arab whore" had been, in a certain sense, a political act.

One day at a wedding party, she met a young man from Bethlehem. Jamal's cousin introduced them, and when their eyes met it was as if they were the only two people left in the world. They talked for three consecutive hours without any of the other guests taking much notice. Hilmi was twenty-two, tall, and dark skinned, with intense, intelligent eyes. He wanted to go to Beirut to study at the American University. Nadia revealed to him that she was already betrothed to another man.

Despite these adverse circumstances, their reciprocal attraction was such that they decided to see each other again two days later. For a while after that, they met secretly in various cafés and restaurants in West Jerusalem and also encountered each other in the Shaheens' home. Fatima and Jamal's mother, an elderly and somewhat naive woman, thought Hilmi was turning up to court her other daughter. Jamal, Nadia's fiancé, occupied with his work at the mosque and busy preparing for his new family, was totally unaware.

Nadia and Hilmi's clandestine rendezvous became more and more intense. One afternoon they made love. Around lunchtime they met at the Damascus Gate and walked to a small hotel. Nadia was tense with fear, and it was obvious that Hilmi, too, was extremely nervous.

Once they were inside the large and handsome room, the couple embraced tightly, ending in a long, passionate kiss. Neither of them had ever been so certain of what they were doing as they were at that moment. Hilmi kissed Nadia's throat and then slowly began to undress her. His movements were awkward, but Nadia thought his the most delicate hands that had ever touched her body. Hilmi gently leaned her back on the large bed. When he saw that she was trembling, he smiled and told her that she should relax, that everything was going to be all right. Nadia didn't stop shaking, and her eyes grew wider. "If you want me to, I'll stop," Hilmi said. He would not force himself on her. Nadia's only response was to take his hand and put it on her breast.

Time stopped for them.

Before they left the room, Nadia embraced him and asked him not to go away. She would have begged him, but her pride prevented it. "You can study here, in any university," she said, but he was adamant. He soothed her by telling her that he'd come back for her soon.

"Please, Nadia, wait for me. Don't get married," he said.

A week later, Hilmi left Jerusalem, and it was difficult for Nadia to keep from showing the great sadness that consumed her. Her disappointment at Hilmi's departure towered over her; once again she felt abandoned. Having lost her faith in men a long while back, she didn't trust Hilmi's promises, and so she decided that she should go ahead with her marriage to Jamal.

She did so a month later, but the day before the wedding she discovered that she was pregnant. She called Jamal and wept as she told him the whole story. It disturbed him profoundly, as he was a good man who had unconditional faith in other people. He rose from his chair and looked incredulous. So many questions were crowding into his brain: Who? And, even more than that, How? How could he have failed to notice anything?

"It would be better for me to go back to Haifa now," Nadia said. "You've been very generous to me, and I haven't been capable of repaying your trust."

Jamal made his decision and broke his silence. "I love you, Nadia. Maybe it's partly my fault, because I've neglected you for my work. I still want to marry you, but you must promise never to see him again."

Nadia felt as though the weight of the world had been lifted from her shoulders. How could she deserve such a good man? "He's gone away, and he's not coming back," she said with tears in her eyes.

"I believe you," Jamal said, drawing near and putting his arms around her. "I love you so much. I've loved you from the moment I saw you."

The first year of their marriage passed in great serenity. Nadia became active in organizing various women's groups. She promoted discussions and hosted parties, encouraged the women to be independent and to demand respect from their husbands. In this sense, Nadia was a genuine pioneer, as haphazard and instinctive as ever but effective in offering a contrast to the marginalized, submissive Arab women who were her neighbors. Her miniskirts, the way she rambled around the city by day or night, her total autonomy from her husband, the fact that she drove a car, that she had both Israeli and Palestinian friends—all provoked a palpable ferment in her part of town.

At the end of that first year of marriage, Hilmi came to see her at the family home. He told her that he had found an apartment in Beirut and enrolled in the university. "The city's modern and full of life," he said. "I know you'll like it."

Nadia flinched, which made Hilmi pause and look at her more closely. A little behind her, he could see an infant a few months old, apparently a baby girl. "You're married," Hilmi observed mournfully, "and you have a daughter." Then a sudden doubt assailed him, a doubt that a quick calculation of the time involved did nothing to dispel. "Tell me the truth, Nadia. Is that baby, by any chance, mine?"

Nadia, who had never expected him to return, was as disturbed as he was, but now it was too late. She fixed her eyes on his and said, with an air of defiance, "No, she's not your daughter. What do you think, that you're the only man in the world?" She wanted to wound him, even though she wasn't exactly sure why. "I've slept with many men, before and after you." As unconsciously as he had broken her heart, she had broken his.

Struck in his pride and his heart, Hilmi leaped to his feet, determined to go away forever. He wouldn't even stay in Beirut, he thought, but rather start over in some distant place, perhaps in Europe.

One afternoon during her second year of marriage, Nadia went to the hammam, remaining in the tepidarium for a long time as she observed the other women, especially those her age, trying to guess which of them wore the veil in public. For many of them, the visit to the hammam was the only time in the week when they were free for a few hours to be what they were, whether good natured or irascible, solitary or extroverted, and not actors performing preordained social roles.

As she was getting dressed again, Nadia looked at herself in the mirror. She was the most beautiful woman there and also the unhappiest. Although Jamal was gentle and kind, marriage had not given her any real sense of equilibrium. One year after the birth of Miral, the daughter born of her relationship with Hilmi, Nadia had brought Rania into the world. Maternity had granted her a new glow and a brief illusion of happiness, but she realized that nothing, not even beauty, could be an antidote to her sadness.

"When a woman is beautiful," she thought, "everyone expects and almost requires her to be happy as well." She could not bear the knowledge that her husband, her sister, her daughters, and even Fatima in her own way, all wished her to be necessarily, obligatorily happy, satisfied with what she had become and with what she was doing. They insisted that she should learn to see the beauty around her. Nadia had continued to conceal her weaknesses from others; she appeared strong and self-assured in public, but deep down inside she was tormented by her past.

She tried to be a good mother, but for her serenity was only a distant oasis, an unreachable mirage.

Nadia got into the car, not knowing exactly where she would go. She drove slowly along the streets of the city. The shops were closing, and the farmers who had come down from the country to sell their produce were returning to their villages, mingling with the few people who were still out and about.

The radio was broadcasting a traditional song, which reminded her of her belly dancing days in Tel Aviv, when she had admirers who would travel across the country to see her. She felt nostalgic for all that attention—the flowers, the compliments, the dinner invitations—and felt anxiety mounting inside her.

She waited on the beach for dawn, accompanied by a bottle of arrack, and thought that there was no continuity in her life. Fatima had tried to pull her out of the spiral of masochism she found herself in and had even succeeded, but only for a while. The reality was that Nadia was groping in the dark, looking for a way out.

She immersed her feet in the cold, clear water and tried to imagine her future: it looked colorless to her, like the last drop of liquor at the bottom of the bottle. A wave higher than the others soaked her skirt from the hem to above her knees. She smiled and then started laughing nervously as she realized that if there was anything missing in her life it was her childhood. She had no happy memories of herself as a child—no pleasant mental images of frolicking on the beach or playing with friends or smiling or receiving a gift. At that moment, she felt a deep hatred for her mother and even a little for her father, who had gone and gotten himself swallowed up by the sea without having raised her, protected her, or held her hand.

She stayed three days with a woman friend in Jaffa, savoring again the freedom of the good old days, and then went back home as though nothing had happened. Jamal forgave that flight, as he did all the following ones, in hopes that her anguish would subside in time, that she would grow more attached to him and her two daughters.

He bought her the liquor she required to combat her attacks of depression and tried not to ask her too many questions. So he wouldn't be recognized while making these purchases, he would go to a café far from his neighborhood. But because he was an imam, people knew his face. The bartender would invariably slip the bottle into the bag, smile maliciously, and say, "Imam, you are a righteous man," following this declaration with a loud laugh that spread among his customers, from table to table. The love that Jamal felt for Nadia made him able to bear even these humiliations.

Nadia decided one day to visit Fatima in prison. It felt strange to walk through those dark corridors again, inhaling the odors of mildew and low-grade tobacco that rose from the cells. Fatima looked as she always did, alert and round faced. Their meeting was warm and friendly, even though they did not speak to each other with the same frankness as when they had shared a cell. Nadia didn't reveal that she had started seeing men other than her husband, or that she drank arrack into the small hours of the morning, sitting in an armchair with a lit cigarette in her hand. Fatima could see that Nadia had not found the peace she yearned for, but she urged Nadia to keep believing in what she was doing for the other women of the community, and tried as always to raise her friend's self-esteem. But it was all useless. Fatima's smile turned bitter when Nadia told her that the three months she'd spent in prison had constituted the happiest period of her life.

Then Nadia asked a question that caught Fatima off guard: "How could you want to kill somebody you didn't even know?"

Fatima, to make her understand that there had been a purpose behind her act, said, "I don't see them as people, I see them as soldiers. Our people are suffering. They have made a war on us and we have no choice. It's either resist or vanish. Their first prime minister, David Ben-Gurion, once said, 'We are people without a land, and this is a land without people.' If this is a land without people, what are we?"

Nadia had already risen to her feet. She moved away toward the door, her long black hair caught up by a red ribbon, her slender figure contrasting with the gray cement cell.

Fatima felt no anguish, neither for herself nor for the fate of her enemies. She had to admit, however, that life in prison had introduced her to a side of the Israeli world she had never known before. The Jewish women who were her fellow prisoners were all thieves, prostitutes, and unfortunate wretches, basically victims in their own right.

Jamal searched everywhere for Nadia. At her relatives' home in Haifa, where she told him she was going for a few days, he discovered that she had not been seen, just as she hadn't been there on the other occasions when she'd gone missing. Nobody knew where she might be.

Jamal returned home and stared at the telephone for a long time; then he removed the stopper from the bottle Nadia had left on the night table and poured a little of the whitish liquid into his cupped hand. He raised it to his nostrils, and for an instant, he had the sensation of reliving the kiss his wife gave him the morning she left.

Nadia had returned to the Tel Aviv nightclub where she had worked as a belly dancer before her arrest. It seemed to her to be the only place where she had really been herself. And notwithstanding her three pregnancies and some added years, within a few weeks she was once again the club's main attraction. She was still very alluring, maybe even more so than before, but hers had become the beauty of melancholy, like a lovely city built in a soulless place.

When Jamal found out that Nadia had returned to her former life, he thought that perhaps he should have been less tolerant with her and that his mistake had been to allow her too much freedom.

Nadia found a way out. For once it seemed so clear. She felt light, and the moment she realized it she had, for the first time, a sensation she recognized as joy: she could spare herself and those she loved a life that was only trouble.

The police found Nadia's body on the beach at Jaffa. Her face was disfigured and her position unnatural. She looked as though she had been trying to reach the sea; her arms were flung out ahead of her, and the waves were licking her hands. High tide was rolling in. One hour more, and the waters of the sea would have swallowed her body up again, as it had swallowed her father's. The authorities called her case a suicide, but neither her husband nor anyone else who knew her well believed that. Nadia had never given up, not even when she was thirteen and her stepfather stole her future. Perhaps she had been the victim of an accident. They refused to let themselves believe it was suicide, the last terrible chapter in a life lived far outside the norms of her time and country.

Jamal decided that his daughters needed to grow up in a serene environment, where they would be in the company of other little girls. Above all, he wanted them to grow up far away from the disturbing dramas that had marked their family. And so Miral and Rania were entrusted to the care of Hind Husseini, who would bring them up in her orphanage, Dar El-Tifel.

PART FOUR

Miral

1

The day Jamal first took them to Dar El-Tifel, autumn had not yet begun, but a thin mist enveloped the hills around the city.

He had left the bathroom door half-open and was shaving, but he wasn't whistling as he usually did. Instead he was just staring in silence at his own weary face in the mirror. He had looked like that on the morning of Nadia's funeral, a month before. As Miral silently watched her father, she saw a tear gleam on his cheek before disappearing into the white foam.

Jamal was a tall, slim man with thin lips and large black eyes. An imam at al-Aqsa Mosque, he had been born in Nigeria and was among the many emigrants from Senegal, Mali, and other Muslim countries in Africa who arrived in Palestine during the period of the British Mandate. In their neighborhood within the walls of their Old City, entered through a green iron gate, nearly all the inhabitants were of African origin. Jamal had a refined stature, a dignity that was evident in his manner, his eyes, and his gestures. He had beautiful hands with long, thin fingers. The district where they lived was more than a neighborhood; it was a genuine community in which all the children played together and relationships, even among adults, were intense and cordial. People considered themselves not merely neighbors but virtually brothers and sisters, like an extended family. Miral's father was one of the most respected people in the neighborhood, a spiritual adviser to many, a wise and patient friend.

They lived in a three-room house whose doorway was framed by fragrant jasmine and a large pomegranate tree. Inside, two steep flights of stairs led to a bright, spacious living room whose floor and walls were covered with rugs. In the middle of the room was a sofa bed where their father now slept, which faced a wooden display cabinet filled with hand-colored drinking glasses that came from all over the Middle East and had been blown by the master glassmakers of Damascus, Marrakesh, and Cairo. They were always perfectly gleaming, for Jamal dusted them every week.

The bedroom, too, was filled with Moroccan rugs and had a low bed covered with pillows. The wrought-iron lamps and colored windowpanes spread a warm light suffused with bluish and reddish tones. The bathroom, though small, had a view of the Old City and a charming mosaic of blue and green tiles. Jamal had taught Miral and Rania that green was the color of Islam, and blue the color of purity, the sky, water, and infinity. One wall was almost entirely occupied by the large sink, which was slightly cracked on one side as a result of a clumsy attempt by Miral to climb onto it a few months before her mother died.

Every time she looked at that nearly imperceptible flaw, Miral could see again, just for a moment, her mother's face.

The day Jamal took his two daughters to the orphanage, he woke up earlier than usual. As he gazed down from his bedroom window at the deserted street still illuminated by the uncertain light of streetlamps and the houses with full clotheslines and windowsills crowded with pots of geraniums, the first call to prayer reached his ears from the minaret of the mosque across the way.

Jamal was attached to his girls in different ways. While Miral had conducted herself like a little adult since her mother's death, continuing to get the highest grades in school, Rania seemed more in need of protection. Whenever Rania couldn't sleep, she would go into the living room, where Jamal had made his bed since the death of his wife, and put her arms around him. Only in this way, lying silently beside her father, could the child manage to fall asleep.

But Miral worried Jamal, as well, because she seemed to be afflicted by a deep anxiety. The night before he took them to the orphanage, she woke up bathed in sweat and told him that she had dreamed about her mother again. In her dream she found herself in a tree whose leaves were moving in a gentle wind. She had resolved to keep climbing all the way to the top. Rania was watching her from the ground, smiling and holding her hands up above her head. Her father was sitting on the grass, smoking, and their mother was walking toward the river. With all her might, Miral tightened her legs around the tree trunk and dug her fingers into its rough bark, which scratched her. She climbed until she reached the topmost branch. Then suddenly the wind stopped blowing and everything became silent. Miral looked and smiled at her father, who waved back to her. She could see her sister joyously hopping around the garden, but she was upset because she could no longer see her mother, not along the river or anywhere else.

Jamal tried to console her, saying that it was normal to have bad dreams after losing someone you loved so much. Miral gave him a look that was difficult to fathom, but it was as if his response had not satisfied her and he needed to offer some further explanation.

He attributed it to her fear of losing the memory of her mother's features.

His decision to place them at Dar El-Tifel had been difficult and, above all, painful; he would never have wished to be separated from his daughters, especially now that his Nadia was gone. But precisely because of her death, and because his family name was still tainted by his sister's attempted attack a few years earlier, he preferred to have the five-year-old Miral and four-year-old Rania brought up in a more protective environment. He had long known Hind and had personally brought her several children who had been abandoned outside the mosque. Now he was bringing her his own daughters. Hind suggested to him that the school could become a second home for the girls. With this in mind, they decided it would be best to change the girls' family name, and Miral and Rania Shaheen became Miral and Rania Halabi.

2

That morning Jerusalem's Arab neighborhoods were teeming with the usual preparations in the souk. A muffled clamor filled Jamal's head as he set out with his daughters, carrying in his right hand a small suitcase with the girls' personal belongings. Rania clutched his little finger on that side as she walked along, and Miral held on to his left hand. Their father stopped at a stall to buy caramels for them. He knew he would visit them almost every week, but even so, he was uneasy. The children tasted the candy's sweetness. It mingled with the bitterness of departure.

Miral looked around as they began walking. Apart from the vendors in the souk, there seemed to be no one on the streets. After a few steps, however, a flood of neighbors appeared at windows, and children who had been their playmates on sunny afternoons greeted them along the way with flowers and even more candy. Miral sensed that she wouldn't be going home anytime soon. Her father had always managed to avoid answering the question of when she and Rania would return, and Miral had never insisted very much, partly because she didn't want to alarm her sister. Ever since their mother died, Miral had looked upon Rania with different eyes: although Miral was only a year older, she felt that it was her duty to protect her little sister.

After they had walked all the way across the Old City, they stopped at Jafar's, the oldest confectioner's shop in Jerusalem. There they ate a *knafeh* in silence. This pastry, made from a mixture of cheese, butter, durum wheat, and pistachios that had been softened and sweetened with syrup, reminded Miral of the happiest moments of her life, when she and her mother would go to Jafar's shop to pick up *knafeh* for the whole family.

Outside the walls of the Old City, they found themselves standing before an iron gate, on which Miral read, somewhat unsteadily, the words DAR EL-TIFEL, JERUSALEM, 1948.

Proceeding through a shady garden, they reached a long drive lined with pine trees. Beyond it was a clearing, and farther on they could glimpse three buildings. "They're decorated in Mudejar style," Jamal told his girls, never missing an opportunity to teach them something new about the historical or artistic tradition of their heritage.

"Mudejar style," Miral and Rania repeated solemnly in unison, their voices sad and serious. Not far off, they saw a lawn where some little girls were playing volleyball.

A middle-aged woman wearing a white suit came toward them, smiling cordially. Her gray hair was gathered at the nape of her neck, and there was a thin coat of pink lipstick on her lips. She greeted Jamal affectionately and then turned to the girls, stroked their faces, and told them that they could join the other children playing.

Miral reached out to take Rania's hand, but her sister was clinging to her father's arm and wouldn't let go, afraid she would never see him again. She stood frozen at his side, silently pouting. Jamal then took both daughters by the hand to the lawn where the other girls were playing, assuring them that he wasn't leaving right away and had to have a little talk with Hind. Rania stared at her father with suspicious eyes for a moment, but in the end she followed her sister. Out of the corner of her eye, Miral saw her father walking away and then turning to look at them, eyes bright with tears. She had never seen him so miserable. Jamal waved to them, but by then Rania was playing and didn't notice. A soccer ball landed in front of Miral, and she simply stared at it, wishing she could kick it back and somehow return to the days when her mother was there and they all were still together.

The school's oldest building, located on the highest point of the hill, overlooking the Old City, housed the classrooms and the administrative offices, including Hind's, a simple room with antique furniture dating back to the period of the British Mandate. On the other side of the playing field stood a more modern building that was built with Sheikh Muhammad bin Jassim Sabah's money and used as a dormitory. At that time, there were already two thousand girls. There, as in the classrooms, Hind had decided that the youngest girls would be assigned to the first floor, where they would live in rooms containing six beds each. The older girls were on the second floor, in rooms with four beds. Finally, the top floor provided single rooms for a few girls in their final year and for the teachers who lived on campus. On the opposite end of the small field was the gymnasium and a little farther down the hill, surrounded by a park, was Hind's residence. As she was getting older, Hind decided that she would move back to one of her grandfather's oldest buildings and would use it as her home. Its spacious terrace looked out over the city, and its white stone walls were almost completely covered with ivy.

That first evening, after dinner in the large cafeteria, a thin teacher with sad eyes accompanied Miral, Rania, and four other little girls to their room. Rania had left her food untouched and never let go of Miral's hand.

Miral noticed that the older girls helped the little ones change into their nightgowns and told them fairy tales to lull them to sleep. Those stories, however, tended to be about other orphans, like themselves. Oliver Twist was a favorite. As Rania listened to one of them, the tears she'd held back all day began to run down her cheeks. Her sister put her to bed, but Rania kept weeping, saying between sobs that they'd lost their mother but she didn't know why they had to lose their father, too.

Miral moved her bed closer to her sister's. As long as they were together, she told Rania, everything would be all right. Then she caressed her little sister's hair and face until she went to sleep. The four other little girls had pushed their beds together, too, making one big bed where they all slept, in that way exorcizing their feelings of loneliness and abandonment. Only Miral couldn't sleep. She thought again about her father walking away down the tree-lined drive and about the stories the older girls had told that evening—sad stories that were perhaps true, just like the story of her own mother, who used to be happy and then one day stopped smiling and disappeared.

While Miral adapted quickly to her new situation at Dar El-Tifel, the same could not be said of her sister. Rania was taciturn and wanted always to be with Miral. After the first night, the other girls joined their beds to the sisters' beds and all six of them slept together, clinging to one another. Such gestures of affection were a means of compensating for the lack of physical contact with their mothers.

The relationship between Miral and Rania had always been intense and was a refuge that helped them to get through moments of despondency. Rania depended on Miral, and Miral sometimes felt suffocated by this constant pressure from her little sister, but with each passing day, she realized more clearly how lucky she was to have a sister nearby and a father who came to visit every week. Some of the other girls were completely alone.

The girls with the worst problems were those who knew nothing of their origins, who had not only no relatives but also no idea of who their parents might have been or where they were born. These girls were the gloomiest but also the most aggressive: sometimes physically violent in the schoolyard unable to accept a simple defeat, usually quarreling over things of no importance. Unable to resign themselves to the uncertainty of their past, to live with questions destined to remain unanswered, they tormented themselves and others.

The school had a custom that every evening before going to bed the students would tell one another stories. Most of the girls maintained that their stories were purely fictional or based on the experiences of their friends, but in many cases Miral could detect, in the veil of anguish that settled over their eyes as they spoke, that the stories were their own. Thus she discovered that Lamá, age ten, had been found by the mufti of Jerusalem as an infant wrapped in swaddling clothes, lying at the door of the mosque. Other girls had been picked up while wandering alone in burning villages, staring wide-eyed into space. Such girls usually turned out to be the most motivated in the school, inspired to affirm an identity for themselves.

During the first month, Miral became accustomed to the sound of the alarm clock, which would ring at six in the morning, and she would slowly get up, go over to the window, and pull the curtain aside. Rubbing her eyes, she would gaze at the Old City: the top half of its walls lit up by the rays of the sun, the bottom half still in shadow, and the low houses packed so densely that they hid the streets that separated them. She would search out her house, which was near the mosque, but her view was blocked by a minaret. She thought about her father, still asleep in his bed, or awake like her, with his eyes fixed on the ceiling, wondering why things had turned out this way. In the background, the Mount of Olives, majestic and reassuring, seemed to protect the city; she imagined the city seen from above, looking like one motionless and magnificent ruin.

Gradually Miral grew accustomed to life at the school and to the constant presence of her sister, who followed her everywhere. Hind allowed them to sleep in the same room for the first year, but in the following years, even when they slept in different rooms, Rania would continue to depend on Miral for many things. When the eleven o'clock bell sounded, signaling the day's first recess, Rania would go out to the playground and sit on the bench under a big cedar. In the meantime, Miral would buy their lunch from the woman who came to the school every day with a basket loaded with sandwiches, flatbreads, fruits, and desserts, and then go join her sister. Filling the maternal role, Miral would feed Rania, who despite being younger had a more robust build and therefore looked to be the older of the two.

For their first few months at Dar El-Tifel, Rania did not speak to anyone else, and the teachers were often obliged to call Miral if they wanted to coax a few words from her sister's mouth.

· · ·

After the summer vacation, the previous year's scene was repeated. The difference was that this time Miral and Rania knew perfectly well where their father was taking them. That morning Miral was excited; she knew she was going to leave kindergarten behind and enter the first grade, and that seemed like a major accomplishment. Above all, she couldn't wait to put on her new uniform and change rooms. As soon as they reached the school, she rushed to the seamstress's room; a long line had already formed outside the door. The seamstress took each girl's measurements and altered their uniforms.

Early that afternoon, Miral received her white blouse, green jumper, red cardigan, and black shoes. With great solemnity, she slipped out of her shorts and took off her favorite blue cotton T-shirt. Then she slowly put on her uniform and polished her shoes, which were already on her feet, before proudly admiring her reflection in the mirror and going to show herself to Rania.

The two sisters were no longer assigned to the same room, which made Rania feel uneasy. She envied Miral's uniform and complained that she had to wait another whole year before she could have one of her own. Nevertheless, the headmistress and the other teachers found Rania to be much less melancholy than she had been the year before. Jamal waited until Miral's uniform was ready, and when she came out wearing it, he took a photograph of the two girls, with Hind standing in the center.

That was the year Miral's fascination with history began. Maisa, a short, stout woman with thick eyeglasses and disheveled curly hair, would narrate the horrors of the French Revolution or the Lebanese Civil War as if she were reading from novels or fairy tales. The entire class held its breath during her lectures, waiting to see how the story would turn out. Nobody spoke a word as Maisa, pacing in front of the classroom, unrolled maps and pointed out distant cities or displayed photographs of leaders and bloody battles. She rarely used the name Palestine, speaking more often about the *ummah*, the great pan-Arab nation; about the Egyptian president Nasser; and about the Ottoman Empire. Miral distilled a basic principle from her teacher's explanations—that history is always written by the winners.

Twice a month, Miral and Rania would spend the weekend at home. They anxiously awaited those Friday mornings when they would spot their father swiftly walking up the long, tree-lined drive.

Before returning to the city with the girls, Jamal would have a long conversation with Hind. The topics they discussed ranged from Jamal's daughters and the orphanage school to the future of Palestine. Jamal always left Hind's office with a smile stamped on his face, and more than once, as he took his girls by the hand and began walking toward the gate, Miral heard him murmur, "What a great woman she is."

Jamal had hung the photograph of his daughters and the headmistress in his living room, above the television set. He would stare at it at length during the interminable nights when he was assailed by sadness, for it imparted a great feeling of peace. Miral's proud gaze, which reminded him of her mother's, Rania's slight pout, and Hind's serene, reassuring expression showed him that he had made the right choice in entrusting his daughters to her.

As soon as they arrived home, the girls would take a bath. Jamal knew how much Miral loved this moment, and he would watch as she heated the water on the fire and then poured it into the copper bathtub. The rising steam dulled the bathroom tiles and made the mirror and the windowpanes opaque. Everything looked blurred and muffled, warm and foggy, as in happy moments in the most pleasant of dreams.

Rania was always a little reluctant to share the joy of this ritual, but she would soon get into the tub with her sister, and the two of them would spend a long time immersed in the hot water, which gradually became lukewarm and then cold. Jamal would suggest repeatedly that they get out of the tub. Then he would try to run a comb through his daughters' tangled, curly hair, covering it with a thick layer of conditioner, but despite these affectionate and awkward efforts Miral and Rania often went back to school with knots in their hair, which the oldest girls would help them undo. After the bath, Jamal would go to the mosque for the midday prayer, and upon his return they would have lunch together, sitting around the little copper table incised with flowers and plants, on ottomans of colored leather.

Jamal usually prepared roasted chicken with curry, basmati rice, and seasonal vegetables. He was a good cook, inventive and patient, and his daughters spent the two weeks between visits anticipating the taste of that meal. The following morning, they would go to the produce market, and then to the carpet souk in the afternoon.

In the fresh-produce souk, Jamal taught his daughters how to choose the best heads of lettuce, which were almost always near the bottom of the pile. The girls learned to evaluate the smell, color, and feel of vegetables and fruits. Jamal could tell whether a tomato had been grown with natural fertilizer or not, and he knew whether the taste of an orange would be sweet or sour. After making his food purchases, he would offer his daughters object lessons in the ancient art of haggling with its most talented practitioners, the vendors in the rug market. Jamal loved Persian rugs and had made the family home particularly welcoming by filling it with them. Many years later, after his death, Miral would count no fewer than thirty-three rugs spread on the floors or hung on the walls of the house's three rooms.

For their part, Jamal's daughters had something to teach their father as well. Having been influenced by the strict rules at Dar El-Tifel, Miral and Rania proudly showed Jamal how to fold his clothes, which had been washed and ironed by a woman in the neighborhood, and stack them in the wardrobe.

Sunday afternoons at home were dedicated to discussion. Father and daughters spoke of the girls' problems and of the importance of their education. Gently caressing the girls as he spoke, he would say, "The uncertainty of our condition puts us in a position where everything is more difficult, where everything has to be overcome with great effort, and a life of freedom is even more difficult for an uneducated woman. You both must study and learn as much as you can. That's the only way you'll be free."

At other times, the girls would eagerly set out for the Esplanade of the Mosques, where their father spent considerable time each day watering his roses, bougainvillea, and olive trees or reading in the shade of a large pine.

On Fridays the faithful would arrive from all over the country to pray in al-Aqsa Mosque and the Dome of the Rock. Miral and Rania would join the stream of people entering through the Damascus or Jaffa gates, having crossed the Old City to reach what Arabs call the Haram esh-Sharif, the Noble Sanctuary, Islam's

third-holiest place, after Mecca and Medina. The contrast between the narrow streets of the Old City, rendered still narrower
by the baskets of vegetables women from the Occupied Territories
brought in daily, and the splendid view of Jerusalem and the Judean
Hills that could be enjoyed from that spot was so great that it often
overwhelmed the faithful, who would linger in the gardens after
prayer, eating Arab bread and hummus while their children played
happily around them, against the solemn background of the Mount
of Olives.

On Saturdays the people who traversed the Old City were
mostly Jews from West Jerusalem, who passed through Herod's
Gate or the Damascus Gate on their way to prayer at the Wailing
Wall. Miral and Rania were particularly entranced by the Orthodox Jews, with their long ringlets of black hair, white shirts, and
short overcoats and trousers of heavy black cloth, which they wore
even on the hottest days of the Middle Eastern summers.

The way taken by the two groups of the faithful, Jews and Muslims, was the same until they came to a fork in the road. There the
Muslims turned to climb up to the Esplanade of the Mosques, while
the Jews continued toward the entrance to ha-Kotel ha-Ma'aravi,
the Wailing Wall, the only fragment remaining of the temple built
by Herod the Great.

Jamal felt that his religion and that of the Jews had many
points in common but one great, fundamental difference. Islam
seemed to be a religion that loved to show itself and hide itself at
the same time. The splendid Qubbet es-Sakhra, the Dome of the
Rock, with its gold roof visible from any point in the city and
the extravagantly colorful tiles covering its six walls, together with
the many minarets scattered around East Jerusalem, seemed to
bear witness to Islam's demonstrative aspect. The interior court-

yards of the palaces and the mosques, on the other hand, with their fountains and their mihrabs, were emblematic of a religion that also loved to conceal its magical beauty.

The Jewish religion, on the other hand, seemed to be fascinated by mystery—or at least that was the conclusion Jamal had reached during long nights of reflection. No other place in the world was so sacred to Jews. The Temple Mount—that open-air synagogue with the Wailing Wall and the steady clamor coming from the religious schools, the yeshivas—made Jerusalem the dominion and destination of an unending pilgrimage of Jews from all over the world. Many who lived there were convinced that the branches of the city's olive trees were moved not by the wind but by the breath of God himself.

Christian pilgrims would walk the length of the Via Crucis— also known as Via Dolorosa—which traversed the Old City. They would make a stop at each station along the way before reaching the Church of the Holy Sepulchre, where they would be enveloped in pungent, intoxicating clouds of incense.

One summer afternoon, when Jamal and the girls were at the vegetable souk, Miral was looking at the chickens hanging in the butcher shops, the cuts of meat dripping blood on the street, the cafés where old men smoked their narghiles and drank mint or sage tea, or cardamom coffee. Then she turned, attracted by a group of people who were passing in front of them. "Papa, where are those tourists going?" she asked.

Jamal, who was intent on buying grape leaves from an old woman seated on the ground with a big wicker basket at her feet, raised his eyes and looked in the direction Miral was pointing. "Those aren't tourists," he replied with a smile. "They're Christian pilgrims on their way to the Church of the Holy Sepulchre."

Jamal and the girls then made a stop at Jafar's shop, where they did honor to their little tradition by eating a *knafeh* each. All the while, Jamal had been thinking that if their city was truly a melting pot of cultures and religions, it wasn't right to know only one part of it. "If you'd like, we can go visit the Holy Sepulchre," he said.

Excited by novelty, the girls enthusiastically accepted. The three of them walked up the last stretch of the Via Dolorosa. When they stood before an iron gate with a sign that read HOLY SEPUL-CHRE, Jamal said, "For centuries before the struggle with the Jews over the city, we had to battle for it with the Christians."

The girls and their father decided to pause for a minute. The heat was stifling, and Rania wanted a glass of water. To their left was a little souvenir shop. Many of the items on sale there seemed mysterious to Miral and Rania, particularly the wooden crosses and the crowns of thorns. An old man sitting on a straw stool looked up from the copy of *Al-Quds* he had been reading intently, signaled Jamal to approach, and gave him a bottle of water. The two men began to talk, while the children watched the groups of pilgrims that thronged the entrance to the basilica. After a few minutes, the old man rose to his feet, and he and Jamal walked toward the church. Miral and Rania, still fascinated by the many souvenirs in the shop, lagged behind and had to run to catch up with the men just before they merged with the stream of pilgrims. The girls followed Jamal and the shopkeeper and remained silent.

Once they were in the church, the old man stopped every so often, leaned on his stick, and talked about the significance of a rock or a lantern. Miral failed to understand much of his discourse—she didn't know who the Copts were or the Syriac Or-thodox Jacobites or the Armenians or the Orthodox Greeks—but she saw priests with long beards and funny hats. They passed by,

swinging lanterns of incense and intoning incomprehensible lita-
nies. All this, combined with the acrid air, which was heavy with
myrrh, incense, and the fumes of oil lamps, made Miral feel disturbed and exhausted when she stepped out again into the sunlight. Then the old man raised his stick and pointed at a minaret a
few paces away.

"That's the Mosque of Omar," he said. "Omar was the second
caliph. The Orthodox patriarch of Jerusalem invited him to come
and receive the keys to the city. Omar arrived at noon, the hour of
prayer, and the patriarch invited him to enter the Church of the
Holy Sepulchre and pray. But the caliph did not wish to do so, from
fear that one day the Muslims of the city might claim a right to
build a mosque on the spot where he had prayed. He was a wise
man, and he would do everything he could to protect the equilibrium of the various religious communities. That is the true spirit
of Islam."

On the way home, Miral thought that her city was indeed a
complicated one, where a mystery revealed itself at every corner,
or at least the next time you came across a place of worship with
an obscure name.

Eventually, a woman's angry voice interrupted Miral's trance.
The woman was blonde, carrying a small child in one arm, and
engaged in a heated discussion with a clothing vendor. In point
of fact, what they were having was not really a discussion, given
that the woman did all the talking while the man stared at her
impassively.

The woman saw the girls and their father and addressed them,
saying in English, "He is a horrible man. I won't spend thirty-five
dollars on a dress."

After the woman left, the vendor finally opened his mouth,

revealing an incomplete, yellowing set of teeth. "She was pretending to be an English tourist, but I heard her speaking Hebrew to her child. That's why I asked her for thirty-five dollars instead of thirty-five shekels," he said, laughing with satisfaction.

It was difficult for Jamal to explain to his daughters the origin of such antagonism without influencing their vision of the world. He wanted them to grow up with respect for people of other races. But he knew he would have to explain to them one day that the situation was the result of many battles fought by religious fanatics for possession of Jerusalem, year after year, century after century. The paths that made them different had sometimes come into being merely for political or economical expedience or for reasons that had long been forgotten. Many believed that their path was the only one, and in the name of that many were sacrificed; while others hoped that even separate paths that were stained with so much blood could move along in the same direction. As he ordered a chicken in a rotisserie, Jamal thought that he belonged to the second group.

The night before they returned to Dar El-Tifel, the girls would always lie down beside Jamal and talk without stopping. They would try to speak in turn, but mostly they babbled at the same time until they fell asleep. Then Jamal would gently lift them up and carry one and then the other to the bed they shared. Often Rania, knowing she had to go back to the school, would be in a daze the next morning, and so Jamal had to put his oratorical skills to work, aided by Miral, who loved to dream up new magical ways to convince her sister to return to school.

4

Within a few years of entering the school, Miral became a spirited child, having shed the melancholy of her early days in Dar El-Tifel.

Twice a year, Hind and the head of the elementary school would visit the classrooms to hand out report cards. This was a genuine ceremony, in which the ten girls with the highest grades in their class would be called up, one by one, to the front of the room, where they would stand in a row while all their classmates applauded. One day, when Miral was in the third grade, to her great surprise she heard her name called out first and was unable to move. Hind beckoned her to approach the teacher's desk, and the other girls burst into applause.

When he learned of his daughter's accomplishment, Jamal was moved and wanted to buy her a gift. Miral asked Rania to choose it for her, and her sister said she'd pick out a new dress and a doll with black hair and dark skin. And so Jamal and his two daughters made their way to the toy market, but it turned out that all the dolls in Jerusalem had blonde hair and very fair complexions. Rania would not yield, and Miral began to feel irritated as well, for she couldn't understand why there weren't any dolls that looked like her. Their father told them not to get upset, for dolls as beautiful as they were, he told his daughters, were rare, and the more time they spent looking for one, the lovelier it would be.

In the end, their aunt in Haifa managed to find a doll with Middle Eastern features, and she truly turned out to be the most beautiful doll that the two little girls had ever seen.

As the years went by, Miral made friends with many girls her age, but more than anything else she loved to listen to the older girls' accounts of their lives outside of school. Fortunately, some of these tales had happy endings, but nearly all of them, particularly the stories of Aziza and Sahar, confirmed her sense that the world outside was a horrible place.

Aziza was eleven when she first went back to Gaza for summer vacation. Her grandmother was waiting for her. Aziza's father had been killed, like many other fedayeen in the bloody civil war in Lebanon. Her mother had remarried, in the process abandoning her three daughters to her first husband's family, an Arab tradition. Aziza's grandmother was very poor, occupying a damp hovel in a refugee camp on the outskirts of Gaza City. Every summer since the reopening of the border, Aziza's uncle, who lived in Egypt, would come to visit his mother, bringing with him a few presents and some money.

Aziza knew that her uncle intended to marry her to his son and was only waiting until she reached the proper age. Soon after her fifteenth birthday, her uncle and cousin arrived in Gaza. Aziza knew the cousin and talked to him a little, but she didn't like him, finding him as repellent as his father, with his greasy hair and bad breath.

The following autumn, the uncle went to Dar El-Tifel to ask

Hind to allow Aziza to leave the school. Hind had him shown into her office, where the man sat down heavily on the chair and crossed his legs. The hard look on Hind's face made him sit up immediately and arrange his legs in a more decorous manner.

After clearing his throat, he announced, "I want to take my niece to Egypt with me."

"Ah, yes?" was Hind's only reply.

"She's a woman now, and I want to marry her to my son. Please understand my position, Miss Husseini. This is a piece of luck for the girl. My son is a very good match, and soon she'll have to get married anyway, so we might as well do it straightaway and keep it all in the family, don't you agree?"

Hind disregarded the question and asked Hidaya to go and call Aziza. When the girl arrived, Hind had the uncle escorted into the hall, telling him to wait there.

The interview with Aziza was brief. The girl was adamant: she had no wish to marry her cousin. Hind smiled and did not insist, because for her the girl's will was the only thing that counted. After dismissing her, Hind asked Hidaya to fetch the uncle and bring him back into her office.

"I'm sorry," she told him, trying to conceal the disgust she felt for him. "Aziza is opposed to this marriage. Now you must understand my position," she continued, using the same words and tone that the man had employed a short while before. "I can't force one of my girls to take such a step if she does not wish to do so."

The uncle flew into a rage, leaping to his feet and clenching his right fist as he threatened to denounce her to the authorities. Hind, unimpressed, was intractable. In truth, the reputation and the fame she enjoyed made the man's recriminations futile. He was immediately shown the door.

After that, Aziza never returned to Gaza. Every so often she would feel remorse that she could no longer see her grandmother, who was too old and weak to visit her. One stifling June day, however, Aziza learned that her grandmother had died on her way to Jerusalem.

Sahar was a beautiful girl who loved to dress up. In the morning, before going down to breakfast, she would spend a long time brushing her hair, and in the evening she repeated the same operation, proudly admiring her reflection in the mirror. She used no cosmetics, because school regulations forbade them, but she kept a box hidden under one of the floor tiles. In that box was a tiny makeup bag she had traded with one of the cooks in exchange for a few English lessons. Whenever anyone asked her about her family, she would say that her mother died during an Israeli attack on her city and that she had never met her father. But her schoolmates knew that her father had left his wife and infant daughter not long after Sahar was born. After a few years, the wife fell in love with another man. This one promised to marry her, but—as he explained—he had many children of his own, and there was no room in his house for a child who didn't belong to him. Sahar's mother didn't hesitate; early the next morning she abandoned her four-year-old daughter in the shack where they lived and went to Jaffa, the home of her new husband.

Sahar stayed shut up in the shack all day, waiting for her mama to return. She found some milk and a bit of bread on the table. She waited and waited, and after night fell, she left the shack and went looking for her mother. She called her name again and again, but the street noises drowned out the child's voice. After a while, she grew hungry and sleepy and decided to turn back. But she couldn't find her way home anymore. Weary and dejected, she gave in to a fit of weeping, and then she fell asleep on the sidewalk.

She woke up in an unfamiliar bed and was about to cry when her gaze was drawn to a figure sitting in an armchair. After wishing her a good morning, Hind asked what her name was and whether she remembered what had happened to her the night before. Sahar wept as she recounted what she knew, what she had understood. Miriam held the child in her arms as Sahar said, "I'm sure Mama has lost her way. She can't find our street, just like me." Then Hind told her, "You can stay here with us until she does."

At Dar El-Tifel, Sahar became infamous among her schoolmates for the haughty airs she put on whenever she felt she was being observed. She was always alone, and whenever she spoke to anyone, it was only to describe the princely life she'd led before her mother died. The other girls regarded her with irritation, but her beauty intimidated them, even though they knew she was lying. And so they would listen to her in silence, pretending to believe her. And they watched her from afar, awaiting the moment when the sandcastle she had built for herself would start to crumble and the real Sahar would finally appear.

In 1982 three thousand Palestinians were killed in the Sabra and Shatila refugee camps in Lebanon, perpetrated by Maronite Phalangists with the protection and cooperation of the Israeli army. After news spread of the massacres, the tranquil atmosphere of Dar El-Tifel was altered. The girls of the senior class wanted to take part in a demonstration that was being organized jointly by Palestinians and by Israeli pacifists to protest the Israeli invasion of Lebanon. The authorities had not forbidden the demonstration, but Hind was undecided and conflicted about the girls' participation. On the one hand, she was wounded by the cruelty of the massacre, which surpassed in ferocity the one at Deir Yassin. And she understood the girls' indignation, which reminded her of her own reactions when she was young. But on the other hand, Hind feared for her school. At the last minute, she decided not to allow the girls to go. She had recently begun to feel that the Israeli authorities were keeping an eye on her and Dar El-Tifel. She had always been obliged to obtain permits from the Israelis when she wished to travel, but what she needed most were documents for the children who had been collected from the streets and who had no known relatives. For several months now, the Israeli authorities had blocked the issuing of documents to anyone who did not have a birth certificate. Through acquaintances in one of the city's hospitals, Hind had nevertheless succeeded in obtaining birth certificates, already signed and made out by friends of hers who worked in the hospital. She understood that she needed to give these orphans an identity so in the future they could obtain a driver's license and work within a legal system. But Hind's righteous nature made her fear that this circumspect method might one day be discovered.

In the end, even the most resolute girls were persuaded to desist, in great part thanks to the intervention of the school's most authoritative teachers, among them Abdullah, the gym teacher.

If for many of the girls in the school Hind was like a mother, Abdullah was like a father. Short and thickset, he was a strong, good-natured man proud of his sportive body. When gym classes were over, he would always reward the younger girls with sweets and caramels, and encourage the older ones to dedicate themselves to athletics as much as they did to their studies. He was Miral's favorite teacher, and she found in him a person willing to engage in dialogue and debate. He was a subversive and provocative force in the mostly conservative community of the school, and Miral admired him for it.

When she ran her four hundred meter, Miral felt happy, in harmony with herself and with the world. She saw only the red earth passing swiftly under her feet and thought of nothing at all until she saw Abdullah, with his stopwatch in hand, urging her on. Some years later, while running away from the Israeli police during a demonstration, she would remember with gratitude her instructor's voice: "Knowing how to run is always useful in life."

In addition to being an excellent teacher, Abdullah was one of the city's leading experts on Palestinian history. The most disparate rumors circulated around him, making him a mysterious figure long before the Halabi sisters entered the school. Miral knew that he had served time in prison for political reasons before Hind hired him. The nails missing from most of the fingers of his left hand appeared to confirm the rumor that he had been tortured while in custody. Contradictory rumors explained why he had ended up in prison: some said he was a fighter in the Popular Front for the Liberation of Palestine, an outlawed organization, while others maintained that he held a prominent position in the inner circles of the Palestinian resistance movement. What seemed certain was that he had refused to provide any information under torture, and that had earned him the esteem of Jerusalem's Arab community.

In the spring, when the heat was beginning to make itself known, Miral loved to spend afternoons reading the books that Abdullah would lend her. In this way she discovered the most beautiful novels of Palestinian literature, including Ghassan Kanafani's *Men in the Sun* and *Return to Haifa*, and began to understand important events in the history of the troubled Palestinian people. The books were engrossing, the stories almost always tragic. Under the big magnolia tree on the east side of the garden, Miral got her first glimpse of the subtle connections and invisible threads that official history does not record.

One day Abdullah came to her and said ceremoniously, "Now you've read enough to know what the *nakba* is." He gazed at his left hand for an instant, drew a deep breath, and went on: "The catastrophe, the disaster. The creation of the State of Israel in Palestine unfortunately caused the dispersion of our people. It's difficult to explain, something that every Palestinian feels inside, like an incurable wound, like a short circuit in our history. What we're living through is a terrible historical paradox."

Miral did not completely grasp the teacher's words but understood that she had, perhaps, found a name for the malaise she sometimes felt.

In the years that followed, after Miral visited the refugee camps and participated in the First Intifada, the Palestinian popular uprising in 1987, that malaise would be transformed into a desire to do something tangible, no matter how small, for her people, who were still waiting.

5

The first time Miral went into a Jewish neighborhood in Jerusalem, she was thirteen years old.

On the afternoon of the previous day, a Thursday, Jamal had gone to Dar El-Tifel to fetch his daughters. Miral had watched the English teacher, a petite woman with short hair, and her father conversing at length. Her father seemed embarrassed, frequently touching his head with the palm of his hand and never looking the teacher in the eyes. Then he turned toward Miral, who had just heard him say, "It seems it was only yesterday that I first held her in my arms."

The last few years had indeed gone by in a flash, but apart from the appearance of a large color television set in the place of the old black and white, and a few new Persian rugs, her father's house had remained almost exactly the same. The jasmine bush had become a tree, and now its branches almost reached the roof. The pomegranate tree had become taller and denser, and on the hottest summer days it provided pleasant shade. And in that same time, Miral and Rania had become two slender and graceful young girls. Miral resembled her mother, with exotic Middle Eastern features, sharp and soft at the same time; Rania had beautiful dark skin and fuller lips than her sister. Until that moment, Jamal had not noticed, or had not wished to notice, the recent changes in his daughters. His mind refused to accept the inexorable passage of time, and he couldn't believe that many years had gone by since the death of his wife.

His daughters, he suddenly realized on that autumn afternoon, were indeed grown up. Miral, in fact, needed a bra.

The following morning, Jamal went to call on Nur, a kindly neighbor who had recently celebrated her fortieth birthday. She had been widowed young and had no children but possessed an acute maternal sense. That was why Jamal consulted her whenever his paternal instinct was insufficient to cope with raising two girls.

Although Jamal considered Nur an intelligent woman, she wasn't particularly well regarded in the neighborhood because she spoke Hebrew perfectly, having worked in an Israeli shop, and had recently begun a relationship with an Israeli man, a Druze. Jamal had always come to the woman's defense, in an effort to counter the increasing animosity toward her, a dislike nourished by a series of rumors that, as they passed from mouth to mouth, became ever more nasty. This peculiar attachment stemmed chiefly from the fact that Nur and Nadia had been good friends but also from Jamal's admiration for Nur's independent streak.

The year before, Jamal had covered the same short distance and, purple faced with embarrassment, knocked on Nur's wooden door. As soon as she opened it, he blurted out, but almost in a whisper, "Miral has got her first period. What should I do?" Nur's broad smile made him realize that there was no reason to worry.

"This time," he said as soon as the heavy door opened, "all I need is some advice about how to buy Miral a bra."

That afternoon Jamal drove Nur and Miral along the street that skirted the walls of the Old City. They were headed for the commercial zone of Jewish Jerusalem, where a myriad of clothing stores, one next to the other, could be found. Greatly curious, Miral gazed at the unfamiliar streets. "How different the buildings are, taller and more modern!" she exclaimed in wonderment. "And so many cars!" After their vehicle crossed into West Jerusalem, she thought, "Everyone seems to be running, not walking. It's as though they're all in a big hurry to get somewhere."

On Ben Yehuda Street, Miral was reminded a little of Haifa, the city where her mother was born and where they went every summer to visit their aunt. Miral was struck by the girls in miniskirts and high heels, by the outdoor cafés where men and women were happily chatting together. The brightly lit shop windows contrasted fluorescently with the darkness of the narrow streets in the Arab Quarter, where the buildings were sometimes crammed so close together that the sun's rays could barely penetrate.

The area they were driving through was just as she'd imagined the cities of Europe would be, but she had never imagined that such a place existed only a few blocks from where she lived. Occasionally, she had seen the western parts of the city from atop the Mount of Olives, but with different eyes, deploring the tall hotels built up against the Old City's walls and the enormous buildings that seemed to besiege the white ramparts of Jerusalem.

Suddenly, Jamal slowed the car and, at a sign from Nur, stopped in front of a shop window filled with brightly colored lingerie. Nur accompanied Miral into the shop while Jamal waited outside; he would go in later but only to pay. Miral chose a simple model made of soft cotton, and picked out three different colors: one white, one pink, and one red. Her father was unequivocally opposed to the red one, and so Miral and Nur compromised with one white and two pink.

Nur had dinner with them that night, and after preparing the coffee, she went back home. Miral watched her father as he waited for the coffee to settle and then asked him point-blank: "Say, Papa, why don't you and Nur get married? You would make a handsome couple."

Jamal seemed flustered and tried to swallow, but his saliva went down the wrong way, and Miral was obliged to pound him on the back to keep him from choking. They began to laugh but eventually managed to regain a somewhat more serious tone, whereupon Jamal replied: "Because I don't love her. She's very dear to me as a friend, but in my life I've loved only your mother. And I still do."

6

Miral became good friends with Amal, a classmate who was a year younger than she was. During warm spring evenings, the two of them would have long conversations in the room they shared, illuminated only by a candle and the pale moonlight filtering through the window.

Unlike Miral, Amal was uninterested in politics and remained steeped in the peasant culture of her family. An intelligent and sensitive girl, she was the only one capable of counterbalancing the restlessness of her friend. Amal, who also had a younger sister at the school, didn't much like going home for summer vacation, which meant leaving her schoolmates and the tranquil atmosphere of Dar El-Tifel to work in her family's fields.

Amal was born in a Palestinian village near Ramallah and given as her name the Arabic word for "hope." Her father died when she was six, and her mother remarried. This second husband was a man who owned and cultivated various fields near the village. Although the family was fairly well-off, Amal's parents asked Hind to take charge of their daughters so there would be more time to devote to their crops and sheep. Hind accepted. She liked the girls.

At the beginning of each summer, Amal's mother came to fetch her daughters from Dar El-Tifel, and would bring them back punctually on the first day of school, turning over to Hind a check for their support, along with a basket of fruit and vegetables as a gift.

Upon her return from summer vacation one year, Amal was suddenly distant. Miral had rushed to tell her that they would once again share a room; then she gave Amal the T-shirt she'd bought in Haifa for her thirteenth birthday, which fell in early September. It read, BE HAPPY. DON'T WORRY. Amal would not look at her, and barely thanked her, then went up to their room and went to bed. Miral felt that she was hiding something, but no matter how much Miral insisted, Amal wouldn't say what was wrong.

Amal's gaiety seemed to have vanished. Her teachers noticed a decline in her scholastic performance; she often fell asleep in class, hardly touched her food, and spent a lot of time in the bathroom. After having been informed of the situation, Hind decided to have Amal looked at by the school physician, her cousin Amir. When Amal appeared at the door of the infirmary, Amir welcomed her with a big smile, in an attempt to put her at ease while trying to hide his own nervousness. The symptoms that had been reported to him did not, in fact, leave much room for doubt.

The tests proved that the girl was pregnant. When she was questioned, Amal replied that she had known a boy but that she would never reveal his name, and then she committed herself to an absolute silence.

Amir went to knock on the door of Hind's office, aware that he was going to confront her with one of the most difficult decisions of her life. In the meantime, Hind had been pacing back and forth nervously for more than an hour, pausing at the window every now and then to watch a group of the youngest girls playing outside.

"She's only a child!" Amir exclaimed as he opened the door. Her cousin's scowl sufficed to make Hind understand that her worst-case prediction had proved true.

Before her cousin could say another word, Hind began to cry out, "Who was it? *Who was it?*"

Amir had never seen her in such a fury. He sat down on one of the leather armchairs before replying.

"She wouldn't give me any details," he said in a grave voice, slowly drawing out the words as though it cost him an effort to pronounce them. "She spoke in vague terms about a boy, but she wouldn't tell me his name or anything else about him."

Hind sank down in the other armchair and asked, "How many months?"

"Two. We still have time, if that's what you intend to do."

Meanwhile, Amal had gone back to her room, her eyes swollen from weeping. Even though the sun was high in the sky, she undressed and went to bed. All she wanted to do was sleep, to sleep and not think. The memory of Mustafa obsessed her. Of all her memories, the tenderest recollection was of the day she met him.

She was returning from work in the fields, carrying a big basket of eggplants on her head. In the past few months, her body, although still immature, had begun to grow shapelier, rounding off, little by little, the angularities of childhood. Even though the sun was setting, the air was still stifling. The intense green of the hills around Ramallah was turning to straw yellow, and the landscape showed itself barer with each passing day.

Amal rounded a bend in the road, and her village came into sight. From where she was, it seemed to be perched precariously on the very top of the hill, almost on the verge of sliding down. The village looked uninhabited; the only sign of life was the smoke rising from the chimneys of the white houses. She stopped to rest a moment. The air was still and hot, and sweat plastered her black hair against her forehead.

Amal heard the sound of a motor approaching: first a barely perceptible buzzing, and then more and more insistent. A boy on a moped rounded a curve a little farther downhill. He was going fairly slowly, skillfully zigzagging in an attempt to avoid the roadway's rocks and holes, leaving behind him a wake of dark dust. When he was a few meters away from her, he slowed to a stop. He was wearing a cap and an oil-stained T-shirt, and when he smiled, he revealed two rows of perfect white teeth. Amal knew him by sight: he was Mustafa, the son of the village mechanic, a teenager two or three years older than she was.

"Do you want a ride? I'm going to the village," he said, smiling the whole time.

Exhausted by the sun and encouraged by his big smile, Amal could see no harm in accepting the invitation, and she gave the boy an affirmative nod. Mustafa tied the basket to the vehicle and re-started it. Amal climbed on behind him, and after a few meters, in order to keep from falling off, she put her arms around his waist.

Suddenly, Amal forgot the heat and her weariness, and she wished that the road were much, much longer. When Mustafa felt her arms around his body and her weight lightly pressing against his back, a thrill of delight such as he had never felt before ran through him.

On the following days, her mother and stepfather were astonished to see Amal, who was usually rather reluctant to go to work, leave early for the fields with a smile on her face. Every afternoon Mustafa would offer to go down to Ramallah to buy some spare part needed in his father's shop. Without ever fixing an appointment, the two young people ended up meeting on the same curve at the end of each day.

One day Mustafa arrived early. He parked his moped on the shoulder of the road and walked down the slope that led to Amal's family's field. He saw her busily harvesting grapes as a light wind tousled her long hair. He knew that she usually bound up her hair with a red kerchief when she worked, but he noticed that every time he came to pick her up she would untie her hair and let it fall loosely on her shoulders.

He liked her as well with the kerchief as without, but when he saw her on that day, with drops of sweat on her brow, and very likely in the hollow between the breasts he could barely make out through the T-shirt she was wearing, his heart beat faster. While she had her back to him, he crept up to her slowly, without making any noise, and tickled her right arm with a blade of grass. Amal turned around at once and was surprised at seeing Mustafa. He moved closer to her, and soon they were looking into each other's eyes from a few centimeters away. Suddenly, Mustafa embraced her, and Amal's arms fell naturally around his waist. Mustafa felt his temples pounding the way they did when he hit top speed as he raced down the last stretch of road before entering the city.

Their naked bodies came together under the shade of a tree, the experience giving new meaning to the deep attraction they felt for each other. On the way back to the moped, Mustafa picked two figs and offered one to Amal, tucking a lock of her hair behind her ear so that he could get a good look at her face. She slowed down and gazed at him, savoring the fruit's sweet red pulp. As they rode home, neither of them said a word. Amal squeezed Mustafa's chest so tightly that he had to make an effort to maintain control of his motorbike. They made their good-byes, as always, with a "so long" and a simple wave of the hand. But their eyes were still embraced in a kiss.

The following evening, Amal waited in vain for more than an hour, sitting on the low stone wall at the roadside, hoping to see Mustafa round the curve at any minute, her eyes fixed on the road below. In the silence interrupted only by the chirping of crickets, she listened attentively, hoping to hear the hum of the motor, which she had learned to recognize when it was still very far away.

When the sun disappeared definitively behind the hill, Amal picked up her basket full of grapes and set out toward the village in the dark, tears running down her cheeks.

She had heard the older girls at school tell stories like this, about boys who disappeared after they got what they were looking for. Even though she and Mustafa had never spoken for very long, she couldn't imagine that he would be someone like that. Trying her best to look straight ahead, she went to the mechanic's shop where he worked and asked where she could find him.

Mustafa's father came out, wiping the grease off his hands. "He didn't give you a ride home this evening?" he asked, smiling tentatively. "He went to Ramallah this morning and hasn't come back yet. I thought he was with you."

The basket Amal was holding fell to the ground, and grapes scattered over the dusty street.

Mustafa had arrived in Ramallah before noon. He'd gone barreling down the ten kilometers that separated his village from the city, reaching such a speed in the final descent that his cap had flown off and he had been obliged to turn back and collect it. The sooner he brought his father the manifold he wanted, the sooner he'd be able to go to Amal. But the parts shop was closed. A demonstration was going on, and the rolling shutters of the shops were all down. Resigned to waiting, he had gone to a stand and ordered an orange juice. After half an hour had passed and no one had appeared at the shop, he decided to walk toward the center of town. In the distance, he heard shots and the screams of demonstrators, among whom Mustafa was sure he'd find the boy who worked in the parts shop, for he was one of the leaders of the resistance in Ramallah.

Mustafa had never taken part in a demonstration. None had ever been held in his village, and he preferred repairing motors to throwing stones. He walked down a narrow lane leading to the main street. Tear gas stung his eyes, and while his breath grew shorter and shorter, he looked to his right and saw, a hundred meters away, a group of boys, some of them very young. Among the slowly retreating group clutching rocks in their hands, Mustafa recognized the boy from the parts shop. His movements were sure and agile, and his nose and mouth were covered by a handkerchief. Mustafa waved to him, but the youth was enveloped in a cloud of smoke and failed to see him. For a moment, Mustafa thought the best thing to do would be to give up, go back to the juice stand, and wait for the demonstration to end. But the thought of not seeing Amal was intolerable, and all he really wanted from his friend were the keys to the parts shop. Mustafa would take the part he wanted, and early the next morning he'd return to Ramallah with the keys and the money he owed.

Mustafa looked at the young shopkeeper, who still didn't notice him. Mustafa decided he was too close to turn away. He started walking toward the boy, careful to hug the walls of the buildings as he advanced. The air had become unbreathable, and the distance still to be covered seemed immense. He saw a narrow side street and decided to turn onto it, but a tear gas canister whizzed past and struck the shutter behind him. He stood still, paralyzed by fear, suddenly aware of the danger he was in. After a few seconds, he could no longer see and breathing became difficult. The soldiers had come closer. One at a time, the boys advanced toward them, threw rocks and Molotov cocktails, and then ran back to where they had started. Less than ten meters away, in the midst of the smoke and dust, Mustafa glimpsed the boy from the parts shop again.

Mustafa broke into a run, determined for all his wheezing and coughing to cross the street, but he had gone only a few meters before he fell to the ground with a tear gas canister lodged between his shoulder blades. A trickle of blood came out of his mouth and mingled with the dust of the thoroughfare. Two boys ran over to him, clumsily extracted the canister, and dragged him along the ground by the feet for more than fifty meters. Together with the other wounded, he was loaded into a car, which sped away, tires squealing, amid the shouts of the crowd. By the time he reached the first-aid station, he was dead. The seat of the automobile that had transported him was drenched with his blood. The doctors told the boys who brought him there that if they hadn't pulled the tear gas canister out of him, he wouldn't have lost so much blood, and then maybe it would have been possible to save him.

The next day, Mustafa was wrapped in a shroud, and someone spread the Palestinian flag over his lifeless body. The funeral procession traversed the village, and there were many mourners from Ramallah as well. The crowd applauded, honoring Mustafa as a hero. The boy from the parts shop asked to bear the coffin together with Mustafa's relatives and fired several rifle shots into the air in homage to the dead boy.

Amal trudged along in the procession, from beginning to end, without enough strength to raise her eyes from the ground.

She didn't want to get out of bed the next day, but her parents, who knew nothing of what had happened, made her go to the fields as she always did. "The fruits and vegetables must be harvested each day," they told her. "You can't wait until tomorrow."

And so she went out and worked the entire day, but it was impossible for her not to think about Mustafa. Taking advantage of her solitude in the fields, she gave herself over to incessant weeping. At the end of the day, she removed the kerchief from her head, loosened her hair, and sat on the usual wall, not far from the curve in the road. She waited until darkness made it impossible to distinguish the line of the horizon from the hills. Only then did she realize that Mustafa was really gone.

When the summer holidays came to an end and Amal returned to Jerusalem, her life could no longer be what it was before. She found herself unable to talk about what had happened, not even with her best friends, not even with Miral. She wanted to forget the whole thing. At other times, however, she would get in bed, hide under the covers, and with open eyes try to remember everything, right down to the tiniest details. She swore to herself that she would never say anything to anyone, that what had happened would be her secret.

During her sleepless afternoons, she would often feel Miral's hand stroking her hair. Amal would pretend to fall asleep, and after a little while, her friend would get up, close the curtains, and silently leave the room. Amal would have liked to speak to her, to explain, but she couldn't.

After Amir left her office, Hind sent someone to pick up Amal's mother and bring her to Dar El-Tifel. There was not a moment to lose.

The conversation between those two utterly different women remained one of the most difficult experiences in Hind's life.

Neither of them had ever liked the other very much. Amal's mother respected Hind but thought that the annual payment of boarding and tuition charges exempted her from the necessity of worrying about her daughters for the length of the school year. Now she had been summoned to Dar El-Tifel and therefore obliged to miss at least a day of work. For her part, Hind was certain that the woman had enrolled her daughters in the orphanage school because she considered it a fairly economical way of getting rid of them, whereas if they had stayed at home, she would have had to take care of them.

Hind began the conversation without beating around the bush. "Your daughter must have had relations with a boy this summer, and now she's pregnant." She observed the eyes and sun-worn face of the woman sitting across from her.

"That's impossible—she's only a child. There must be some mistake."

"Madam, we've taken all the steps necessary to verify her condition, and unfortunately there is no mistake. Do you by any chance know who the boy could be?"

"Now that I think about it, she did act strangely this summer. It was like she was—well—happy. That's it, happy." She seemed about to add something but then stopped talking with her mouth half-open.

"And then?"

"And then, I don't know. She turned sad all of a sudden. She didn't want to go out to the fields anymore, and she would hide under her sheets and cry."

"And you didn't ask her about the reason for this sudden sadness?"

"Look, my daughter's mood changes are no affair of mine. I already have enough to think about, what with my work and my other daughter, to say nothing of my husband."

Hind stiffened, but she forced herself to remain calm. "In other words, you didn't notice anything. No boy in Amal's company, nothing like that."

"No. However, if you really want to know, someone did tell me they always saw her coming home from the fields on the back of a moped, and the driver was a boy from the village. Maybe it was him. We sure won't be able to ask him, though."

"Why not?" Hind inquired, increasingly astonished and offended by the woman's attitude.

"Because he's dead. He went to a demonstration and wound up dead. The sort of thing that happens to people who don't mind their own business."

"I understand. Now, in regard to your daughter, we have to—"

"I don't have to do a thing, dear lady. I don't want to see that daughter of mine again. She has dishonored us!" Amal's mother exclaimed, as she jumped to her feet.

Hind could no longer tolerate the paradoxical situation. She stood up and poured herself a glass of water. "Fine," she said. "Then you certainly won't have any difficulty signing this document authorizing the abortion."

The mother merely shrugged and signed the paper in an uncertain hand.

"And now please go away. I don't wish to see you anymore," Hind said, addressing the woman as firmly as she possibly could.

Amal's mother looked at the headmistress with something like supplication in her eyes. "Try to understand," she said. "I don't want to ruin my reputation for someone like her. And if the boy's dead, we live in a little village, and—"

"A child," Hind said, interrupting her. "Your daughter is still a child. She doesn't even realize what she's done. And you want to punish her and take away the affection she needs now more than ever. That's unforgivable. I'll take care of her future. And now please go away, and don't bother to come back for Amal next summer."

And so the woman abandoned her daughter to her fate, and Hind decided that Amal should have an abortion. This was not an easy choice to begin with, and it was made more difficult because several members of the school council were opposed to it. In the end, Hind succeeded in imposing her will and ordered that the matter be kept a closely guarded secret. "The girl's reputation depends on us. No one must know what has happened. Believe me when I tell you that this is a painful decision for me, too, but we have no alternative," she said at the end of the meeting.

When Miral awoke the next morning, she noticed that Amal was already up, putting clothes into a little suitcase. Hind came into the room and said, "Are you ready, Amal? The car is waiting for you in the courtyard."

Miral watched the automobile slowly disappear down the drive. Her friend was inside and so was Dr. Amir.

A few days later, Amal returned to the school. Her face was hollow and her eyes even more so. She had recovered none of her former lightheartedness. Miral, who had been told that her friend had gone into a clinic because she wasn't well, often saw her put a hand on her stomach and one day asked her why she had needed to be taken to a clinic and what had been done to her there. Amal said it was appendicitis.

In the following weeks, she became more and more reclusive, as if she wanted to distance herself from everyone. By the time winter was approaching, the two friends were exchanging only fleeting glances. In January, Amal left for Germany, where she completed her studies thanks to a scholarship that Hind had obtained for her.

Miral would learn Amal's story only many years later, when she saw her again in Berlin. Amal was teaching architecture at a university. There she'd met her husband, who was also an architect. They had three children, and she'd named their firstborn Mustafa.

That winter was one of the coldest in years. One night it began to snow and did not stop until the following afternoon. Miral looked out over Jerusalem, covered totally in white; the snow had softened the contrasts between the Old City and the buildings in the modern parts of town, and the distance between the Arab and Jewish quarters seemed to have been shortened.

Miral continued to worry about Amal. The only news she had of her friend came through Hind. "There must be a lot of snow in Germany, too," she thought; maybe that would bring them closer together. Rania was obsessed by the fear that because of the snow their father wouldn't be able to come the next day, and yet she was also leaning with her elbows on the windowsill, staring dreamy eyed, like her sister, at that magnificent white blanket that covered everything.

On the next afternoon, the lobby of their building, which at that hour was usually crowded with students' relatives, remained silent and deserted. Many of the girls, after waiting for more than half an hour, went sadly back to their rooms, for no one had passed through the gate at the bottom of the drive.

Miral and Rania decided to wait a little longer. After all, they thought, their father didn't live all that far away. Their patience was rewarded, because even though the snow had started to come down again, Jamal appeared at the gate shortly before the custodian closed it. Their father's hair was white with snow, and he was wrapped in a black overcoat. His daughters watched as he ascended the drive with uncertain steps, his black shoes sinking into a fresh drift.

Miral and Rania's joy was uncontainable. They began to skip back and forth around the room, and the clamor they made could be heard throughout the dormitories. Their papa was the only one who had braved the storm to visit his daughters.

PART FIVE

—

Hani

1

Three times a week, a group of girls from Dar El-Tifel traveled to the Kalandia refugee camp, just outside Ramallah, where they would distribute food to children and keep them company for the afternoon. Some of the girls gave lessons in Arabic or mathematics, while others organized group activities like drawing or sports.

As soon as the children in the refugee camp saw the bus turn onto the camp road, lifting up a cloud of red dust, they would abandon the little soccer field, which was covered with holes and puddles, and go to meet their visitors. Miral always brought sweets and caramels and distributed them carefully, making sure that no one remained without. Her assignment was to teach a bit of English to children between four and twelve years old.

A cracked blackboard had been set into a ramshackle wooden structure that stood within a semicircle formed of rocks, bricks, and gasoline cans. There the children took their seats with composure that seemed out of place given the surroundings.

One of the boys in the first row was Hassan, an emaciated child of eight, smiling despite the casts on both his arms. Israeli soldiers had caught him and broken them by pressing down with their heavy boots. Hassan couldn't wait for the day when his casts would come off and he could start throwing stones again, even though his father had warned him to stay away from the soldiers and his desperate mother had run after him to try to bring him back home whenever there were demonstrations.

Next to him sat Said, nine years old, with big black eyes and hair covered, like the rest of him, with mud. He, too, was a regular among the rock throwers, despite the beatings he received from his father, who had already lost one son that way.

Despite the shacks of rusty sheet metal, the hovels of earth and straw, the open sewers and piles of garbage that formed a backdrop to the makeshift school, the children dutifully repeated the words Miral wrote on the blackboard, and smiled happily. "They seem almost serene," Miral thought in amazement.

The girls from Jerusalem were the camp children's only contact with the outside world—a world that otherwise seemed to have forgotten them. Indeed, the only regular visitors to the camp were Israeli soldiers, whose reception was altogether different. The children, no matter how small, would collect stones and throw them incessantly, while older boys and young men aimed slingshots at the armored vehicles and jeeps. They knew every escape route, and when chased they would display remarkable agility.

The children told Miral that when the soldiers came at night to arrest someone, the entire camp would awaken, and the refugees would do everything they could to hamper the soldiers' efforts and to keep the wanted person from being caught. "Those are the kinds of games camp children play," Miral thought. Brutal games that left many players stretched out on the ground.

The women of the camp did their part as well. Often, during the Israelis' nocturnal blitzes, they would defy the rigid Muslim sense of modesty by going forth from their houses half-naked to distract the soldiers and gain a few precious seconds for whoever was trying to escape by running over roofs and out into the fields.

At the end of her lesson one day, Miral went up to a boy who always stood apart from the others, leaning on a gasoline drum. At thirteen he was one of the oldest of them, with broad shoulders and a clump of long black hair that totally covered his forehead. At the end of the lesson, he would always remain motionless for a few moments, staring at Miral while the other boys ran to the muddy lot they used as a soccer field and resumed the game that had been interrupted by the arrival of the English teacher.

The boy wore a pair of wrinkled military trousers several sizes too big for him. As he watched Miral's approach, he extracted a cigarette butt from a side pocket and lit up.

"Is it me you don't like, or is it English?" Miral asked with a smile.

The boy took a long drag on what was left of his cigarette. His eyes were half-closed, and little wrinkles formed at the sides of his mouth. "It's not your fault," he said, repeatedly shifting his weight from one foot to the other. "You're great, but I don't want to learn English. I'm the one with problems, not you."

"If you want, we can talk about them."

"No, it's a long story. Besides, you have to get back to Jerusalem."

Miral was intrigued by the assured tone of the boy's response and by the expression of defiance she could read in his face, the look of one whose eyes have already seen too much suffering. She knew very little about him—only that he refused to study English, and that he had turned down a scholarship Hind had managed to find for him and four other boys from the camp to study at a school in Damascus.

"I have a little time," she said, holding his gaze. To underline the seriousness of her words, she sat down right in front of him, on a block of cement that was part of the wall of a demolished house. Khaldun calmly put out his stubby cigarette and contemplated the other boys, who were running after a soccer ball made of rags. Then he stared into Miral's eyes, drew a long sigh, and told her his story from start to finish, hardly pausing for breath and never lowering his gaze.

"My great-grandfather died in a British prison, where he was put for joining the Arab revolt of 1936. My grandfather and grandmother died in Jordan during Black September, in 1970, when—as you must know—many Palestinians were killed there by the bedouin soldiers in the service of King Hussein. Palestinians were oppressed everywhere by Arab regimes. They killed us in Lebanon, in Jordan, in Syria, and here in our homeland. My father was a fedayee with the Popular Front for the Liberation of Palestine. He met my mother in a refugee camp in Jordan, where they were fighting against the Jordanians. Then they went to Lebanon, where I was born, and where my father was killed during one of the clashes between Palestinians and Israeli soldiers during the invasion of Lebanon. All I have left of my father's are these trousers I'm wearing and a little red book with the sayings of Mao Tse-tung. My father underlined one of them: 'Political power grows out of the barrel of a gun.' I also have a photograph of him standing next to George Habash, one of our leaders, holding an automatic weapon and smiling. My father was a brave man. Now I've been living in this place for the past three years, in a tin shack with my mother, her sister, and her sister's family. Why should I learn English or go off to study in Damascus? I don't need that. I love to write stories, but what I need is a rifle, so I can fight and help to take back the land my ancestors have cultivated with olive trees for centuries."

A moment later, they heard a muffled sound, a sort of sharp thud, and Miral saw the shape of a little boy not more than ten years old emerge from a cloud of dust. The boy had climbed up the side of a shack made of a couple of dry brick walls and rusty sheet metal. A brick gave way, taking down with it about half of the unsteady wall. As Miral and Khaldun ran to the shack, they heard shouts and curses coming from inside; the hovel was inhabited. The door opened and an old man appeared, crying out, "Why didn't you warn me that you wanted to bury me alive?"

Khaldun burst into noisy laughter, while Miral looked around her in search of some explanation.

After the old man calmed down, Khaldun shouted at him, "Don't worry, Yassir. The Israelis aren't demolishing your shack. It was only that idiot Said, trying to climb up on your roof again." Then Khaldun resumed laughing, with all the joviality of his thirteen years, as he pointed to Said, who was still groaning and gasping for air amid the rubble and the dust, while shaking off bricks. As she helped Said to his feet, Miral couldn't help but smile.

Old Yassir, however, having realized what had happened, showed no inclination to joke about it. He took a few labored steps toward the boy, lifting his stick with the intention of striking him. But without the support of the knotty olive branch, he teetered and seemed on the point of falling over backward. The sequence repeated itself with each step the old man took: he would brandish his stick and totter, and Said would limp out of his range. In the meantime, Khaldun was holding his sides and howling with laughter. A dense crowd of children, women, and old men gathered, and soon the hilarity had become infectious. Yassir, his skin wizened by age and the sun, continued his improbable pursuit, and Said kept trying to get away, but the other boys prevented him from breaking through the circle of onlookers, throwing him back each time he tried to escape.

The little comedy came to an end when Yassir finally managed to give Said a blow on the head and then fell over backward. Some people ran to assist the old man, helping him up and placing him on a straw chair. Others went to fetch a few pails of water, which they poured over Said's head in an attempt to wash away the dust that covered him so completely he looked floured. When it was ascertained that the boy had survived the ordeal with only a bruise on his calf and a lump on his forehead, most of the curiosity seekers returned to their own shacks. The old man remained seated, still loudly complaining about his house. This litany was interrupted by Khaldun: "Don't worry, Yassir. Tonight you'll sleep at your grand-daughter Fatima's, and tomorrow Said and I and a few other boys will fix up that wall for you so it's better than it was before. At least that'll give us something to do."

"Thank you, my boy, thank you. You're a real prince, just like your father. You always think of others first," Yassir said, giving him a pat on the cheek, whereupon Khaldun turned toward Miral, his eyes filled with pride.

She smiled at him with sincere admiration. "I have to go now. I'm already late," she said. "Otherwise I'll be punished, and then they won't let me leave the school grounds for a week."

On the bus to Jerusalem, Miral gazed back at the refugee camp and thought about Khaldun. Smoke from kitchen fires, over which women were preparing falafel or couscous, rose lazily into the sky. The boy's manner was that of a prisoner shut up in a narrow cell, who with the passage of time has grown so accustomed to reducing the rhythms of his life that he responds to external stimuli with nothing but automatic responses. More than anything else, Miral was struck by the lack of rhetoric, the absolute clearheadedness with which he summarized the dramas that had afflicted his family. There hadn't been the least trace of fatalism in his words. His proud face expressed fortitude and a focus on redemption that Miral had never seen in anyone else. Khaldun's greatest fear was not the possibility of dying in a clash with the Israeli army but the possibility of failing to do his part in his family's century-old struggle for their land. He had worked out—perhaps unconsciously—the project of his life, fashioned in every detail after the model of his father and his grandfather and his great-grandfather and focused on the struggle to drive out the foreign occupiers of Palestine, be they British, Jordanian, or Israeli.

"His intelligence is a more effective weapon than a rifle," Miral thought.

Khaldun, too, thought about Miral after she had gone. He followed her with his eyes as she got on the bus for Jerusalem and wondered why such a beautiful, intelligent girl would waste her time teaching English to kids who would probably never use it. He'd been struck by the way she had looked at him as he was telling his story. She'd gazed at him without the pity he usually read in the eyes of the girls who came to teach at the camp. Khaldun had felt at ease talking to her, and that was a sensation he rarely experienced when he didn't have a rock in his hand and an Israeli tank within range.

The following Monday morning, Miral hurried back to school after a weekend at home, arriving just in time for history class. That afternoon the minibus took her back to the refugee camp. Miral looked at her work there differently now. On the bus she saw

Muna, one of the new girls, a robust teenager who was a year younger than Miral and had long, curly hair and cheerful, calm brown eyes. She hummed continually, and when she wasn't doing that, she would speak about any subject at all and asked a great many questions, so many that the other girls complained about her. But Miral liked her.

"What made you decide to sign up for work in the refugee camp?" Miral asked Muna.

"Do you want to know the truth? There's a boy I like a lot. I met him at Dar El-Tifel and he lives in that camp. So I can see him and make myself a little useful at the same time."

"What a noble motive!" Miral said, laughing.

Muna replied, "You have to be able to lighten up in life. Everything's too serious. I'm tired of that. I want to live, I want to have fun, and you should, too."

"Well, here's your chance to have fun. We've arrived!"

The girls exchanged complicit glances, but Muna's smile vanished at the sight of the refugee camp. "Wow, what a dump."

Miral remarked, "It's a real miracle just to be able to smile and have fun here. You think you can amuse some of these kids? We've brought poster paper and colored pencils. Take some, go on, and try to get them to draw a little."

Children were already running up to the Dar El-Tifel bus to embrace the girls and welcome them. Miral took a group of five or six and started writing English sentences on the blackboard, while Muna, getting over her initial shock, gathered together about ten little ones and led them to a eucalyptus tree. There she spread a cloth on the ground, laid out the white paper and the colored pencils, and invited them to draw whatever they wanted.

Miral tested her imagination, trying to give the children a temporary escape and make them concentrate on something other than what she saw: houses of corrugated metal, where families of seven lived in rooms of only a few square meters, and open drains whose contents mingled with rainwater. The girls' visits were the only moments of normality in the refugee children's endless days.

Miral watched Khaldun, who was sitting on a big rock, with a cigarette that had gone out between his lips. He seemed to be paying attention to the lesson; the usual mocking smile had disappeared from his face. A short while later, the rumble of tanks became audible.

"Soldiers! Soldiers are coming!" one boy shouted.

"They're only passing through, stay calm," Miral replied. However, she soon discovered that they were there to demolish the house of a leader of the intifada.

"We won't let them do it," Khaldun remarked. "It won't be easy for them to knock down that house." He snatched up a stone and started running toward the tanks. A call to alarm shivered through the whole camp, transmitted from shack to shack. Women came running, looking for their children; men gathered in groups. Shouts came from everywhere: "Go away, you bastards! Leave us in peace!" Some panic-stricken children started running to their homes; others hid behind the schoolgirls, covering their faces with their clothes and crying out in fear.

Miral and Muna tried to calm the youngest children, who started trembling and clinging to the girls more tightly. Every incursion of the Israeli soldiers traumatized the young ones, and it would take weeks to make them smile again.

The first sharp explosions could be heard. Tear gas canisters began to fall everywhere. Some were fired high and came down in slow parabolas; others flew horizontally, a couple of meters above the ground. The inhabitants of the camp started throwing stones at the tanks, and the soldiers responded with plastic bullets and tear gas. But after a little while, the plastic bullets gave way to real ones. All that was needed to produce a massacre was one frightened soldier. Soon the air became unbreathable. Miral and Muna picked up the smallest children and began to run, looking for a hiding place. Khaldun turned back to help the girls reach safety.

Although the battle did not last long, it was exceedingly violent. Before they withdrew, the tanks fired a few rounds from the top of the hill that dominated the camp. After the resistance leader's house was leveled, a cloud of dust mixed with tear gas settled over everything. Miral and Muna, together with a group of the youngest children, were running to take refuge inside a big Dumpster. Before they reached it, however, a tear gas grenade grazed Miral and exploded a few centimeters away. The gas stung her eyes, and the frightened children continued to scream. Miral was unable to calm them down. She wondered what kind of adults these children would become after taking in so much terror and violence.

When the barrage was over, the inhabitants of the camp began to dig through the rubble, using their bare hands and makeshift tools. Two bodies emerged from beneath the ruins.

After an interminable wait, an ambulance finally arrived. The two people recovered from the wreckage were seriously injured, both of them with several broken bones, but at least they were alive. Miral cried out when she saw Khaldun nearby, clutching one of the smallest children. He had saved the child by shielding it with his body. An old man had been less lucky; his corpse lay motionless in the dust. The women wept and despaired, and their cries were lost in the unreal silence that had fallen upon the camp. Miral saw one of her little pupils, a seven-year-old boy, sitting on a pile of rubble that used to be his house. He stared into space.

Later, still shaken, Miral and Muna set out for Jerusalem. That evening Hind decided to suspend the teaching initiative in the refugee camp for a few days.

Little by little, Miral felt the anger inside her mounting. She couldn't get the memory of one family she had seen out of her head. After their dwelling had been destroyed before their eyes, they had tried to recover from the ruins their few intact possessions— some children's notebooks, toys, photographs.

"What kind of war is this? A regular army against children with rocks?" Miral thought, as the red sun sank behind the Mount of Olives. "What sense does it make to teach English to children who may not ever become adults?"

A few weeks later, the bus that was once again bringing the girls from Dar El-Tifel to the refugee camp was stopped at an army checkpoint. The Israeli soldiers weren't letting anyone through because there had been clashes in the camp that morning. Miral still wanted to go; she was afraid for Khaldun, Said, and the other children and wanted to make sure they were all right. She got out of the car and approached a soldier who was leaning against a jeep. He was around twenty, with black hair, dark brown eyes, slightly olive skin, and fleshy lips. He could have been an Arab. He smelled strongly of cologne, and he looked her over, head to toe, hesitating here and there along the way, attracted by the charms that were beginning to bloom in her young body. Finally, he lit a cigarette and said, "If you give me a kiss, I'll let you pass."

Miral watched him inhale a mouthful of smoke from his American cigarette. His hands were smooth and perfectly manicured. She looked him in the eyes and said no before walking away.

Then she remembered a path the camp kids had shown her one evening when she stayed past curfew. It would take her at least two hours to go that way, but she'd get there without having to kiss a soldier. Making her way down an embankment covered with weeds, she found herself with a view of Ramallah, and it seemed to her as though she were seeing it for the first time. Everything appeared compressed, the living space reduced to a bare minimum. "How can anyone live in such a place?" she wondered, tripping over a crumpled Coke can.

That morning Khaldun had taken part in the clashes with the Israeli soldiers, and he had gotten closer to the tanks than anyone. Contrary to his practice during English lessons, he was always in the front rank during battles. The hail of stones had been intense and had continued for several hours. Said climbed up on the roof of Yassir's shack—it offered the best view—so that he could follow the soldiers' movements and communicate them to the other boys by a series of coded whistles. He noticed Khaldun creep toward a tank until he was a few meters from it, take cover behind a mound of garbage, and raise his slingshot, which was made from an olive branch and the inner tube of a bicycle tire.

Khaldun was so close that he could have looked into the eyes of the soldier standing in the turret of the tank. On his third try, Khaldun struck the soldier's helmet, slightly denting it on the left side. The boy's movements were casual, almost insolent, and even though he was creeping through dust and garbage, he looked almost elegant, as if he were another combatant in one of the many wars that had left a mark in history books during the course of the twentieth century.

In response to the thick volley of rocks, the soldiers launched tear gas missiles and then sent several shots into the air; but when these measures persuaded few of the camp boys to stop fighting, the Israelis lowered their sights and fired on their adversaries. A few meters from Khaldun's position, Hassan was cut down, having been foolish enough to get up and try to run to a heap of stones while exposed to Israeli fire. Two other boys were wounded, one in the arm and the other in the leg. Said had to crawl across the rusty metal of Yassir's roof and drop to the ground because a sniper posted on the hill in front of the camp had got him in his sights. One bullet missed his right leg by a few centimeters, the same leg that was still aching from the fall he'd taken the previous week. In the meantime, Khaldun threw all the rocks he had and waited for the tanks to complete the operation of withdrawing from the camp; then he got to his feet and began slowly walking home.

A grim silence had settled on the camp. Khaldun carefully approached the clearing that divided Kalandia from the city of Ramallah, and he was surprised to see the column of armored vehicles once again ascending the dirt road. In that instant, he realized that the Israelis had set a trap for him and his comrades. Signaling to the other boys, who were still huddled on the ground, he started running toward the shacks.

First he heard the roar of a jeep engine, and then he saw the jeep itself come out from behind the peeling wall that marked the boundary of the camp. He cursed his own foolishness, which had brought him to his present position: exposed, with his line of retreat uncovered and a hundred meters between him and the first shack—an easy target for the Israelis' bullets. He zigzagged as he ran, trying to avoid the piles of garbage, and did not turn around at the sound of gunshots. The Israeli soldiers managed to capture at least five of the younger boys but didn't seem satisfied.

Khaldun knew what would happen to him should he fall into the soldiers' hands. Since he was a minor, they wouldn't be able to put him on trial, but in the best possible scenario they would break his hands and his wrists—if not his arms—to make it impossible for him to pick up a rock again for a long time.

A soldier in a jeep spotted him when he was no more than twenty meters from the shack and pointed his rifle in Khaldun's direction, but his vehicle hit a hole in the ground and he fired into the air. Nearing exhaustion, Khaldun dashed into the little street formed by two rows of shacks, but the jeep driver apparently had no intention of letting him go. Khaldun was out of breath. It had been hours since his last drink of water, and the heat had become unbearable. He slowed from a run to a lunging walk. All of a sudden, an arm seized him and hauled him in. Too weary to offer resistance, Khaldun found himself inside a shack. It took his eyes several seconds to adjust to the darkness of the small room, which was only a few square meters and had no window. There was a mattress in one corner and a washtub stood in the middle of the floor; some laundry hung to dry on a cord that crossed the room diagonally. The only chair was propped against the wall. A woman stood before him, not much taller than he and dressed in traditional robes that must once have been blue but were now faded and threadbare. She could have been forty or sixty.

"Take off your clothes and get in the tub," she said decisively. Her eyes, accustomed to the darkness in the shed, were two slits. Khaldun did not understand what was happening but obeyed, guided by instinct. He felt he could trust the woman, and anyway he had nothing to lose.

When the Israeli soldiers entered the hovel, they found only a mother giving her little boy a bath.

Meanwhile, hands in his pockets, Said walked along, whistling in the direction of the battlefield where everything was over by now. He wanted to ask Khaldun to teach him how to use a sling-shot. Suddenly, he became aware of the approaching jeep and heard the unmistakable sound of gunfire. He turned and ran, limping toward home. After a while, he stopped and, flattening himself against a mud-brick wall, cautiously stuck out his head. Everything seemed calm, but as soon as he drew back, he heard the jeep again, followed by a rumble he recognized as the sound of an advancing tank. He peered out to see an enormous tank headed straight for the place where he'd been hiding.

By the time Miral reached the top of the hill overlooking Kalandia, dense clouds of smoke and dust were rising from the refugee camp and drifting on the wind.

The previous days' rains had made a host of yellow flowers bloom, forming a strip that ran along the crest of the hill and then down one side, among the rubble and wrecked automobiles scattered on the slope. Miral hurried along that flowery trail, a sad path that seemed to be created just for her, especially since she was named after a flower—yellow on the outside and red at its heart—that blooms in the desert after the rain. Its fragrance is sweet and delicate but intensifies with the heat of the sun.

When she finally reached the open space where classes were held, she saw no one at all. Directing her steps to the center of the refugee camp, she soon made out a large gathering of people standing in front of a pile of rubble and twisted metal. As she got closer, she recognized Said and Khaldun, who were busy rummaging around in the debris, which, Miral now realized, was what remained of Yassir's house. Khaldun saw her coming and went to meet her. His eyes were more alert than usual, as if lit from within by strong emotion.

"What happened?" she asked.

"Big fight this morning: one dead, ten wounded, and six arrested. They almost got me, too," he replied, pointing to the cartridge cases strewn about.

"What about Yassir?" Miral asked, as she watched the crowd digging among the remains of his shack.

"Unfortunately, this time he was buried under his roof for real. Just think, it was only yesterday that we finished rebuilding his wall. Said feels guilty about it—he often used Yassir's roof as an observation post, and he thinks that's why they knocked the house down. Maybe he's right, maybe not. But what difference does it make now?"

Staring at Khaldun as he lit a cigarette, Miral wondered how he could be such a fatalist, but then she considered the probability that embracing fatalism was the only way to survive when death and suffering formed such a constant part of everyday life.

"Why don't you accept the scholarship to study in Damascus? I know I've been asking you that question for some time now, but you should give some thought to accepting. It could be an alternative for you." Miral spoke to him firmly, sure that she was right; she had no doubt that they would all have happier lives if they lived anywhere other than the refugee camp. "Yesterday I talked to a girl from Dar El-Tifel who studied in Damascus for a year," Miral went on. "She said it's a very beautiful city. And after you complete your studies, there will be a lot you can do. You could come back here and teach." She felt certain that this was Khaldun's weak spot: his desire to feel useful.

"No, Miral," he said. "The alternatives are for you. My place is here, in the midst of my people. I'd wind up putting on a tie every morning, and slowly but surely, day after day, I'd forget about the refugee camps. I'd even forget they existed. I don't want that to happen, and, besides, I'd rather stay here and throw rocks."

"Stupid jackass," Miral said, under her breath. Khaldun was very hardheaded and had his own implacable logic. She played the only card she had left. "I fight my battles, too. I go to demonstrations in Jerusalem or Ramallah. But that's no reason for me to give even a moment's thought to dropping out of school. Khaldun, we were born in the wrong place at the wrong time, but we mustn't give up on trying to make a life here. A people that can't see a future for themselves or their children have already lost."

Khaldun didn't appear to be listening to her. He was looking around. He saw that the rubble was about to yield Yassir's remains; he saw the laundry hung out to dry, the minuscule patches of cultivated land, the soccer ball made of rags; and they all evoked the miserable nature of the everyday life everyone inside the refugee camp pursued so avidly. "Maybe," Khaldun thought, "it would not be an act of cowardice to leave this place and go to Damascus."

But that wasn't what he wanted. How could he think about studying mathematics if what he felt inside was hatred? What animated him was a rage at once focused and blind, a hatred that made him dream every night of being a hero and wake up every morning with the hope that this was the day. That was difficult to explain to a privileged city girl. He turned to Miral and said, "You see? After all, you risk your life every day, too, and you think you're doing the right thing. No one forces you to take part in demonstrations or to sneak around an army blockade so you can come here. That's simply what you feel you have to do. It's the same for me."

The other boys called out to him: they needed a hand to extract Yassir's body from the rubble. Khaldun looked at Miral, and a moment before he left her his face lit up in a smile that struck her with wonder. How could anyone be capable of smiling in a place like this? One thought remained fixed in her mind: "I must save this boy."

2

On afternoons after visiting the camp, Miral would meet with other young activists in Ramallah or Jerusalem. It was 1987, and the First Intifada, the Palestinian uprising against Israeli rule, had begun. It started after four workers in Gaza were run over by a military convoy. The whole Arab population in Jerusalem, the West Bank, and the Occupied Territories, incensed by this event and years of military occupation, took to the streets in a protest that became a violent struggle, rocks and Molotov cocktails against tanks. This created a revolutionary solidarity among the young population.

Occasionally, she would ask one of her Dar El-Tifel schoolmates to take her place for the children's English lesson so that she could participate in an important demonstration. In her first year of high school, when the intifada began, only she and two other girls from her class took part. Two years later, the intifada was still going on, and by then a total of seven Dar El-Tifel girls were participating.

On several occasions, she and her comrades circumvented Hind's prohibitions and left the school grounds clandestinely, mingling with the day students who went home to their families every afternoon. Most of the time, the custodian was reading a newspaper and failed to notice them or pretended not to. When they returned, the girls would climb over the surrounding wall at its lowest point, in the rear of the school grounds, just opposite the American Colony Hotel. Miral would help the more hesitant girls, and then would nimbly pull herself to the top of the wall and jump down on the other side. After making sure that no one was about, the girls would dash to the dormitory, generally arriving a few minutes before dinnertime. One evening one of the senior girls, who was running in the dark with her head down, collided with the mathematics teacher and, as punishment, was confined to the school grounds for a month. But she won her comrades' esteem by refusing to give up the names of the other girls who had also participated in that day's demonstration.

The demonstrations, organized on a daily basis so as not to alert the Israeli authorities, would begin with the singing of patriotic songs and chanting of slogans against the military occupation, which slowly but surely drowned out the clamor of the souks and squares of various cities in the West Bank. The young demonstrators would wave the Palestinian flag, which was strictly forbidden, as they faced the charging Israeli army, fancying themselves fedayeen in the Jordanian forests. When the police and soldiers began throwing tear gas grenades or firing rubber bullets, the demonstrators, in turn, would throw rocks, taking cover in narrow streets. Some protesters used Dumpsters to improvise barricades and slow the advance of the army; others launched stones with slingshots or lit Molotov cocktails and hurled them in the direction of the Israeli jeeps and armored vehicles.

Often some of the bravest boys, the ones who got within a few meters of the tanks, were cut down by machine-gun fire or got their brains blown out by snipers posted atop the highest buildings. The most intrepid were usually—and unfortunately—the youngest, kids whose school day had ended just a few hours before and whose schoolbags were still on their backs as they lay in pools of their own blood.

The inhabitants of neighborhoods where the guerrilla skirmishes broke out, along with shopkeepers, craftsmen, and street vendors, did their best to help the protesters, hiding them in their houses, giving the wounded first aid, showing them escape routes, and inventing ways to hinder the soldiers from arresting the young demonstrators, many of whom defied the asphyxiating tear gas with uncovered faces, fueled by adrenaline, their eyes burning with hatred.

Some Israeli soldiers were troubled and embarrassed at the idea of pointing their weapons at such young targets, aware that their victims were more or less the same age as their own children or, in some cases, their own comrades. Others, however, squeezed their triggers without a second thought, carrying out their orders and squelching any scruples with the conviction that the saying *mors tua, vita mia*, "your death is my life," was the best philosophy, particularly in the Occupied Territories, where the laws of the Israeli state were not accorded the slightest consideration.

After running down a narrow street, Miral and some other girls from Dar El-Tifel stopped in a quiet little square. The sound of gunfire steadily receded. "My God," she said to her comrades, all of whom were younger and less experienced than she. "It's getting harder and harder to avoid getting hit by a club or a bullet, especially when you're in a cloud of tear gas. Those madmen are becoming more violent to stop us from protesting! But they don't understand that our people's anger is fueled by injustice, by marginalization. It's as though they're deaf and blind; they don't want to hear, and they don't want to see."

Miral paused for a moment, then added a warning. "Running through the streets isn't easy, but staying on your feet if you're in a crowd is even harder. Never stand in the center of the demonstration, and stay close to one another. Don't trust anybody else, and as soon as the police arrive, be the first to run away."

That afternoon, before starting her homework, Miral stopped in a café to get a glass of water and saw on a television screen images that would not leave her mind.

Rage deformed the faces of two Israeli soldiers while they broke a young boy's arms as naturally as if they were oiling their rifles. One soldier had three English words on his helmet: "Born to Kill." The bones of Palestinian teenagers, stone throwers, creaked and broke under sharp blows delivered by soldiers just a few years older than they. In the instant before the victims began to scream, two dreams were shattered: that of a peaceful state, which had been yearned for and dreamed of for two thousand years, and that of a people who had seen its future prospects destroyed.

When the First Intifada broke out, the Israeli soldiers found themselves unprepared to deal with a popular revolt. As a general rule, during the various wars conducted by the State of Israel, the armies were never seen on the streets, but now, in its effort to quell the protests, the Israeli government, caught by surprise, had its army play the role of the police. As the months passed and the protests, instead of fading away, progressively intensified, the authorities began to react more harshly, dispersing crowds of demonstrators with tear gas and rubber bullets. The rock barrages moved from the open squares to the narrowest streets, where residents often opened their front doors to boys running at full speed and then let them slip out a rear exit and vanish into the courtyards.

The first time she was pursued, Miral, in the panic of her flight, got lost. Not finding any better possibility, she threw herself into a full Dumpster and remained there, buried in garbage, for several hours, until the shots, the cries, and the sirens became distant and finally faded into silence.

The next time, she wasn't so lucky. She ran into an Israeli soldier, who seized her arm in a powerful grip and dragged her to the vegetable souk, where they awaited the arrival of the jeep that would take her to the police station. But the women of the souk abandoned their stalls—their displays of mint, carrots, and tomatoes—and approached Miral and the soldier. In a few moments, they surrounded him and pushed Miral out of the circle. Stunned and unexpectedly free, her heart in her throat, she began to run toward Dar El-Tifel. Only then, as she ran, did she fully grasp what being arrested would have meant for her, and she felt shaken but relieved. She had barely passed through the gate and onto the school grounds when she saw her sister, Rania, coming toward her, her eyes swollen with tears. One of her classmates had told her that she had seen a soldier capture Miral and lead her away. Rania hugged Miral in a desperate embrace. Having already lost her mother, she was afraid that Miral, too, would be taken away from her. After a little hesitation, Rania declared that she would tell their father everything if Miral didn't stop taking part in the demonstrations.

3

The arrival of spring in Jerusalem was magical. The hills became covered in green, the trees were in bloom, and fragrances of wild herbs and exotic fruits wafted from the markets. Arabs compare the spring to a bride, dressed in green and pink garments, who has awakened from her wintry torpor and rides into the city. When Miral returned to school after a weekend at home, she would always bring something for her friends. In the first days of spring, she brought sweet almonds and cherries, and during recess she distributed them among a group of students sitting on a bench in the sun. One of them, Hadil, a diminutive girl with soft, pretty features and a smile punctured by dimples, Miral had known since they were both six years old. They often swapped novels and made fun of some of their teachers. Hadil was especially good at imitating the mathematics teacher, with her French r's and her continual sneezing.

Miral signaled to Hadil to move to a more private spot, where they could talk alone. A student demonstration was planned for that afternoon, and Miral was eager to participate in it. She asked Hadil to join her, having already made arrangements with some twenty other girls from the school. They would leave one by one, so as not to draw attention to themselves, and then, around three o'clock, they were to meet at the Damascus Gate. But ever since one of the girls from Dar El-Tifel had been arrested—at the first demonstration she'd ever attended—the girls' comings and goings had become subject to much stricter controls. Miral knew that many teachers suspected her of being one of the instigators within the school, but they had never obtained any proof. Not even her classmate Nissrin, when she was arrested, had revealed Miral's name.

They had gone to a demonstration together, but then Miral lost sight of her. Later she learned that Nissrin had met a boy during the march. With friendly smiles and a knowing manner, he had persuaded her to follow him, in spite of Miral's earlier warnings that she should have nothing to do with anyone she didn't know. With the excuse that he was bringing her to a safe place, the boy had taken Nissrin by the hand and led her to a police van. He was, it turned out, one of the secret police. His fluent, accent-free Arabic was as false as his smile. They put Nissrin in the van and handcuffed her, and then the van drove away. She tried to remain still, even when the jolts and bounces became heavier and harder, probably because they were getting increasingly farther away from the city streets. After about twenty minutes, which seemed like an eternity to Nissrin, the vehicle stopped. She could tell that they were in open country, but they didn't let her out. Instead, the driver of the van got in the back, and now there were six men sitting in front of her.

The interrogation began. Who was she? Was she a student? If so, where? What was she doing at the demonstration? With whom had she come? And above all, who was the leader of her group?

Nissrin was afraid. Fear clenched her stomach, made her go weak in the legs, and set off a buzzing in her head that made it impossible to think. She started to reply in an uncertain voice, giving her personal details and declaring that she was a student at Dar El-Tifel school in Jerusalem. At that point, the five men looked inquiringly at one another, and the young man who had trapped her met the oldest man's eyes and made a brief sign of mysterious complicity.

When she saw this, Nissrin wondered what exactly they wanted from her. There had been so many girls at the demonstration—why was she the one they had chosen? It had been a coincidence, but she was overcome by a profound sense of anxiety and paranoia. Her heart kept pounding, and as she vomited up the entire contents of her stomach, one thought was humming in her head: They had brought her out there for a reason, there in the middle of nowhere. If she didn't talk, she told herself, she would probably never go back home. Nissrin was committed to dying right there and she wouldn't give any information about the other girls. Maybe it was the mention of Dar El-Tifel, but something guided that van back to Jerusalem, even though Nissrin would spend three months in jail.

Nissrin was the daughter of a spice merchant. Her mother had died when she was ten, and her father had enrolled her in Hind Husseini's school in accord with his wife's last wishes. It couldn't be said that Nissrin was Miral's friend. Although they were the same age and attended the same classes, Miral had come to know her well only recently, since the day when Nissrin expressed her desire to participate in the student demonstrations.

There was a close bond among the girls of the orphanage school, who thought of themselves as sisters. Despite their minor disputes, Hind had managed to make them all feel like members of a family bound by something more than blood. Miral was one of the most active and admired girls, excelling both in her studies and in the organization of extracurricular activities, but beyond her dedication to the refugees in the camps it was her kind heart and political passion that made the other girls look upon her as a leader.

Although many of the girls sought her advice regarding their problems, Miral herself placed a high value on the opinions of Hadil, whose calmness and serenity made her Miral's opposite. She was able to soothe and pacify Miral in her moments of anxiety and always found the right words to say, but otherwise she preferred to remain silent. Miral was very fond of Hadil and wanted her to get involved politically, so she persuaded Hadil to take part in the demonstration.

Normally, the protests started small and grew only gradually, as the protesters marched through various neighborhoods and people spontaneously joined them. But that day the police had learned about the gathering place in advance, since the demonstration had been organized expressly in memory of the intellectual Ghassan Kanafani. When the demonstration began, Israeli tanks surrounded al-Manara Square in Ramallah, where students from all the schools and universities in the West Bank had gathered.

Snipers had been posted on the roofs of the surrounding buildings, and at the first sight of the soldiers the young protesters started throwing rocks and chanting, "Free Palestine! Get out of our land!" Immediately, a cloud of tear gas enveloped everything; shouts, shrieks, shots ensued, and the protest turned into chaos. Miral instinctively began to run, dashing away so as not to be arrested, and at the same time trying to hold on to her friend Hadil's hand. But after running some three hundred meters, she was knocked down by someone. She discovered that Hadil had fallen on her. Miral tried to lift her up, and she realized that her hands were covered with a dense liquid. She didn't know where it was coming from or whether she or her friend was wounded, but then her hands came upon a hole in Hadil's head. Miral tried to scream, but her voice wouldn't come out; it was trapped in her throat, as in a nightmare. No one would ever know if Hadil was shot intentionally or struck by a stray bullet intended to eliminate one of the leaders of the intifada.

Hadil's body was lying supine, her arms stretched out over her head as though in a desperate effort to escape the bullet that was so much faster than she.

Miral could hear the sirens of approaching ambulances and the soldiers' footsteps as they combed the neighborhood streets, but she hadn't the strength to move yet; she felt chained to that spot and to Hadil's body. Death had made a violent entrance into Miral's life, and her tears flowed without stopping, a mixture of desperation, rage, helplessness, and—especially—guilt.

A warm hand clasped her shoulder, and she felt no fear. Even if they should arrest her, she would offer no resistance. But the voice that spoke to her was not that of an Israeli soldier. And sure enough, when she turned around, she saw a man of about thirty, tall, athletic, and light skinned, with dark, intense, kind eyes. With a few decisive movements, he raised her to her feet, put his arm around her, and drew her away from the square. Miral tried to resist, but he told her that they had to get away from there at once, and that men from the Red Cross would see to recovering her friend's body. But Miral still resisted: "Please, let me go, please! I can't abandon her! Please let me stay here!"

"We have to get out of here. Come with me, you'll be safe," the man said convincingly. Miral recognized his Jerusalem accent and realized that she had no choice.

She could no longer feel her own body; it was as if she were paralyzed. The man held her close as they crossed the square and got into a car that took them directly to Jerusalem and dropped them off in the Old City, in front of the Jaffa Gate. The man, still holding her tightly, walked at a rapid pace, as if he knew by heart that mysterious sequence of steep narrow lanes. They must have entered the Armenian Quarter, because Miral, before she fainted, caught a glimpse of the Cathedral of Saint James.

When she regained consciousness, it was already dark, but a pinkish light was filtering through a little window. After her eyes adjusted to the darkness, she could see that there was another person in the room, a man, who sat reading a book in a low armchair.

"Where am I? Who are you?" she asked, trying to raise herself.

"You're finally awake! Now, take it easy, you're safe," the man replied, putting down his book.

"Oh my God, it's late. It's almost night! I have to go back to the school. They'll be furious at me! This time they'll expel me for sure!" Miral complained, once again trying to get to her feet but immediately falling back onto the couch. She was still too weak.

At that instant, in the mirror across from her, she saw her purple face, her disheveled hair, and her dusty, bloodstained school uniform, and she immediately understood what had happened. Anguish and panic racked her as she recalled that she had been the one who persuaded Hadil to go to the demonstration. Now she would have to face them all: Hadil's family and friends and the angry teachers at school. And so, weeping, overcome by desperation, and without even looking at the man, she said, "I have to go. I have to go now. . . . Oh my God, what have I done? Hadil! Hadil!"

"Calm down, Miral. Don't worry about your school. I've already alerted them," the man replied.

"What do you know about my school? Who are you? Are you a spy?" Miral cried hysterically, raising her voice and trying to give herself courage. Just then a middle-aged woman entered the room, carrying some cups and a steaming teapot. The fragrance of mint tea filled the room.

"Don't insult me!" the man said, coming closer to her. "But you're right, we haven't yet introduced ourselves. My name is Hani. I saw you at the demonstration, and I'm the one who brought you here."

"Him, a spy?" the woman said. "That's all we need." She poured the tea and told Miral, "Drink a little. It'll make you feel better. . . . You're in our house now. Don't worry."

"I took the liberty of checking your papers, and that's how I saw that you lived at Dar El-Tifel. I called the school and told them what had happened. It seemed the right thing to do," Hani said, sipping the hot tea. He had a deep, gentle voice.

In an effort to apologize, Miral said, "No, yes, it was right . . . it's fine. You did the right thing."

As soon as she had recovered somewhat, Hani called a cab and accompanied her to the main door of the school. On the way there, neither of them uttered a single word. Miral was still in the demonstration, thinking of Hadil and of her absurd death; Hani gazed at the walls of the Old City and then the elegant white and pink stone houses of the Sheikh Jarrah district, which stood in such contrast to the atmosphere of violence and cruelty people were breathing only a few kilometers away.

When the taxi stopped, Miral got out, managing to say no more than "Thanks" before Hani disappeared.

. . .

In the course of the following days, Miral fell into a state of deep depression. She felt responsible for Hadil's death. Some girls, among them Aziza, tried to console her, but others kept their distance, avoiding her as a way of underlining their disappointment and fear.

The faculty of the school was in a state of agitation as the administration wanted Miral to be expelled. She had broken all the rules and put the school itself at risk. For Miral, the worst possibility was that she would be sent to live with her aunt in Haifa, which would mean giving up her political activity, her teaching job at the Kalandia refugee camp, and her friends. Hadil's death had not slowed, but rather had strengthened, her growing desire to take an active part in the struggle. It was difficult for her to give her teachers a rational explanation of what was going on inside of her. She belonged to that portion of humanity that would not accept resignation. And even though she knew that from that day forward it would be increasingly difficult for her to leave the school in order to teach at the refugee camps and to help the children dream, her thoughts continually returned to Khaldun. The boy was too restless, too imprudently courageous to survive in this world.

Miral also understood what Abdullah, her old gym teacher, had said to her years before: "If you want to comprehend this conflict in its full extent, to realize its local and regional implications and understand who its real movers are, you must get to know it thoroughly, from the bottom up." At the time, they seemed to be nothing but abstract, distant words, but now they proved prophetic.

While she waited for the school's decision, Miral spent the days stretched out on her bed, staring into space. It was a struggle for her to wash or eat. Aziza brought her yogurt and fed it to her, tried to embrace her and caress her the way they had done when they were children, as though to make up for the physical affection they weren't getting from their parents. Aziza's familiar hands relaxed and comforted Miral, but a feeling of embarrassment mingled with shame often arose in her when she looked Aziza in the eyes, for fear that her friend could read her firm intention to continue her political activity. She constantly asked Aziza about the children in the refugee camp and especially about Khaldun—how he was, what he was doing—and when Aziza revealed that he was deeply worried about her, Miral realized that the time had come to act. She had already decided on the one person who, more than anyone else, would be able to help her on that road: Hani.

In the meanwhile, an emergency meeting was held at the school, and there Miriam and the other members of the school council voted unanimously to expel Miral. She was held to be directly responsible for the unrest in the school, which had led to several students' skipping classes in order to participate in demonstrations, thereby endangering the general security. The Hadil episode was the last straw.

Hind intervened to block that decision, explaining to the gathering that the present moment was one in which the students, all of them, had the greatest need for the council's support and understanding. She maintained that the girls should not be punished for their civic passion, that she herself was the person directly responsible for what had happened, and that therefore the final decision would be up to her alone. The vice-principal, Miriam, attempted to object, pointing out that Hind was ill, that Miral would be hard to handle and difficult to control, and that there was a strong possibility that her presence would compromise the school. Hind replied that she would talk to Miral immediately.

And so she called the girl into her office.

"Miral, do you know how I've managed to keep this place open?" Hind began. "I've convinced everyone that education is the best means of resistance. Do you have any idea how often we've had to start all over, from scratch? When I found the first orphans on the street, I had only 128 dinars. As far as I'm concerned, you're all my children, and I love you all very much, especially you. This school is the difference between you and the children in the refugee camps. I've invested a great deal in your future, and your father has done the same. Don't waste this opportunity. This is your chance."

Then Hind informed Miral that two possible courses of action remained open to her: she could either sign a pledge never to leave the grounds of the school without precise authorization to do so, or she could pack her bags and leave immediately for Haifa, where her father had agreed to take her. Should she remain at school, the slightest violation of the rules would result in her immediate expulsion.

Miral nodded her acquiescence with tears in her eyes; she understood that she really had no choice, but at the same time she tried to explain to Hind that the anger and the sense of injustice fermenting inside her compelled her to do something. "We can't stand around with folded arms, waiting to be liberated by someone else. It's not fair to delegate the struggle to the young people from the refugee camps—we're called to do our part, too," she declared.

"You're right, Miral," Hind replied. "Each of us is doing something for Palestine. I'm responsible for making sure that this school remains open. Thousands of families depend on me. Many girls would be on the streets otherwise, and that's something we can't allow to happen. You must keep in mind that political involvement on the part of any one of you could seriously compromise this place. By and by, you'll see that there will be ways for you to do your part. Our future state will need pragmatic, intelligent young women, not martyrs."

They stared at each other for a long time. Hind's stern eyes betrayed the love she felt for her rebellious "daughter," while Miral's glowed with impatient pride.

4

Miral had been too stunned and confused by her friend's death to remember the exact location of the house where Hani had taken her after the demonstration, but she was sure she could find someone to show her where Hani lived. She went to the Armenian Quarter—one of the most fascinating in the Old City, despite the wounds inflicted on it during the heavy fighting in 1948—and tried to get some information from a group of children playing ball in a square illuminated by the lukewarm morning sun.

"Sure, we know him," the oldest of the group replied to her question. "But who are you? And what do you need him for?"

"Tell him Miral's looking for him. He knows me."

The boy kicked the ball, which shot away over the smooth stone. Then he sized up Miral with what was, despite his youthful age, the scrutiny of an adult.

"Wait for me here, I'll go and call him," he said, going off with his hands in his pockets. His oversize trousers gave him a comical appearance.

Left to wait, Miral gazed up at the white roofs of Jerusalem, which provide a kind of contrast to its bloody history. "God, how I love and hate this place," she thought. Perhaps one day, the city would become the capital of two states, one Israeli and one Palestinian. Although her birthplace was Haifa, as she contemplated the Dome of the Rock, gleaming in the rays of the sun, she longed to merge with her adopted city.

After a few minutes, the boy returned with Hani, who looked thinner and much taller than Miral remembered. He had brown, tousled hair and was wearing a pair of blue jeans and a gray sweater. Despite his melancholy eyes, he possessed a radiant smile.

"I can see that you've recovered very nicely," he said, squeezing her hand. "I'm glad. Have you had breakfast? Come with me, I know a place near the Damascus Gate where they make the best hummus in town."

"No, thanks, I don't want to disturb you. I just need five minutes of your time to talk to you about something important," Miral replied.

"So let's take a little walk. We'll have a better discussion on full stomachs," he said.

The Old City was in ferment, filled with tourists in town for Passover and Easter. It was a mild day, and a fresh, pleasant breeze caressed the undulant Judean Hills.

"So what's this important matter?" Hani asked.

"Well, it's about a person I know, a boy who lives in Kalandia refugee camp. He seemed very sharp and articulate. I've read one of his stories, which shows real promise, if he has the chance to do something with it. He's received a scholarship to go to school in Damascus, but I don't think he'll accept it. He doesn't want to abandon the intifada. He's always the first to throw stones or use his slingshot against the Israeli tanks, and I'm afraid he's going to come to a bad end." Miral stopped, and they stared into each other's eyes for a few seconds. Hani seemed to have the ability to read people from the inside, to understand what they were feeling. He started walking again, slowly.

"What makes you think I can help your friend?" he asked in a low voice, almost a whisper.

"I saw the way you moved. Even when the fight was going on, you seemed sure of yourself. Please, could you talk to him? He needs a father figure—his own father was killed many years ago."

"Do you love him?"

"No no, where did you get that idea?" she replied, blushing in embarrassment.

"What's this boy's name?" Hani asked.

"Khaldun."

Hani smiled and raised his eyes to heaven.

"What's going on? Do you know him?"

"Miral, we have to trust each other. And if we want to keep talking seriously about these things, we must get to know each other a little better. Come with me, I'll take you to a safer place than this," Hani said, turning onto a narrow street where the houses were so close together that only an oblique ray of light was able to filter past them. They entered a café that occupied the corner of a low building and consisted of a single large room filled to the ceiling with smoke. Several old men were inhaling slow, endless lungfuls from their narghiles, while the younger patrons of the establishment drank cardamom coffee or mint tea. There was a large counter covered with colored ceramic tiles in red, yellow, green, and on it stood a large silver tray filled with oriental sweets. Behind the counter, two young men prepared the infusions and other beverages. Hani was apparently very well known in this place, because everyone greeted him with a nod or a smile and the proprietor shook his hand.

Miral and Hani sat at a table that was somewhat removed from the others. "I see you're very popular here. Wouldn't it be better to talk outside, in the open?" Miral asked.

"How suspicious you are. It's good to be like that in these times, but you can relax now," Hani responded ironically, continuing to smile as he placed a hand on hers. "These people here can be trusted—they're my friends and comrades," he added.

"Do you belong to the Popular Front for the Liberation of Palestine?" Miral asked, speaking very softly.

He looked directly into her eyes. "Yes, Miral, I'm the PFLP officer responsible for Jerusalem—the secretary—and I know Khaldun well. His father was one of the best men we ever had, and he would have been very proud of his son. I didn't know he liked to write. I saw him in action once, during an Israeli raid on the camp."

Miral smiled. She'd been lucky to find Hani. "Super!" she said. "What part of Palestine do you come from? Your accent is a mixture of Jerusalem and other places."

He thought for a moment, as if Miral had asked a hard question.

"I was born in Lebanon. We are Christians. My parents were Palestinian refugees in 1948, forced to leave their lands and their house in Jaffa. We were able to reenter Jerusalem through Jordan a few months before the 1967 war, so at least we're refugees here, in our homeland. Now I believe only in our cause. Do you know what *intifada* means?"

"Sure. It means raising your head up, rebelling to preserve your dignity."

"That's right."

He had the same look of melancholy that had struck her the

first time she met him. Miral added, "I'm frightened to think that a lot more blood is going to flow, and even after that, God knows how many sacrifices we will still have to make."

Ever since the death of her friend Hadil, Miral had felt a need to talk about politics with an adult. In fact, Hani was her senior by about ten years, but she felt he had great authority.

"Of course, it won't be easy, Miral, not for us and not for them. They've built their happiness on our unhappiness, on our diaspora, and that can't get them anywhere. Now our destinies are intertwined. A great many of us will still be compelled to leave the country, and some of us will die, but in the end the international community will force the Israelis to sit down and negotiate with us."

That was just what she wanted to hear. "I'd like to do something more than what I'm doing now. It's frustrating, what I see every day in the refugee camps and in the villages, the continual humiliations at the checkpoints—I feel so helpless in the face of all that. It's not enough for me anymore to go to a refugee camp three times a week and teach kids a little English. I'm angry. The whole world should know what's going on here."

Before he spoke, Hani ran a hand through his hair, pushed the bangs from his forehead, and took a deep breath.

"Miral, you're young, but this struggle is making your generation grow up in a big hurry. You have to think over a decision like this carefully before you make it. You're talking about going down some roads there will be no turning back from. Besides, what are you going to do about your school?"

Miral, too, seemed to weigh her response for a while, thinking her way to the bottom of her heart. "I know it won't be simple, and after I graduate it will get even harder. I don't even know if I'll be able to stay in Jerusalem, but for right now, I think our struggle is crucial, and I want to be part of it."

Hani considered Miral's words and found them sincere, free of rhetoric, and he could tell that she was not just blowing off some passionate steam. At the same time, however, he was afraid to give her too much hope. He had already seen too many young people fall in the struggle or wind up in Israeli prisons.

"All right. As you must know, you're going to have to be very well informed politically, so I'd like you to think about that, at least for a little while. When you've made your decision, let me know. As far as Khaldun is concerned, let me speak with my organization. We'll try to get him out of the refugee camp. Let's meet again, you and I, in a week, okay? I'll get in touch with you through a girl in your school."

In her heart, Miral had already made her decision and didn't need a single minute more, but it still seemed reasonable to take a few days to reflect. The two said good-bye in front of a white stone wall that dazzled in the sun. Hani stood still for a few moments and watched her walk away, gracefully slipping through the crowd of people returning from the souk and heading for their villages. As he walked back to the Armenian Quarter, he considered her qualities. "She'll be a good politician," he concluded. "She's a little excitable and impulsive, but with some training, she'll learn to control herself."

Miral couldn't stop thinking about the words Hani had said to her, or about his dark eyes, which seemed to look into the bottom of her soul. They shared a passion for politics and a commitment to social work; they both admired the left wing of the PLO for the moral rigor it had demonstrated. Hani, however, was critical of the left's intransigence, especially regarding peace negotiations with Israel.

On the way home, Miral felt more serene, more solid somehow, and, more than anything else, physically attracted to that young man. On her way home the following weekend, she decided to pass through the Armenian Quarter and enter the Old City through Herod's Gate. She felt as though she were entering a new phase of her life, filled with energy and enthusiasm, and as she crossed the gate, she again went over her choice in her mind, knowing that she would have to live with that choice in secret. "I'm not turning back," she thought.

The man was staring into Khaldun's eyes. He had just made the boy a proposal, one that could change the course of a life. Khaldun looked around at the shack where he had spent the last three years, at the muddy streets, at the garbage, at the children running after one another in the midst of open sewers. What was there left for him to do in this place? Sure, it was his home, his land, but it was also his hell. What future could he have here? He would grow up and grow old in a shack, and maybe he would die prematurely, but for useless reasons, and he wanted to be of use, to do his part. He felt the adrenaline rising in his veins; he would have liked to play soccer whenever he wanted and to be a real combatant when he grew up. Khaldun nodded in agreement.

The man standing before him squeezed her shoulder. "Good, then it's done. Be sure you're there at seven o'clock tomorrow morning," he said, before slowly walking away.

Khaldun thought about Miral, about the last time he'd seen her, as she was walking up the path that led to Jerusalem. She was the only person he would have been glad to talk to before he left. That night, stretched out on his cot, he remembered the stories the older people in the camp told about Deir Yassin and Tal el Zaatar, about the mutilated bodies lying in heaps and decomposing in the sun. He thought about his father, dead in Lebanon—Khaldun didn't even know where he was buried—and for an instant he considered the possibility that Miral was right, that he should accept the scholarship to study in Damascus. He would be able to live in a house, a real house. The other inhabitants of the camp, his friends and neighbors, came to mind, and he reflected on the cruel destiny that united them. He wouldn't be worthy of his family if he didn't fight as his father, his grandfather, and his great-grandfather had done before him. That night he fell asleep certain he had made the right choice.

Said had awakened hoping that Khaldun would have enough time that day to teach him how to make a slingshot. He had waited for half an hour at the place where Khaldun usually played soccer with the older boys, but when Khaldun didn't come, he headed back to his shack, kicking every empty can and bottle he found along the way. He saw Khaldun's mother outside the shack, busy hanging laundry on a frayed clothesline.

"Good morning," he said. "Do you know where I can find Khaldun? He's not at the soccer field."

When she heard her son's name, the woman flinched. She carefully adjusted a threadbare sheet before turning to the little boy. "Hello, Said. Khaldun's not here. He went to study in Damascus, and he couldn't say good-bye to anyone because he had to leave this morning at dawn, but he asked me to give you something."

Said watched the woman disappear behind the rusty tin panel that served as her front door. After a few moments, she reappeared and handed the boy a plastic bag. He took it, thanked her, and slowly walked away. As soon as he turned the corner, he sat down on a rock and opened the bag. To his great surprise, he found himself holding the military trousers that Khaldun always used to wear, the ones that had belonged to his father. Said was pleased to receive those pants as a gift, because he knew how proudly Khaldun had worn them. There was another package in the bag, something wrapped up in old newspaper. When he saw the slingshot, he was touched, and as he ran to the place where the other kids were playing soccer, his eyes were bright with tears.

Miral had spent the whole morning thinking about the demonstration that was to take place that afternoon in Ramallah. Before she went there, she decided, she'd make a quick trip to the Kalandia camp to distribute some books to the kids and, with any luck, say hello to Khaldun. During lunch she announced that she was not feeling well and that she was going to lie down for a while. She hurried to her room, took off her school uniform, dashed down the stairs, crossed the park while the teachers were still at lunch, and climbed over the wall.

Miral ran to the Damascus Gate, the point of departure for buses to the Occupied Territories. When she finally reached the path leading down to the camp, Miral saw Said, who was using a slingshot to launch rocks at the carcass of a vehicle, as boys of various ages stood around him admiringly. When Miral got closer, she noticed that Said was wearing Khaldun's trousers—he'd had to roll the cuffs way up and tie the waist with a cord. His decidedly small stature contrasted with his serious, military-style movements as he manipulated the slingshot.

Miral greeted him as soon as she joined the group. The kid was busy taking aim at the only portion of window still intact in the tangle of scrap metal that must have once been a jeep. When he heard Miral's voice, he gave a start, causing him to shoot so wide that he struck one of the other children in the back. General laughter broke out immediately and infected Miral as well, while Said, red with shame, was the only member of the group who wasn't laughing.

After the laughter died down, Miral turned to Said. "Why did Khaldun give you his pants? Did you win them from him in some kind of bet?"

"He gave them to me before he left for Damascus. But I didn't see him. His mother gave them to me."

"Damascus?"

"Yes, he left this morning at dawn. He didn't have time to say good-bye. But you must know more about it than I do. You're the one who kept pushing him to go study there."

Miral was undecided about whether to reveal that she knew nothing about Khaldun's decision and didn't think it was possible, but then she chose to act as if nothing was wrong. "Well, of course I knew he was supposed to leave, I just didn't think it would be so soon. Would you mind taking me to his mother's house?" she asked, trying to hide her surprise and satisfaction. Her grateful thoughts went to Hani, who had, it seemed, succeeded where she had failed.

When they arrived at Khaldun's shack, Miral waited for Said to leave before knocking on the door. When Khaldun's mother opened it, Miral said, "Good day. We've never met, but I'm a friend of Khaldun's, one of the girls from Dar El-Tifel school. And I . . . I'd like to know how you're doing . . . and how did Khaldun's departure go?"

"You must be Miral. Come in and sit down," the woman said, pointing to a straw chair.

Miral was surprised to discover that Khaldun's mother knew her name. She instinctively liked the woman, whose sad eyes gave way to a lovely smile.

"Khaldun has spoken to you about me?" Miral asked as she took her seat.

"He told me a very beautiful girl might drop by and ask what had become of him. Would you like some coffee, dear?"

Miral nodded and the woman got up to prepare it, placing two tablespoons of cardamom coffee and one tablespoon of sugar in a small saucepan, adding water, and setting it on the fire, stirring slowly as she did so.

Miral watched her as she spoke. "I had a feeling this moment would come, but his departure caught me off guard anyway. Your son is a wonderful boy. I just hope he really goes to Damascus to study and doesn't stop in Lebanon like the rest of the PLO. Would it be all right if I come to visit you from time to time so I can get news of him?"

"Of course, come and visit whenever you want. I've accepted my son's moving far from me so that he can have a better future. I've got a letter for you. He asked me not to open it. From the way he talks, I know he has a very high opinion of you."

Sitting in front of the shack, the woman and the girl drank their coffee in silence. Both knew it was impossible to change Khaldun's mind once he had made a decision. In his mother's eyes, Miral could read the sorrow of immense loss and the resignation of someone who had never had a choice.

"I have to go now," Miral said when she had finished her coffee. "I'm glad to have met you." The two embraced affectionately.

"Khaldun was right—you're a smart girl and very beautiful, too," the woman said as she handed Miral a yellow envelope.

By now it had grown late, so Miral decided to return to Dar El-Tifel and skip going to Ramallah, thus reducing the chances that the teachers would discover her absence. But when she mounted the wall and dropped down onto the school grounds, she realized that someone was sitting on a bench a few meters in front of her, beckoning her closer. It was Hind's adopted daughter, Hidaya.

"I'll bet you've been to some protest rally, as usual. You know how fond my mother is of you. I feel the same way. So I won't say anything to her about this demonstration, but forget about the next one."

Hidaya had always treated Miral and Rania kindly, feeling great affection for them, she who had grown up in the school and had enjoyed the good fortune of being raised by Hind personally.

"No, I swear," Miral said to her. "I've only been to Kalandia refugee camp. I wanted to see this boy, Khaldun. Maybe you remember—Hind got him a scholarship to study in Damascus. But in any case, I arrived too late."

"He's already left for Syria? Hind told me he refused the scholarship. She said she'd give it to one of the girls from the school."

"I don't know. His mother gave me a letter. Maybe it says where he is now," Miral said, extracting from her bag the yellow envelope with the simple inscription "For Miral."

"I'm afraid he's made the wrong choice," Miral went on. "He's smart, but he's impulsive, too, and too young to choose wisely. He often flirts with tragedy."

Hidaya cast a glance at the school, at the well-tended garden and the girls' athletic field. This place had been her whole life, and she had dedicated herself to it entirely. It was to her a fixed point, an oasis in the middle of a devastated land. "The intelligent boys are the ones who feel that they bear the heaviest burdens, because they're able to understand. Sometimes that's not much of a privilege," Hidaya said. "Go to your room, and remember the agreement you made with Mama Hind."

When the other girls were outside in the schoolyard and Miral was alone in her room, she sat down on her bed and opened the envelope. The handwriting, although shaky, was elegant in its way.

> *Dear Miral,*
>
> *When you get this letter, I'll be far away. But I'm not leaving forever. One day I'll return to my land as a free man. I'll cultivate the fields of my village or take up my studies again. I have no intention of running away. I know that I could, but I don't want to. I feel like a man who has never had a chance to be a boy. Life in the refugee camps isn't normal, as you know; here you grow up throwing stones, without reading books. The past comes back to me every night and wakes me up, and I lie there, sweaty and angry. Here I'm alone, but where I'm going, there will be many other boys like me. I don't want to become a hero. It's enough for me to be a soldier fighting for a country that doesn't exist but is still mine.*
>
> *What can I do with my life, with my time, with my future? This is a question I've often asked myself during sleepless nights in the camp, and it's only now that I think I've found an answer: I am prepared to do the*

right thing, to fight for the things I believe in, whatever
the cost may be.

I want to thank you because you were the only person
who brought joy into my life. Your smile will keep me
company on this difficult journey.

See you soon,
Khaldun

A big demonstration was scheduled for a few days later, a rally
in which both Palestinians and Israelis were to participate. The flu,
compounded by the prohibition imposed on her by Hind and Hidaya, kept Miral from going. She was dozing in her bed when she
heard her name.

"Miral, are you awake?"

Hind was standing in the doorway, her white hair gathered at
the nape of her neck, her features as calm as ever. Still groggy from
sleep and medicine, Miral was surprised to see her and managed a
wan smile. Then she remembered the demonstration and the fact
that she was forbidden to take part in it, and her face darkened.

"I know you're angry with me," Hind said, entering and sitting
down on one side of the bed. "And I know how much you wanted
to go to the demonstration. That's why I've come to tell you that it
went well. There were a few minor incidents, but in general things
were peaceful."

Miral could not suppress a smile of satisfaction.

"A large number of people turned out," Hind continued.
"Many foreigners, and especially a great many Israeli pacifists, who
marched side by side with the Palestinians, chanting the same slogans, singing the same songs. If I didn't let you go, Miral, it is be-

cause I want to protect you. When you graduate and leave here, you'll be free to do whatever you think is right, but for now, I just hope the situation has changed and intelligent girls like you don't have to throw rocks anymore."

Miral observed her. Hind had aged a great deal in the past two years. She seemed more fragile, yet in her eyes the pride of her family was intact, along with the legacy of its ancient strength.

6

Khaldun had been on the road for two days, hidden in a truck that was transporting oranges, with a boy two years older than he as his companion. Jostled about by the potholes in the road, they hardly spoke but smiled weakly at each other every time their eyes met. Khaldun had found a small crack between the metal sheets that covered the sides of the truck, and through this tiny opening he could get a glimpse of the landscape. He saw first a parade of endless orchards, villages perched on the slopes of hills, and meadows where flocks of sheep were grazing. Then the vegetation disappeared little by little, the grass became scorched, and the landscape appeared rocky and barren. He mused that one day he, too, would have a piece of land to cultivate, and in the meantime he was happy that he wouldn't have to wake up the next morning in the squalor of the refugee camp.

Somewhat farther on, the truck made a hard, sudden stop, flinging Khaldun face-first into a mound of oranges. When he lifted himself up, the other boy started laughing at him as he watched the bright juice dripping down from Khaldun's forehead. Khaldun made a sign to him to be silent, as the driver had warned them to do in case of unexpected stops. They heard voices outside, speaking in

Hebrew. It seemed that they had arrived at the frontier. The two boys had been assigned to a space deep inside the truck, close to the driver's cabin and covered with some planks that, in turn, were covered by a thick layer of oranges. Khaldun and his companion were practically lying down, with very little room to move. If a soldier had cast a hurried look their way, he wouldn't have been able to see them, but in the case of a more detailed inspection they would have been detected. The rear door of the truck was open and some oranges must have fallen out, because Khaldun heard the driver complaining about his load. Instinctively, Khaldun picked up a few oranges and used them to block the opening in the side of the truck. The other boy did the same on his side. An Israeli soldier ran his hand all along the edge of the canvas covering. After a few minutes they heard the sounds of the door closing and the engine starting up again, and the boys breathed sighs of relief.

At last the truck reached the quay in the port of Acre and drove into the hold of a small cargo ship from Cyprus.

Khaldun felt the ship rolling. He wanted to get out of that truck, go up on the bridge, see the ocean, and inhale its smell. For more than two days, he and his traveling companion had seen little more than oranges. He was very fond of that fruit, of its delicate fragrance and distinctive taste. It was the symbol of his country, and one day he would own a big orange grove. But right now, in the heat and stench of the hold, the smell of oranges was like the smell of garbage. The sea was swelling, and the ship began to rock. Khaldun felt what little there was in his stomach rising, but he fought the nausea down and tried to think about something beautiful. It was impossible. The reek of ripe oranges was sickening. "I wonder when I'll get my first rifle," he thought, trying to escape from his surreal situation. A little straggly beard made his features look even harder. All things considered, he was happy; the day after tomorrow he would be a refugee no longer. He would be a political partisan, perhaps even a warrior, in a struggle that would sooner or later bring him back to Palestine as a liberator. In the end, he had chosen not to flee, not to go to Damascus to study mathematics or to Kuwait to work for the Arab oil tycoons. He was going to Lebanon, to study and to train.

"A new war will come, and this time it won't last six days," he said in an undertone, but no one could hear him, because the roar of the engines drowned out his voice. The ship disembarked its load of oranges and desperation in the port of a small city in the south of Lebanon. The fruit, by now quite ripe after its long trip, would end up being squeezed into juice by shiny steel machines and then sold in various parts of the world. For their part, the two boys would be fed into a different apparatus, the machinery of war, which in a few months would turn them into men, transforming their resentment into hatred, their adrenaline into courage, their adolescence into daring, and their sweetness into resolution. Khaldun lit a cigarette in an attempt to get the bitter taste of oranges out of his nostrils. The moon cast a long wake of light over the sea, like a bridge.

"First of all, I want all of you to bear in mind, always, that there is a great difference between the violence our people are compelled to utilize as a means of obtaining the land to which we are entitled and massacres such as those in Deir Yassin and Sabra and Shatila. If you understand this, you are already on the right path. I know that you will miss your homes. But look across the sea—that's Acre, and beyond it Haifa—and you'll feel closer to home."

The military instructor, despite this gentle introduction, had no intention of being indulgent with the small group of boys, almost all of them minors, who had assembled on the training field for the first time. Khaldun looked around. Without uniforms, without weapons, more sheepish than strutting, they looked readier for a boat trip than for a battle. The man who was speaking was the only one wearing a military uniform. At the end of his brief speech, he made a sign to Khaldun, whose comrades in arms were moving in disorder toward the tent that served as a mess.

"You must be Khaled's son," the instructor said. "I'm the one who insisted they look for you, you know. I was at your father's side when he was killed. He was one of the bravest men I've ever met. If we'd had a thousand fighters like him back then, we'd be drinking coffee on the seafront in Tel Aviv right now. You have his eyes—let's hope you have his courage, too. If you do, you'll get a chance to show it. Now you'd better go and eat, because soon the only thing left of that soup will be its smell."

Khaldun felt stupid for not having said anything, for not having asked how his father died, but at the same time he was filled with a liberating sensation. Maybe he was badly dressed and undernourished like most of the other boys, but he felt different. He was Khaled's son, a hero's son. A fighter by birthright.

7

*H*ani was already seated at a table, drinking cardamom coffee and reading *Al-Quds*, Jerusalem's Arabic daily newspaper, and from the expression on his face, Miral divined that the news wasn't good. She stood still and observed him from a distance for a few moments. The young man seemed a mixture of calm, charisma, and dignity. Customers in the café approached to say hello and pay their respects to him and, especially, to hear his opinions.

His eyes met Miral's, and he beckoned her closer.

Before she could even sit down, he smiled and asked her, "You've made up your mind so soon?"

"Well, you've moved pretty quickly yourself. You know what I'm talking about. But in any case, I wouldn't have come back otherwise. I want to do my part! I can't just stand and watch and twiddle my thumbs anymore. Have you seen what's happening in Gaza? There were five people killed there only yesterday," she said, her voice firm, speaking aloud the words she had repeated so often inside her head.

"Yes, I'm reading about it now. Unfortunately, these are the same crimes we read about every day, not only in Gaza but also in Jenin, in Nablus, and in many other Palestinian cities. The most disturbing thing is that these events are taking place against a back-drop of worldwide silence. Other countries are too preoccupied with their economies and debates over government corruption to pay attention. Anyway, Miral, there's something urgent to be done. Are you up for it?"

"Of course," she replied without hesitation.

Hani smiled and folded the newspaper. "Let's take a walk."

When they were outside, he started talking again. "I wanted to tell you that Khaldun's already in Beirut, where he'll study and receive his training." Without thinking of the consequences, Miral gave him a big hug and a kiss on the cheek. They were passing in front of the Damascus Gate, and the other pedestrians stared at them, scandalized. Hani gently detached himself, took her by the arm, and said, "The curfew has just been lifted in one of the refugee camps near Ramallah. Soon we'll go out there and help the farmers harvest their olives before it's too late." Her expression of surprise and disappointment amused him, and he added, "Look, what you're going to do is extremely important. That's how our people live, and even the smallest things are meaningful. But first I have to introduce you to the rest of the group."

The meeting took place in an old apartment in the Armenian Quarter, near the Jaffa Gate. This was the highest part of the Old City, and from there one had a view over the roofs, red to the west and white to the east, sloping down to the Esplanade of the Mosques. The bell tower of the Cathedral of Saint James soared majestically over the expanse of lower buildings and the luxurious foliage of the public gardens, which served as a meeting place for the young people of the neighborhood. The owners of a shop across the way kept a close eye on the apartment, and if they caught a glimpse of the police, they would warn everyone by hanging a piece of white fabric on their door, signaling that the apartment was to be evacuated immediately.

In the front room of the apartment, about ten people were busy photocopying and xeroxing flyers; in the second room, which was larger and more comfortable, six others were seated around a large wooden table, deep in discussion, the smoke from their cigarettes swirling about before collecting under the vault of the stone ceiling.

One of the people at the table, a young man named Ayman, spoke first. "Here's the secretary!" he said, pointing to Hani. "We were talking about finding some secure means of putting the local leaders of the intifada in touch with PLO men in other countries."

Before replying, Hani signaled Miral to come closer. "We also have to create new channels for sending and receiving messages," he said. "The old ones aren't secure anymore, and that's why we need new faces, faces the secret service doesn't know. Let me introduce Miral, a new comrade."

And so Miral greeted them. Their smiles told her that she was part of the group already, and they invited her to sit with them at the table. They formed a clandestine cell, and as such, they would hold their meetings in different apartments from time to time and occasionally in public parks. Miral would be notified about them directly, either by Hani or by a girl in her neighborhood named Jasmine.

Hani began passing by the school on alternate days, arriving at the same time, shortly after classes were over. Without attracting attention, he would post himself behind a big tree near the rear gate of the campus. Miral would join him there, and the two would exchange only a few words in order to avoid being seen by the porter. Hind had an inkling of something, but she thought that Miral was just being carried along in the general adolescent whirlwind.

For her part, Miral was very careful to avoid getting caught. She seemed to have lost her cheerfulness and vivacity, and always looked distracted. Her grades were no longer as spectacular as they once had been. But she tried to behave as usual, at least with the littlest girls. On evenings when the girls asked her to tell them stories before they went to sleep, Miral would stand in the middle of the room and ask them to put their heads on their pillows and close their eyes, and then she would start telling them stories from *Thousand and One Nights*, the tale of a king who killed his wives on their wedding night, one after another, for fear that they might betray him, until a young girl named Scheherazade saved herself by telling him a different story night after night. This storytelling was Miral's favorite moment of the day.

Although Hind seemed unaware of what was happening, she knew Miral too well and sensed that the girl was only pretending to obey the rules; but since Miral risked immediate expulsion for any infraction, Hind acted as though nothing was amiss. She loved the girl too much, and she believed in Miral, who, like all the boys and girls of her generation, was forced to grow up too fast.

Miral kept her promise to meet Hani and go with him to the refugee camp near Ramallah. Since the visit fell on the weekend when she was back at home, she simply told her father that she was seeing a girlfriend for the day.

"Have you ever read *My Home, My Land*, by Abu Iyad?" Hani asked her as they were getting into the car. Miral shook her head.

"He was one of the most enlightened minds of our people," Hani continued. "The Mossad assassinated him. He was poisoned."

As they drove along, bouncing over holes in the asphalt, Miral let out all the anger she'd held inside since her last visit to the Kalandia camp. "The clashes in the camp convinced me that teaching English to children isn't enough. I'm willing to help the farmers with the harvest, but I want to do more. I'm talking about a real response, a fitting response, one that will make a lot of noise. You all belong to the Popular Front, Hani—you're supposed to be the party of deeds, not words, damn it!"

Hani was driving with great concentration, intent on avoiding as many potholes as possible on the strip of pavement that divided those harshly contested hills. "Miral," he said, "you have to understand that the goal of the struggle is not to give vent to our rage but to free ourselves from the occupation. I understand and appreciate your enthusiasm. I know you're a brave girl, maybe too brave, and, trust me, you will be very useful to the PFLP and the Palestinian cause. But there's no way I'm going to allow you to join the armed branch—you're too impulsive to be a part of that." After a pause, Hani continued. "Instead, you'll work inside the political structure. We need new perspectives, smart individuals who can raise our people's awareness and help them understand. Ignorance is a trap it's too easy to fall into. I've decided that you'll work as a courier in the organizational sector. You'll see, it'll be an exciting assignment. And I want you to come to the weekly section meetings so you can listen and learn."

Hani squeezed her hand, and when she felt the heat emanating from his grip, she grew pleasantly agitated. As for Hani, he was quite taken by this girl, by her freshness, her silences, the defiant look he sometimes saw in her eyes. He felt that her eagerness to do her part, if properly channeled, would be very useful.

When they arrived at the camp, they saw a group of farm workers, together with some younger boys and girls, all busily gathering olives. Some workers were in the trees, detaching olive clusters, while women piled them in crates or gathered them on plastic sheets spread out on the ground. Miral and Hani joined the group and began working alongside the others. After a while, Miral began to feel excruciating pains in her arms and legs; Hani handed her a bottle of water and told her to stop for a minute or two.

In the afternoon, after the first morning of the harvest had come to an end, they were invited to lunch with the farmers. The meal was arranged on a blue and red rug that had been spread on the ground behind the farmhouse and surrounded by hassocks stuffed with coarse wool. It included skewers of grilled lamb, saffron rice, sautéed vegetables, and salad. While the others were sitting down to eat, Hani, carrying a plateful of food and a jug of fresh lemonade, headed for a small, isolated house. Miral was able to glimpse a man about thirty years old who spoke with Hani while devouring the contents of the plate. She couldn't imagine who he might be, but guessed that the little house was his hiding place.

Hani returned about half an hour later and sat next to Miral, who was chewing a mouthful of lamb. Noticing that a few strands of her hair had strayed into her mouth, he removed them affectionately, smiling and bringing his face close to hers. Miral felt her heart beating crazily and lowered her eyes to hide her embarrassment; the rest of the group, immersed in conversation and joking, paid no attention. Hani leaned toward her again, offering her some food, but this time Miral was distracted by the lateness of the afternoon and suddenly jumped to her feet, exclaiming, "Oh God, I have to go!" She was afraid her father would begin to worry, so Hani offered to accompany her home.

Once they arrived in Jerusalem, they left the car in a parking lot outside the Old City, and together they set out, crossing the souk to the place where they would have to part. They were filled with a happiness that had no need of words. They walked along hand in hand, almost embracing, exchanging looks of mutual understanding and desire as they made their way through the crowd that was coming down from the Old City and heading for the villages on the outskirts of Jerusalem. In the midst of this confusion, Miral failed to notice her father, who was at a stall purchasing coffee. Stunned and incredulous, Jamal watched his daughter go by. In his anger, he forgot about the coffee and ran to catch up with her.

"What are you doing here, Miral? And who is this man? No, I don't want to know," he said, blocking his daughter's response with a gesture of his hand. "Come home with me, this instant!" he yelled, yanking her by the arm. Hani tried to explain, saying that he was terribly sorry. But there is nothing more obstinate than the anger of a father who believes he's protecting his daughter.

Hani watched for a few moments as Jamal dragged Miral away down the Via Dolorosa. "What a fitting name for it," he thought, then started walking in the direction of his apartment.

Miral turned around for an instant and saw that Hani had vanished. She was afraid this would be the end of everything, that she would not see him again.

"What the devil were you doing? That's what I'd like to know! Have you gone crazy?" Her father barraged her with questions, not so much seeking answers as exorcising his own fear and anger. "What were you doing with that man? Do you have any idea who he is?"

As Jamal kept shouting furiously and pushing her ahead of him, Miral found the strength to reply: "He's a friend of mine, Baba. He's a good person. It's not a sin to be politically active. He's a true patriot!" Jamal had never heard her voice vibrate with such pride.

"Patriot?" he replied, opening their door. "You have no idea what you're talking about! How long have you known him?"

"He's a friend of Jasmine's. I met him by chance—" Before she could finish her sentence, Jamal slapped her across the face.

"Don't look me in the eye and lie to me!" he said, shouting at the top of his voice. "Do you think I'm stupid? Now listen to me closely. You're too young to understand the situation you're getting yourself into, so before you do something irreparably stupid, I absolutely forbid you to see that man again! Are you listening to me? I've seen this before. Our family was destroyed by the same thing. My sister spent ten years in prison and then was thrown out of the country. She won't see her home again. I don't want this for you. Violence is not the way."

"You don't understand anything because you have been hiding in the mosque your whole life!" The words exploded automatically from Miral's mouth. Then, seeing how deeply she'd wounded him, she said, "I didn't mean that, Baba." But a sea of disappointment suddenly lay between them. Jamal was truly distraught. Miral had never seen her father in such a state, and the words stuck in her throat as tears slid down her cheeks.

She felt humiliated and confused, but she couldn't stop her thoughts from returning to the past few weeks. They had been the most intense of her life, and she couldn't imagine turning back to the life she'd led before, as if nothing had happened. She had to figure out some system for communicating with Hani and continuing her political activity.

Miral spent a day in bed, without touching food or speaking to anyone. Her sister, Rania, tried to distract her by telling her amusing jokes. Then she listed the sacrifices their father had made for them, reminding Miral of how much he loved her. But it was only when Miral saw her father's tearful eyes—he had been weeping in private—that she changed her attitude. It was the first time he had ever imposed anything on her or treated her in an authoritarian manner. Her sadness grew, and along with it frustration. She knew she could never give up Hani and her ideals. More convinced than ever of the rightness of what she was doing, she realized that now she would have to deceive not only her school—as if that weren't enough—but also her father.

She decided to use cunning. In the course of the following days, she tried to put on an appearance of serenity, so the school authorities would believe that she was bending to their will; but as soon as she could, she met Hani in the café in the Armenian Quarter. Together, they agreed on a series of precautions that would head off future incidents. They would see each other much less frequently—never in public—and they would communicate through Jasmine.

"I don't want to stop seeing you. I can't. If you want, I'll speak to your father," Hani said.

"No no, for the time being it's best to wait," Miral replied. "Maybe you can do it later on. I don't want to stop seeing you, either." Their eyes met, and they embraced each other tightly.

"I understand why your father's worried," Hani said. "We're all targets. Shin Bet, the Israeli secret service, isn't just standing around watching—every day they arrest one or more of our comrades. You have to be careful, too. Don't keep flyers or other compromising materials in your home. Unfortunately, the young man who was our contact with the PLO in Jordan has disappeared. He left two days ago and never arrived. Nobody knows where he is, and I'm afraid he's been arrested."

"Maybe he's just gone into hiding for a while," Miral said. "I don't want to seem naive, but we're all becoming paranoid."

"I hope you're right, *habibti*. William Burroughs once said, 'Paranoia's just having all the facts.' The big problem is that he was carrying documents, including a detailed report on our activities and a complete list of the operations we've carried out in the last three months. He was last seen trying to cross from Israel to Jordan on the Allenby Bridge."

A chill ran up Miral's back when she heard the tension in Hani's voice. Before she went back to the Dar El-Tifel campus, she got rid of all the flyers she had by burning them in the bathtub and hid her books in the manhole in front of her house.

8

The following week was calm. Miral saw Hani only once. She carried flyers printed by the PFLP's clandestine press to various bazaars outside the Old City, where some of the group's other activists would collect and distribute them. When the weekend came, Miral, as usual, went home to her father. Their relationship seemed more tranquil. In his heart of hearts, Jamal was worried, particularly at the sight of his daughter's evasive, enigmatic eyes, but he had resolved to let things ride, at least for the present. And while he prepared a lunch fit for a special occasion, he scrutinized Miral, who seemed to be suffering from a severe case of nerves. He didn't know whether to attribute this to her upcoming examinations or to something she was hiding, but he decided to talk to her about it the following day rather than disturb the atmosphere of harmony that was currently visiting his home.

Miral fell asleep happy that night, because she was going to see Hani again the next day. They were to meet in the Church of the Holy Sepulchre, where they'd been leaving messages for each other during the past few weeks, hiding notes under the black stone behind the altar in the Coptic Chapel. She missed Hani inexpressibly.

The next morning, Jasmine came to her house to tell her that everyone was waiting for her at a demonstration the movement had decided on at the last minute. Miral asked Rania to cover for her and went to the demonstration. When she arrived, she wove through the crowd until she reached the PFLP detachment. Hani was in the middle. A red scarf covered most of his face, but Miral immediately recognized his eyes; she had never known anyone whose gaze was so deep and intense. A thrill went through her, and Hani, too, seemed happily surprised. They embraced as the crowd surged past them, shouting slogans. Hani and Miral allowed themselves to be hauled along by that multicolored mass, like branches in a flooding river. They were holding hands when they heard the first tear gas canisters hissing through the air. Part of the crowd began running madly, while some of the younger protesters started throwing stones and launching marbles with slingshots. Others improvised barricades with garbage receptacles and set automobile tires on fire. Some PFLP militants were carrying Molotov cocktails and began lighting them and hurling them at the Israeli tanks. Miral was overwhelmed by adrenaline. This time, unlike during the attack on the refugee camp, she wasn't afraid; all she felt inside was a dense black hatred rushing through her veins. She barely noticed the tear gas and was breathing deeply and normally. A young protester was distributing Molotov cocktails. Miral went up to him. She lit the incendiary bomb he gave her, ran toward the Israelis, and flung it at them.

Miral turned and saw Hani. He seemed shocked and bewildered. His eyes were sad now, but not with his usual melancholy. He went to Miral, grabbed her from behind, and tried to drag her out of danger. "We're going away right now," he said as he clung to her. "This isn't for you. We're not like this, Miral. This won't get us anywhere."

Miral looked at him in amazement. "What are you saying? This isn't what you wanted? The struggle grows in proportion to the people's anger. This is the only path left for us to take, and we can't turn back now." At this point, Hani led her away by force, and when they had almost pushed through the crowd of demonstrators, swimming against its current this time, Hani pulled down his scarf and turned to her.

"Miral, you have to listen to me. All this violence—it makes no sense anymore. They're militarily superior to us, whatever we do, and this imbalance of forces will lead us to barbarism. I'm afraid of what we may become. If we reply to every one of their attacks with yet more violence, we're going to activate the classic mechanism known as 'the dog biting its tail,' and we'll all become prisoners of its doomed logic. We have to compel them to sit down at the negotiating table, and we have to come up with other ways of responding to them."

Dismayed and angry, Miral replied, "What do you suggest we do? Resign ourselves? Burrow down and live like rabbits? What's up with you? You scare me when you talk like this. I don't recognize you."

"After the arrests of the past several days, I'm convinced that a violent struggle will wind up playing into the hands of the Israelis who don't want negotiations—the settlers, for example, the religious right, the Orthodox right. Don't you understand? It's a political strategy they're using to discredit us, to make it appear to the eyes of the world that *we're* the occupying force and *they're* the ones who are defending themselves. Our hope lies in the portion of Israeli civil society that is becoming more and more convinced that peace must be reestablished between us. Think about it and you'll see that we need to start going down paths that will yield rapid results, because our people can't go on this way. We have to leave room for negotiations, and arriving at a political compromise is crucial. Violence is a trap we're stupidly setting for ourselves. We must use our brains, not our guts. We are two people fighting over the same little stretch of land. We both have our reasons, and we're both victims. They've suffered the Holocaust, and we suffer because the world felt guilty and used us as a bargaining chip."

Miral gazed at him and had no reply. She felt that there was something true in his words, but she hoped he was just blowing off a little steam. "The truth is always inconvenient," she said, "especially when you say it out loud. You shouldn't talk like that publicly, Hani, not in these times. It's too dangerous. You could be misunderstood, and you know it doesn't take much for someone to get branded a traitor."

Hani didn't feel like talking anymore, either. He moved his face closer to Miral's, so close he could feel her warmth. Their lips met in a passionate kiss. It wasn't their first kiss, but it was their most desperate, abolishing time and space despite the acrid taste of tear gas and the confusion going on all around them. Clinging to each other, they walked off in the direction of the Old City.

Month after month, as the conflict grew, so too did the divisions among the Palestinian factions, largely due to the secret peace negotiations, whose aims were widely shared by the civil society. But the radical leftist and religious groups believed such efforts to be a concession, a compromise, and—above all—a betrayal. Hani especially feared collaborationists; that is, spies who passed information to the Israelis because they needed money or work permits. Because of them, suspicion reigned everywhere. One had to be very careful; nobody could be trusted. You couldn't talk on the telephone for fear of wire taps, and every document had to be burned after it was read. Hani said that everyone was a potential spy, and that the enemy took advantage of people's weaknesses to lure them into the trap. Every week flyers appeared listing the names of collaborators; they and their families were repudiated by Palestinian society.

Ever since 1948, the Israeli secret services had been constantly perfecting their strategies for countering the wave of protests. The current unrest was not at all weakened by traditional methods of repression, and the great echo set up by the international media, including television and daily newspapers, which described in detail everything that happened in the Occupied Territories, was causing the Israeli government more and more embarrassment. This pushed the authorities to seek new methods of crushing the revolt while making as little news as possible outside the country. Among these methods, the bloodiest was surely the widespread recourse to sharpshooters, who were employed in the most sensitive places and prevented any gathering of young people in the street. The appearance of tranquility and peaceful coexistence had to emanate from the capital, Jerusalem, at any cost, and so soldiers became a permanent presence at every corner of the city's narrow streets, as well as along the roads leading to the city. The leaders of the Palestinian resistance likewise made adjustments in their methods, constantly varying the locations of their rallies and avoiding areas where there was no cover, such as public squares.

The most underhanded system developed by the Israelis involved using Arab shopkeepers, particularly hairdressers and beauticians, to recruit informers and stool pigeons from among their young female customers. The owners of the shops were threatened with losing their licenses or told that fiscal pressure would soon force them to close. The proprietors therefore cooperated, and with their complicity, their young customers were drugged and then, while under the influence of narcotics or sleeping tablets, photographed in obscene poses. Some days later, such a girl would be contacted and summoned to the shop with the excuse that she had forgotten some personal item. A couple of Shin Bet agents would be waiting for her. The secret service men would show her the photographs and, by threatening to divulge them and thus dishonor her and her family, compel her to spy on members of the resistance and sometimes to mark their automobiles with a phosphorescent liquid that was invisible except to the X-ray equipment in military helicopters, making the cars and the people inside them potential targets for fatal missile strikes.

During the First Intifada, this method was used to force dozens of girls to become informers. Some months later, one of them had the courage to relate her experience to one of the leaders of the resistance, whom she had been seeing for some time. This man, knowing that he would have to make the matter public, first of all asked for the girl's hand in marriage, so as not to dishonor her, and then had flyers printed and distributed in all the Arab neighborhoods of the city, asking the girls who had been blackmailed not to collaborate with the Israelis and to get in touch with the resistance. During the following days, a great many young women, students who lived in Jerusalem and the surrounding villages, turned up. Those who confessed were guaranteed confidentiality and pardon. Young men in the resistance married them so they would not fall into dishonor when the photographs were published. In the most delicate cases, they went to live elsewhere in order to avoid retaliation. This network of solidarity involved all those who in one way or another participated in the disturbances and allowed the First Intifada to continue until 1992, despite harsh Israeli repression.

Shops belonging to the barbers and hairdressers who had participated in the blackmail were burned down; their names were made public, and they were banished from the city. Those whose cooperation had resulted in the death of a leader of the resistance were condemned, sentenced, and executed; others were spared, in consideration of mitigating details, but were obliged to apologize publicly and visit schools, telling their stories and informing girls of the dangers that might beset them.

There was a deep hostility toward the Israeli secret police and the Israeli army, but perhaps even more intense was the loathing reserved for any Palestinian who collaborated with them. Strictly speaking, what was going on was not so much a war as an ancestral, visceral conflict between two peoples. On one side was a well-trained, well-armed national army; on the other was a mob of young people that followed its instincts rather than any strategy or military art. Reciprocal hatred made up for the lack of prospects in this struggle and provided the background for a mutual, tenacious obsession over the same land. Hani feared that a solution would be long in coming and that, meanwhile, his people's response would become increasingly radical and perhaps fall under the control of bordering countries that had a score to settle with Israel.

Miral suspected that some of the girls in her school were being blackmailed. In fact, she had noticed that two students no longer took part in the demonstrations. They had isolated themselves even in the classroom, were eating less, and seemed depressed. She decided to explain to her schoolmates the proper conduct in case of blackmail and held some impromptu meetings. The two girls—together with a third, who was evidently a more talented dissimulator—paled noticeably at her words. A few days later, the three confessed.

However, there was another girl who particularly aroused Miral's suspicions. Fadia was tiny, pretty, and ambitious, with delicate skin, light eyes, and straight hair. She never confessed to having collaborated with the Israelis, but Miral distrusted her nonetheless, even though they were in the same class and Fadia was always very nice to Miral. Although Fadia's family was decidedly poor, she was one of the most elegant girls in the school, and when she left the campus in the afternoon, she always brought back a small gift for Miral, sweets or a notebook or some ice cream.

One day, during a demonstration, a friend presented Miral with a list of girls who were collaborating with the Israelis. Because of the delicacy of the situation, and because of the particular attention given to not dishonoring the girls, such lists rarely contained errors. Next to the names of the three girls from Dar El-Tifel who had confessed, Miral read Fadia's name and understood the motive behind the constant attentions, the gifts, the forced smiles. She suspected that this apparently ambitious girl had not even been blackmailed but had voluntarily offered herself as a collaborator in exchange for money. Miral felt endangered: Fadia could give her name to the Israelis at any moment, and if she hadn't already done so, it was probably because she wanted something more from her. In all likelihood, she wanted to meet the resistance leaders with whom Miral had become friendly.

Miral decided the only thing to do was to distance herself from her classmate, not abruptly, but slowly, trying to avoid arousing Fadia's suspicions and to keep her from giving Miral's name to the Shin Bet. Fadia asked several times to attend demonstrations with her, but Miral replied that she didn't intend to take part in them anymore because the time had come for her to think about her future. After this it was Fadia who distanced herself, little by little, having realized that her "friend" had become wary and that she wouldn't be able to get any more information out of her. Aware that the game was up, Fadia also knew that she would be the prime suspect if anything happened to Miral. She therefore dedicated her attentions to someone else and at the end of the scholastic year transferred to another school.

9

To all appearances, Miral's life went on in a normal fashion, and she went home to her father's house every weekend. But in fact, she was living two parallel lives: the regular school life she had led for years, in which the bulk of her time was given over to study and her only distraction was the nightly bedtime story she told the littlest girls; and the secret life bound up with Hani and the Intifada. She thought about him constantly, about their moments together and their growing love. Now, whenever they had a chance, they would meet at his house and spend hours embracing and chatting, and as their passions mounted, Miral discovered the secrets of love. Hani was very gentle; the veils of childhood and innocence fell away, and Miral's physical awareness grew. At the same time, her voracious reading of political books and newspapers broadened her intellectual horizons. For the first time, she began to turn on television news programs, to the great annoyance of her sister, who wanted to see action movies. To make it up to Rania, Miral sometimes brought her along to Hani's house, where they would all stretch out on the roof and watch the sunset.

She felt that she had finally escaped being managed by others and was now the author of her own choices. If she slept at home more often during the week, she'd have even greater freedom of movement than she did at school, where it was becoming harder and harder to find new excuses for leaving the campus.

In a certain sense, time had inverted Miral and Rania's roles. In their first years at Dar El-Tifel, Miral had been protective of her sister, acting almost like a mother to Rania; after Miral became one of the most politically active girls in the school, it was Rania who took on the protective role, covering for Miral with the teachers while at the same time trying to dissuade her from exposing herself to such frequent danger. As the years passed, the temperamental differences between the sisters had grown more conspicuous. Rania became increasingly intolerant of school life and its attendant rules and was not at all fond of study. She wanted to go to Haifa to live with her aunt and, eventually, get married. Miral tried to convince her that she should continue her education, telling Rania that she had observed her while she was giving mathematics classes to the camp children and that she thought she had a great talent for teaching. "Knowledge is freedom," Miral told her, trying to persuade her sister by repeating their father's words. Miral loved both her school and her political activities, believing that her emancipation would result from her studies and her growing awareness. These days all her conversation revolved around history and politics. Rania loved pop music, the kind she could dance to, and found her sister boring and repetitious; Miral listened only to patriotic songs performed by Jordanian or Lebanese singers, and she became particularly emotional when such anthems were broadcast on television as the soundtrack to the intifada demonstrations.

Rania preferred to wear skirts or dresses, and her great passion was brightly colored high-heeled shoes. Miral loved tight jeans, loose-fitting T-shirts, and gym shoes, substituting sandals for the latter during the summer months. Although the two sisters often quarreled, and found themselves in disagreement on practically every subject, they loved each other deeply.

At their weekend family dinners, Jamal and Rania liked to talk about what they had done during the previous week. One evening Rania described the new brassieres she had seen her friends wearing (which she was sure would make her look less flat chested) and then addressed the topic of what she wanted to do that summer. Miral was distracted, her eyes vacant, her appetite nearly gone. Hani was moving farther and farther away from the party; everyone was complaining to her about him. He was deserting everything; he was making speeches advocating moderation, just at the moment when panic had spread through the entire group because of the hundred arrests that had been made all over the Old City in the past few days. It was only a matter or time for Hani and perhaps for her as well.

"What's wrong, sweetheart?" her father asked, stroking her head.

Miral remained silent for a few seconds, searching her brain for the right words so as not to alarm her father; then she described what she had seen during her most recent visit to the refugee camp. Jamal gazed at her with mounting concern.

"Do you understand, Papa? Our people can't continue to rot in the camps. What future can there be for those kids? The world's indifferent, and we're faced with the injustice and arrogance of a military occupation. You know, Papa, for refugee-camp children, the Israelis are either soldiers or settlers. That's the only face of Israel they know."

Jamal looked out the window at the clear blue sky over Jerusalem. "Miral, I know how you feel, but we have to find nonviolent ways of making our voice heard. We won't obtain what is ours by right with stones or even with rifles, and we risk triggering a vicious circle of violence that will be very hard to break out of. Please, I do wish you would spend more time thinking about school and your final exams."

But Miral had other things in mind than her diploma. Later that evening, as she walked through the streets of the Old City on her way to a PFLP section meeting and inhaled the intensely fragrant Middle Eastern spices in the souk, she sensed all the fascination of the city, all the mysterious force that enveloped it. Her thoughts turned to some of Khaldun's comical gestures, which were still vivid in her memory, and she wondered when she would hear from him again. She had promised to write to him. She thought about the gratitude of the people in the villages around Ramallah. Simple, proud country folk subjected to continual humiliations, determined to hold on to their traditions and their culture. As soon as she saw Hani, she lit up like a candle. He came to her, kissed her on the forehead, and whispered in her ear that the section was being watched and that no more meetings would be held in that place. She must go back home, he said, and he would contact her.

At three o'clock the following morning, someone began knocking violently on her front door. Miral understood at once what was going on; she had heard some comrades in the Popular Front talk about such visits. Jamal, surprised and half-asleep, went to the door.

"Police! Open up!" The speaker was a man dressed in civilian clothes. He held out a shiny badge to the incredulous Jamal. "Where is your daughter Miral?" the man asked. "She has to come with us. Here's the warrant," he added, handing Jamal a sheet of paper.

"Why do you want to talk to her? What has she done? There must be some mistake," Jamal said, his voice husky with anxiety.

"There's no mistake. We have a precise warrant. Your daughter must come with us for questioning. Now go and call her—we're in a hurry," the man said, stepping into the living room. Two uniformed policemen stood at the front door, awaiting orders.

Miral, already dressed, came out of her room. "Here I am," she said, feigning a self-assurance that in fact was nowhere to be found inside her.

"Well, I see that you're ready. Let's go, then," the man said, seizing Miral by the arm. She was repulsed by the touch of his cold hand. When they passed in front of her father, Miral said, "It's all right, Papa. I haven't done anything wrong. I'll be back soon, you'll see," and she left him, an old, devastated man in pajamas.

When he saw his daughter being roughly shoved into a police van, together with some other young people from the neighborhood, Jamal ran into the bedroom for his shoes, thinking that he would follow on foot. Meanwhile, a small crowd of furious, worried parents had gathered in the street; someone said the police had rounded up a great many people that night. Jamal saw many of his neighbors embracing one another and weeping. Soldiers were coming out of houses, carrying books, documents, and computers, as Jamal started running desperately after the van.

It rolled through the streets of the Old City, heading for the Mascubia police station, inside the New Gate, where the interrogation center was. So many young Palestinians had been brutally tortured inside the walls of that macabre facade that every Arab who passed in front of it felt uneasy. The deserted streets gave Jerusalem a sullen aspect. The new city, with its towering buildings, seemed to be laying siege to the ancient and tormented Old City.

The van came to a stop in the courtyard of the station, and the prisoners were escorted to their various cells. With the exception of a trembling and weeping girl from her neighborhood, Miral knew none of the others. She was brought into a large room. It was dark except for the light shed by a bulb hanging from the ceiling over a rusty desk with an old black telephone. The rest of the furniture consisted of three wooden chairs and a metal locker. The walls bore stains of every color and dimension, some of them recognizable as dried blood. It was very cold, but Miral's anxiety prevented her from feeling the external temperature. Her hands were sweating, her heart was beating uncontrollably, and she kept thinking, "I must stay calm. They're trying to frighten me, to upset me. I must stay calm." Despite her efforts to bolster her spirits, her legs were getting weaker and weaker. She heard far-off sounds, the thudding of slammed doors, footsteps in the corridors. That waiting period, which in reality lasted no longer than half an hour, seemed immeasurably vast to Miral. Every minute increased her distress. Finally, the metal door behind her opened, startling her.

"Come here. Sit in front of me," a police officer ordered her, pointing to a chair that faced the desk. Except for a lock of hair that hung down over his forehead, he was almost completely bald. He sat down and arrogantly lit a cigarette. Then he took a file out of a drawer. Miral caught a glimpse of her name and some documents in Hebrew. The man began to turn pages with his chubby fingers, all the while holding the cigarette clamped between his lips. "We've had our eye on you for some time now, Miral," he said, chuckling in a reproachful tone. "You've disappointed your father, and you've disappointed all of us." There was a singsong quality to his voice.

"I beg your pardon?" Miral replied, feigning ignorance. She had decided to limit herself—if she could—to giving only vague and evasive answers.

As the policeman slowly put out his cigarette, his lips curled in a sneer. "Very well," he said. "If you answer properly, I'll let you go back home before nightfall. Otherwise, you'll force me to keep you here longer. Who gives these orders?" As he asked this question, he showed her a leaflet. Miral shrugged her shoulders. The leaflet came from the PFLP; it was one she herself had delivered two days before, carrying them from place to place in a straw purse under a few bunches of wild mint. The leaflets bore the central orders to the Bethlehem section. Jasmine was supposed to deliver them but had asked Miral to do so in her stead, and Miral had complied unbeknownst to Hani, who, when he found out, became quite angry and accused her of being reckless and impulsive. Miral had resented this, but he explained that the whole area was full of collaborators. She should have told him first, he said.

"Look at it closely," the officer said. It sounded like an ultimatum, and it snapped her out of her thoughts. "And don't make me waste time with little games."

After an initial moment of confusion, Miral replied, "Do you want me to say what you want to hear, or do you want me to tell you the truth? I don't know what that leaflet is."

"Don't give me that shit! If you want to play the naive innocent, do it with your daddy, not with me. Now take a good look at this photograph and tell me which of these is the one who gives the orders."

The photograph showed almost all the members of the PFLP,

including Hani, at the last demonstration. Miral found the strength for another denial: "I don't have the slightest idea who these people are." She spoke in the firmest voice she could summon up.

The policeman leaned back in his chair and lit another cigarette. "It would be a shame for a pretty girl like you to spend the best years of her life in prison. A real shame." His voice resumed its singsong lilt. "Give me the names, and I'll let you go home immediately." He handed her a pen. "If you don't like saying them, write them down. Or take the pen and make a circle around the faces of the persons who print these flyers. Who are they? Who brings them their orders? Who's their contact with the outside?"

The man's fake courtesy rekindled Miral's anger. "It's no good putting on the paternal act. I don't know who these people are. I don't know who printed the leaflets. I don't know anything at all." And she added defiantly, "Beat me if you have to. I don't know anything."

He laughed and pushed a button. "So you want to play with the grown-ups. Keep provoking me and you'll see what happens to that pretty face of yours. You won't recognize yourself when you walk out of here!"

Miral gave him a defiant look. "If beating up a girl makes you feel more like a man, do it."

"You're mistaken. I personally will not lay a finger on you. But I've got a friend who can't wait for the chance."

"I'm an Israeli citizen," Miral asserted. "If this is really a democracy, I have the same rights you do."

The man smiled as he spoke: "Not when it's a matter of national security. Now, will you make up your mind to cooperate, or shall I call my friend?"

Miral looked at him. "I have nothing to say."

He fell silent and continued to smoke, without saying another word and without looking at her, as if he were alone in the room. Suddenly, Miral heard the heavy door behind her screech on its hinges. She turned around and saw a woman a little older than thirty, blonde and powerfully built. She was wearing a black T-shirt, sand-colored camouflage pants, and a pair of heavy combat boots.

Without a word, she rushed at Miral, seized her by the hair, and dragged her out of the room. Miral screamed as she was yanked along a corridor made dazzlingly bright by innumerable fluorescent lights. Her cries mingled with those of other young people who were being beaten. Those howls of pain seemed to shake the whole building. The woman flung Miral through an open door, into a room that was practically dark. It looked like a bathroom, completely covered with white tiles and divided by transparent curtains. The woman tied Miral's hands with plastic handcuffs and shoved the girl's face against the wall. Miral felt the plastic cord cutting into her wrists and her heart beat wildly, as she waited for the torture to begin.

She did not have long to wait. Blows from a riding crop began raining down on her back, on her legs, on her neck. The pain quickly became unbearable, and Miral could not keep from crying out every time the whip struck her. She could feel her T-shirt ripping, and shortly after that she felt blood running down her back. After a few minutes, she fainted, and when she regained consciousness, her T-shirt and trousers were gone. She felt ashamed and tried to cover herself, but her hands were still tied behind her back. Stunned as she was, she had no idea how much time had passed. Two female soldiers ordered her to kneel on the cold, dirty floor. "You mustn't sit down. If you do, the blonde will come back. She's not finished with you yet," they told her, laughing. After an hour, Miral could take no more and fainted again. This time she woke up lying in an extremely small room. Behind a grate, the same policeman as before repeated the same questions, over and over, but without success.

"I want to go home. I want to wake up from this nightmare," she kept telling herself. "I just have to hold out a few hours longer."

But it wasn't long before a new torturess entered the cell. As the hours passed, the torments became more and more refined. At one point, a hood was put over her head and removed after half an hour. Miral found herself surrounded with blinding light and deafening music interspersed with other detainees' cries of pain. The sound and light prevented Miral from sleeping. To escape mentally from her situation, Miral began envisioning some of her life's happiest moments. She thought about the warm room she'd had as a child, about its bright blue walls, about photographs of her friends, about her sister on the beach where they played games in the water. She couldn't remember when she had hidden Hani's gifts, especially that book, *My Home, My Land*. As she kept searching her mind for a way out, for an escape from that place, she imagined the colors red and yellow, the colors of the big carpet that hung on the wall of her family's living room. "That carpet's much older than you, Miral. It's at least eighty years old," her father would remind her proudly.

As she was traveling in a dream to escape the physical pain that throbbed in her wounds, a different police officer came by every half hour, shook her, and asked her the same questions. Her answer was always the same, too: she knew nothing. Her collapse began several hours later, when she asked for permission to go to the bathroom and was denied. She could go, they said, if she gave them something, and at that point Miral started crying hysterically, over-whelmed by shame and humiliation at the sight of her wet legs and the puddle of urine under her.

She was unable to calm her anxiety. Weariness hung over her, but she wasn't through yet. She was brought back to the first room. "How disgusting! What a smell!" the officer said. "Do you want to wash up? Do you want your clothes?" When she said yes, he asked, "So will you cooperate, or shall we continue?"

"But I don't know anything!" Miral replied. "You've got the wrong person." At those words, he struck her violently with the back of his hand, knocking her to the ground. As Miral was trying to get up from the floor, using one hand to wipe away the blood that was flowing from her nose, two female soldiers entered, raised her up, and handed her a wet towel so she could clean her face. Then they roughly helped her into a sweatshirt and a pair of pants.

It was time to go before the judge, as the law regarding minors required.

10

During those same hours, Jamal was sitting in the waiting room of the police station, asking every ten minutes for news of his daughter, but no one knew anything about her. Miral was in another building, the interrogation center, which stood across the way. The entrance to the station was a long corridor, spartan but fairly accommodating. Jewish music filled the air, perhaps to prevent the most piercing screams from reaching the ears of the detainees' relatives. Jamal waited together with other parents, some of them still in their pajamas, sitting in chairs and trying to console one another. Someone announced that an important person had been arrested carrying compromising documents and trying to get into Jordan. Jamal realized that it was useless to remain where he was and that he had to do something more than wait. When he saw the first light of dawn spreading over the Galilean hills, he decided in desperation that the best course of action would be to leave the station and find a lawyer. He realized that to stay in that waiting room, where he was helpless, was nothing but an exercise in futility.

He found a lawyer. Although still young, this man had acquired a great deal of legal experience since the outbreak of the intifada, and he was quite familiar with cases involving Palestinian militants who were under arrest. "Don't worry, Jamal," the lawyer told him over the telephone. "If your daughter's a minor, she'll go on trial today, and if she doesn't have anything on her record, they'll let her go with a warning."

And as the lawyer had predicted, Miral, escorted by two police officers, was brought into court on the afternoon of the following day. The courtroom was empty except for a small number of people, one of whom was the judge. He never looked at her but kept his eyes on the documents he was perusing. She caught a glimpse of her father in the corner, sitting next to two other persons, and as soon as the judge raised his head, looked at the prosecuting attorney, and asked, "What do we have here?" the man next to her father approached and declared himself Jamal's lawyer. Instinctively, Miral saw that this was her chance and resolved to act innocent and submissive, casting aside all defiance. And when the prosecutor began to state his case to the judge, Miral took off the sweatshirt that covered her bruises. The officers glared at her threateningly, recognizing her attempt to display for the judge's benefit the marks of her mistreatment, which were clearly visible, including those under her white, bloodstained T-shirt. Jamal had seemed dejected, but when he saw Miral's condition, he had to make a great effort to keep from crying out. The lawyer gripped his arm and told him to remain calm. He could see that Miral had been beaten and probably tortured, but the lawyer whispered that this was practically routine procedure for extracting information, and that nobody was spared, not even the youngest.

Miral was trying to avoid her father's eyes, but out of the corner of her own she saw him trembling in his chair.

The judge very brusquely asked the prosecuting attorney if

Miral had made a statement of confession or if there was any evidence of her involvement in the disorders of the intifada, and the prosecutor replied that he needed another twenty-four hours before he could produce such evidence and offered the judge a photograph that showed Miral, in profile, at a demonstration. The judge gazed at Miral for a moment before turning his attention to the dialogue between the two attorneys. Miral's lawyer asked the prosecutor if there was any other evidence or if there were any witnesses against his client. The prosecutor contemptuously avoided answering him and continued talking only to the judge, but the judge told the prosecutor to reply to the lawyer's questions. That same morning, the Israeli daily newspaper *Haaretz* had published a long denunciation of the abuses committed by Israeli officers in charge of interrogations, some of whose victims were minors, all in the name of national security. The title of the article was "How Far Are We Willing to Go?" and a copy of the paper lay on the judge's desk. After listening to the arguments on both sides, he said that since the accused was a minor who had not confessed and had committed no prior offense, he would grant her the benefit of general mitigating circumstances. Jamal's lawyer gave him a satisfied smile.

"You're free to go," the judge said, specifying that she pay a fine amounting to three thousand shekels, or about seven hundred dollars. Then, with a stern look in Miral's direction, he added, "I don't want to see you in my courtroom again. The next time, the sentence won't be so light. Therefore you had best make sure that you stay far away from trouble from now on."

A weight lifted from his chest, Jamal gladly paid the fine and waited for Miral to be set free. When the gate opened and he saw her appear, his heart leaped into his throat, and tears rolled down his cheeks as he embraced her with all the strength he had. The tension of those interminable hours was finally dissolved. Miral could not suppress a cry of pain because of the burning wounds on her back. She was brought at once to an outpatient clinic, where a doctor dressed her wounds, and then she was finally able to go home.

Jamal understood that danger still hung in the air. He couldn't take a repetition of such events. Miral washed and went to bed, and as soon as she fell asleep, Jamal asked Rania to stay with her sister and went to Dar El-Tifel. He wanted to discuss with Hind his decision to remove Miral from Jerusalem for a time in order to keep her safe for the immediate future. Hind received him in her office, and after an exchange of cordial greetings, she asked him for news of Miral.

While Jamal told her the story, recounting what had happened and describing Miral's physical state, tears filled his eyes. With every detail he added, Hind's face showed greater distress and worry. She agreed about the necessity of sending Miral to her aunt in Haifa for a time. Until exams began, Hind said. Jamal asked if a few weeks would be long enough. When Hind said yes, he wanted to know if it would compromise Miral's grades. Hind told him not to worry. Miral knew what the syllabus required and would be fine if she studied on her own while she was at her aunt's. Jamal left with a knapsack full of books and notebooks to take home to his daughter.

Haifa was an ideal place, a calm city free of the heavy political air that one breathed everywhere in Jerusalem. The city of Haifa was considered something of a civic laboratory, where Israelis and Palestinians managed to live in peaceful coexistence.

. . .

Miral's departure was fixed for three days later, and she remained in bed during that time, letting her wounds heal—those that had marked her body, but also her dignity. She seemed like an injured bird; any movement cost her great effort, and she hardly spoke. She asked Rania for news of those who had been arrested in the neighborhood, and Rania told her that many were still in jail, while others who had not been found that night—Hani among them—were living as fugitives.

This news landed on Miral heavy as the whip, and after listening to her sister, she pulled the covers over her head and began to weep. Rania tried to soothe her, rubbing her sister's feet and assuring her that she would do just fine in Haifa.

Several hours before the scheduled departure, while her father was in the mosque leading the morning prayer, Miral received unexpected visitors: two of her former PFLP comrades, Jasmine and Ayman. For the first time in days, Miral smiled, but when she tried to embrace them, they seemed cold and aloof; then, when they started firing questions at her, Miral understood that this was not just a visit from some old friends but an interrogation. They asked her to tell them exactly how her arrest had been conducted, what methods had been used to make her talk, and whether she had been confronted with anyone else. Above all, they wanted to know what evidence and what names the Israeli agents had in hand. This was a standard procedure utilized by the PFLP to compare information and to determine whether any of their members had confessed under questioning, or even worse, had been forced to collaborate. Saddened and disappointed, Miral told them everything. She revealed that she was about to be sent to Haifa to study and prepare for her final examinations. When she asked for news of Hani, her two questioners exchanged enigmatic looks and informed her that he had been relieved of his post as secretary of the Jerusalem section of the PFLP. They warned Miral to be on her guard against him because of his turncoat attitudes and his speeches in favor of negotiations with the Israelis, which the Palestinian left considered high treason. Finally, before leaving, Jasmine and Ayman asked Miral not to try to contact any of them and to await a future communication. Immediately after they left, Miral asked Rania to leave a message for Hani with the proprietor of a certain café in the Armenian Quarter; Hani was to know that she had gone to Haifa, that she would be back in a few weeks, and that if he wanted to communicate with her, he would have to do so through that café. On his way home after the prayer, Jamal saw Jasmine leaving his house. His face darkened, and without saying a word to Miral, he advanced the time of their departure and personally accompanied Miral to Haifa.

At the moment when they passed the city limits of Jerusalem, Miral was choked by the sensation that she was abandoning everything dearest to her. And while the bus, puffing and snorting, crossed the dusty roads of Samaria on the way to Haifa, she felt a rising anguish. To keep her father from seeing her tears, she spent the whole trip with her forehead glued to the window.

Miral knew that Haifa was near when she spotted the white and red flowers of the oleander bushes that lined the last stretch of road before the bus entered the city. The vehicle's windows seemed almost caressed by those plants, and then the first houses appeared, scattered along the edge of the beach. For an instant, Miral caught a glimpse of the Arab cemetery and its sand-beaten gravestones. That was where her mother was buried, a few paces from the sea and the beach she had loved so much, and where she used to bring her friends in summer to take long walks on the shore.

The sight of that cemetery strangely brought a hint of serenity to Miral's mind.

$\mathcal{M}$iral felt at home in Haifa, where she and Rania had spent most of their summers at Aunt Tamam's house rejoicing in the slower rhythms that replaced their strict school schedules. The girls were always curious to see their mother's native city again and discover how it had changed since the previous year, how much their cousins had grown, and how many new buildings had been constructed on Mount Carmel. But their preferred place was the beach, where they passed entire days swimming and chasing each other.

The atmosphere in Haifa was completely different from the climate that prevailed in Jerusalem, for in Haifa, the new and the old mingled together in harmony. The city was always in motion, searching—like its inhabitants—for an identity. Despite the fact that the Arab neighborhoods with their picturesque alleyways, pot-holed streets, and peeling plaster had been partially razed and re-placed with modern residential buildings, life in Haifa was more pleasant than it was elsewhere. The city was sunny, convivial, joy-ful, with its colorful shops always open and the long green stretch that ran from the sea to Mount Carmel decorated like a Christmas tree with restaurants of every kind, one after the other on both sides of the street, where songs could be heard in every language. On paper, Arab and Jewish citizens of Israel had equal rights, but in Haifa coexistence between Arabs and Israelis was a reality, not a utopia, and it was the result of the courageous decision to include the Arabs who had remained there in the State of Israel. Here the wounds left by the war and by the Arabs' abandonment of their homes—homes that were immediately assigned to Jews who immigrated to Israel from the ruins of Europe after World War II— seemed to have the ability to heal.

Whether due to the cosmopolitan character that the port gave the city, the fact that its annexation went back to the distant past of 1948, or the warm, bittersweet sea air, there was a cultural ferment in Haifa that made the place open and welcoming to diversity of every kind. A lot of people spoke both Arabic and Hebrew, and people mingled with one another not only as work colleagues but also as friends.

But this time, Haifa represented for Miral a place of exile from her world. She didn't know how many hours she had spent on the bus, but when she saw her aunt, who had come to the station to welcome her, Miral understood that her immediate fate was sealed. Jamal left the following day. Miral had watched him as he whispered to her aunt Tamam and had seen the worry and sorrow in his face.

Miral fell into a trancelike state. She spent entire days lying on her bed with the windows closed, eating very little. There was apparently no one she wished to see, not even her beloved cousin Samer, who ordinarily kept her occupied for days on end with his singing and chatter. Tamam tried to distract her, lying on a nearby bed and telling her stories about her mother. Nadia, Tamam said, had been fascinated by Israeli women and their style of life, by their independence, their clothes, their beach parties, and she recalled how Miral's mother had been capable of understanding linguistic nuances that others missed in the songs performed by the bands along the seafront. "Your mother always used to say, 'When I watch people dancing, their swaying bodies look to me as if joy is possible in this world.' Your mother loved dancing."

Tamam noted how much her niece had grown since she last saw her, and it seemed to her that she could detect in Miral's eyes the same lively curiosity she remembered in her sister Nadia. Similarly, Miral could glimpse—in certain attitudes her aunt assumed, in the imperceptible movement of her hand before she said something she considered important, in her way of smiling—traces of her mother, of the little that she remembered of her. What Miral appreciated most about her aunt was her open mind, which sometimes led her to drop her traditional woman's values. While speaking to Tamam one day about a neighbor notorious for having extramarital affairs, Miral was stunned to hear her aunt declare that such behavior was the result of unhappiness and loneliness, not wickedness.

Tamam described to her niece what life had been like for the family after 1948. She related amusing anecdotes about herself and her husband, in hopes of persuading Miral to leave her bed and take a walk, or perhaps to go shopping, but the girl refused. And so Tamam turned to her son, Samer, for help. Cousin Samer was in his first year at the university, a young man of twenty-two, with a sleek, muscular body and long lashes that emphasized his black eyes, whose radiant appeal did not pass unobserved. He had become quite popular in the family for his good nature, helpfulness, and good looks, but his most endearing trait was his clumsiness. He was continually breaking things at home, to the chagrin of his mother and the general amusement of the rest of the family.

Samer and Miral were cousins but really bound by a relationship of friendship and deep affection. It therefore saddened him to see her in such a state, and he resolved to intervene. Entering her room with a cup of coffee, he opened the windows, snatched off her covers, and said, "Get up now, or I'll be forced to pick you up and carry you to the bathroom! Come on, get up, I'm taking you to a place I know."

"Leave me alone!" Miral shouted. "Stop it, please! I'm not in the mood. I'm too tired to do anything and my back still hurts."

"Get over it," Samer said, and then he lifted her off the bed forcefully and carried her into the shower. As the jet of cold water drenched them both, Miral started laughing, "All right, let me wash up and I'll go with you. But get out of here and leave me alone!"

Samer, dripping, exited the bathroom, calling out as he closed the door, "I'll give you ten minutes and then I'm coming back in. Consider yourself warned!"

Tamam was overjoyed to see them going out together again. Once they were in the car, Miral asked, "Now where?"

"We're going to a beach party," Samer replied. "You have to meet some friends of mine."

Miral said, "Let me out! All this so I can meet your stupid friends?"

"Miral, I want you to see my fiancée."

This declaration stopped Miral, and she smiled as she thought about her friend Maha, who had had something of a fling with Samer the summer before. Miral hadn't realized that things had gotten serious. Maha was a girl from Dar El-Tifel. As she was an orphan and had no other relatives, she spent her summers at the school. But the previous year, she had graduated and gotten a scholarship to study at the university in Haifa, and had accompanied Miral and Rania there. Miral thought back to her long walks with Maha through the streets of the commercial district, behind the port, where most of the clothing stores were located. She remembered her friend's sensitivity and shyness, and how she had become embarrassed when she saw young people kissing in public or observed the scanty clothes favored by the women of Haifa, who wore miniskirts and even bikinis to walk around town. As the days passed, Maha, who had been pale and always sad-eyed, seemed to be reborn. The sun and the sea air had done her good, giving her a healthy color and what seemed like a permanent smile. Now Miral understood why.

As happened whenever she was in Haifa, Miral's curiosity was aroused by everything around her. She noticed even the smallest changes that had taken place since the previous year—a freshly plastered house, a bar with a new sign, a bench on the seafront that hadn't been there before. Her body, too, seemed to respond positively, not just to the warmth of the sun but also to every facet of her native city, which constantly revealed some new, iridescent marvel, like a meadow after a summer shower.

Samer parked his car far from Carmel beach, and so they had to walk for a good distance along the seafront to reach their destination. It was a warm spring evening; the sun had not yet completely sunk behind the horizon, and a light breeze was stirring the branches of the tall palm trees. The two young people walked along slowly, chatting about this and that, until Miral suddenly stopped and stood still, pricking up her ears and listening to a song that was coming from a bar on the beach.

A girl with delicate features and loose, shoulder-length blonde hair was setting the tables and moving to the rhythm of the music. She was a couple of years older than Miral and appeared unaware of her surroundings, transported, following a harmony that seemed to come not so much from the radio as from inside her. Leaving Samer, who had stopped to greet some other friends, Miral went up to this young woman and asked, "What song is that?"

The girl looked up, saw Miral, and smiled at her. Then she placed the last glass on a table and said, "'Here Comes the Sun,' by the Beatles."

"It's wonderful," said Miral, who had never heard a song she liked so much. "You know, the music I'm used to is a little different," she added, and then she quickly bit her upper lip. She didn't want the girl to ask her too many questions. This evening she didn't want to think about Jerusalem and the demonstrations; she just wanted to be like a normal teenager on her way to a party.

Perhaps sensing Miral's embarrassment, the other girl made no inquiries and simply introduced herself. "I'm Lisa," she said, holding out her hand, which was pale as alabaster. Miral, surprised by this unexpected familiarity, shook the extended hand with some force and stated her own name in the same tone of voice she used in school at roll call. Then she said good-bye and went back to Samer and his friends.

"Where were you?" Samer asked.

"Do you know that girl? I think she's an Israeli."

"Of course I know her. Very well, in fact. I'll tell you all about her later," Samer replied.

"I'm sorry I walked away. It was just that I heard that sweet song and I wanted to get closer to it."

"Well, look, it's about time for you to discover that patriotic hymns are not the only kind of music in existence," Maha exclaimed, embracing Miral and greeting her affectionately.

The two young women looked into each other's eyes for a few seconds and then burst out laughing. Samer hugged them both and said, "Dinner's all ready! Ron's been grilling!"

Miral noticed that almost all the guests at the party were Israeli Jews, but after her initial embarrassment, she stopped paying attention to that fact, and everyone had a good time. Maha told her how her life had changed since she came to Haifa, but the music, which was very loud, prevented Miral from hearing much of what her friend said. After they had eaten, Samer invited them to dance. Miral didn't feel like it, but she was dragged onto the floor by Maha and Lisa. At the end of the evening, they all sat around a fire, chatting, their voices mingling with the general babble. It became clear to Miral that everyone either intentionally or obliviously avoided any reference whatsoever to politics, right up until the moment when a boy questioned her about a pin she was wearing on her dress. "What does that symbol stand for?" he asked, coming closer to her so that he could see it better.

He must have already guessed what it was, because she could hear that the tone of his voice had changed. "It's the Palestinian flag," she replied, as naturally and ingenuously as she could.

"Ah," was all he said in front of her. But as he moved away, she heard him muttering: "Hard to believe. We give them citizenship and they don't appreciate it."

The girls started laughing, and despite this little incident the party went very well.

. . .

Maha's presence during those days changed many of her friend's habits. Miral had never spent so much time talking to anyone, not even her sister, and now the afternoons seemed too short to contain all their conversations. Maha helped Miral study for her final examinations; she knew all sorts of memorization techniques and was able to remember the questions that she'd had to answer the year before. And although Miral wasn't able to concentrate very well, Maha's help obliged her to make a greater effort. Within a few months, she would have to decide what course of study she would pursue in college. Maha suggested that she enroll at the University of Haifa, but that would mean distancing herself from Hani forever. She wasn't ready for that. Observing the other girls her age, watching them serenely joking among themselves, she thought that perhaps they made fewer problems for themselves than she did, that their blissful ignorance spared them from the cruelty of life outside Haifa. Besides, a few weeks before she hadn't a trace of her current lightheartedness, which in reality had little to do with who she was.

Miral consoled herself by thinking about the great inner freedom she had gained, imagining that many of those girls would marry men chosen by their families and would accept those arranged marriages without complaint. They would stand by their husbands even if they didn't love them, and they would be as faithful to them as dogs to their masters, not by choice, but of necessity. As she was slowly walking home one evening, and the sun was turning a stretch of the sea's horizon an intense red, she realized that she—like her mother, who had always been an independent woman—had no intention of following a track laid out for her by someone else.

Samer appeared more and more evasive and nervous, especially if Maha was around. Miral could see that something between them had been lost. One night he confided to Miral that he had fallen in love with an Israeli girl. The shock made her jump. "Are you serious? Your mother will have a heart attack!" Samer replied that Tamam already knew and that the time had come to move beyond prejudices. He told Miral that he had invited the girl to lunch the following day.

Miral's aunt was in a state of profound agitation. She was walking back and forth in the room, straightening the sofa cushions, shining the silver; she asked Miral to help her with the preparations. Miral had risen very early that morning and found her aunt already busy in the kitchen. Miral could read in her movements an uncharacteristic anxiety, bordering on hysteria, as she dashed about the kitchen preparing the most traditional Arab dishes: couscous with fish for a first course, then chickpea soup, salads, and falafel followed by walnut-stuffed dates, with lemonade and mint tea to drink. In the end, it turned out to be practically impossible to help her in any way, seeing that she wanted to supervise everything, including the setting of the table, dictating literally to the millimeter the position that every object must occupy. Then she put on the traditional garb for festive occasions, thus causing her niece even greater amazement, because Miral's aunt Tamam, like many of the women of Haifa, always dressed in Western clothing.

Shocked by the long black galabia and the scarf covering her head, Miral wondered what her aunt was trying to demonstrate, what message was hidden behind all that industrious preparation. Was she prejudiced against the girl, or did she just want to underline their differences? When Tamam noticed her niece's bewilderment, she explained that she had never met her son's girlfriend. She knew only that Samer was very much in love, and that she was the daughter of a general in the Israeli army. For a moment, she looked at Miral with a peculiar expression on her face, as if to say, "What's happening to us? They kill our people in the West Bank, and my son's dating a Jewish girl? Just wait and see how people are going to look at us!"

Tamam's penthouse apartment, with its big roof terrace offering a view of the sea, was located in the Halisa neighborhood, in a building where both Arabs and Jews lived. She had cordial relations with her Jewish neighbors, some of whom had even become her friends. Nevertheless, it would not have been easy for any Arab woman willingly to accept her son's love for a Jewish girl, especially one who was the daughter of an army officer.

This realization made Miral feel uncomfortable, too. As she waited for Samer and his beloved to arrive, Miral reflected that the girl's father might have headed operations that led to the death or disappearance of some of her friends. Maybe one day he would lead his men into the Kalandia refugee camp, where they would kill the most daring kids, including some of the pupils from her English class.

When the doorbell rang, Miral and her aunt, who had each been lost in her own thoughts, jumped in their seats. They exchanged glances for an instant, and each of them almost absentmindedly arranged the other's clothes.

12

Great was Miral's surprise when she opened the door to find Lisa standing there, her blonde hair reflecting the sunlight. She, too, was openmouthed with surprise.

The two girls hit it off right away and chatted with the familiarity of old friends, although they were both aware of the profound difference that divided them. When they had first met, Lisa noticed the pin with the Palestinian flag on Miral's chest, but Miral didn't seem to Lisa like one of the fundamentalists her father was always talking about. Lisa ate her couscous with relish, and between one mouthful and another, she complimented Tamam on the lunch she had prepared. But after various attempts to initiate a conversation with her—attempts at which her hostess seemed to flinch—Lisa realized that Samer's mother was mistrustful, and she sensed what an effort it must have cost her to receive Lisa as a guest in her home. Miral, on the other hand, had to acknowledge that she couldn't help being fond of this girl, and Lisa told herself that maybe Miral was just a person who was proud of her own people, unlike Samer, who, like many of the young men of Haifa, didn't care about politics.

For Lisa, it was hard not to think about politics and all the problems it entailed. She adored her father, a strong, brave man in whom she had taken great pride when she was a little girl. Lately, however, a kind of uneasiness had grown alongside that sentiment as she watched the violence on the daily news programs. He never allowed his daughter to forget that they were on a mission in Israel; throughout her childhood he had repeatedly reminded her of her good fortune in being alive at the most important moment in her people's history, when they could finally live in their promised land. During the last two years, with his promotion to general, their talks had become increasingly tense. Every time she saw him, he seemed harder, wearier, and driven more by intolerance than by his old resolve.

During those same years, Lisa had discovered in her mother a woman who was much more interesting than she had ever believed, while her father's sporadic visits had become more of a nuisance than a pleasure. Her mother would tell her about her youth in various kibbutzim, where the socialist ideal was very strong, the people believed in justice and equality, and everyone worked the land, lived, and ate together. Lisa's mother had started at a university but quickly withdrew to get married. Ever since she was a little girl, Lisa had loved to watch her mother put on her makeup before a mirror. Her eyes were of an intense blue; her chestnut hair showed golden highlights in the sun; her face was oval, her lips full.

Lisa's childhood had resembled her mother's in many ways. Even though with the passage of time she had begun to feel a sense of disquiet that had no name, Lisa had led a tranquil life until she met Samer. Despite their evident cultural differences, they were bound by a strong, reciprocal passion. They loved to do the same things; she had immediately felt comfortable with him, and she had told herself that there was no reason not to go on seeing him. They were frequently and openly together, not just careless of the disapproving stares of the people around them, but feeling a bond in their complicity.

Lisa's mother, Rachel, had heard some gossip about her daughter, but she decided that Lisa was merely going through a period of adolescent rebellion. After all, she was the one who taught her daughter to be open. In any case, it was clear that her husband must know nothing about this. She was sure he would never accept it.

And so Lisa and Samer always met in Arab neighborhoods, to avoid the possibility that some relative or friend of her father's might spot her and tell him all about it. She tried not to give Samer the impression that she was ashamed of him, but it was still too soon for her to challenge her father's authority and prejudices. Samer was not at all bothered by the circumstances; he told her that they had led him to discover many delightful places that he would surely have never seen otherwise, even though many of them were frequented by Arabs as well as Jews.

Lisa wanted to get to know Miral better. She felt that they could be friends, since they both were curious, loved challenges, and were animated by a restlessness that would open up lines of communication and weaken any convictions they possessed more out of a sense of duty than out of personal beliefs.

During lunch Tamam, too, tried to be cordial, but Miral could hear in her voice the great effort she was making to seem at ease.

Samer, on the other hand, appeared satisfied with the way the afternoon was proceeding. Perhaps more than anything else, he was motivated by a certain childish desire to test his mother, who had always raised him to believe in mutual respect between Arabs and Jews. At that moment in his life, showing her that she was deficient in following the lessons she had taught him was more important than the lesson itself. He loved Lisa, but he knew all too well that "mixed" relationships often fostered an initial illusion of happiness and equality before the weaker of the two parties, if not both of them, plunged into an abyss of incomprehension and racism. Two girls he knew had been engaged to Jewish boys. After a little while, the boys broke up with the girls, and ever since then, neither the girls' families nor their lifelong friends had ever really accepted them back into the fold, considering them living evidence that such utopias were forever destined to remain wishful thinking.

After the lunch at Tamam's, Miral and Lisa began to see each other frequently. Samer took them for long drives in his car, and they spent afternoons on the beach together, all three of them. One day they set off without any particular destination in mind and wound up on the shore of Lake Tiberias, in the northern part of the country. It was an unseasonably hot day without a breath of wind, and they would gladly have taken a dip, but none of them had brought a bathing suit. However, that part of the lakeshore was deserted, and after first looking around, Lisa removed all her clothes with the utmost naturalness and plunged into the tepid water. Miral, shocked, watched her and then began to laugh, fascinated to witness a degree of daring she would never be capable of imitating, one that would always be impossible for someone of her culture.

Conversations between the two young women remained superficial, never touching on politics, and in any case they avoided it, almost frightened at the idea that their different heritage might cause the invisible wall that divided them to materialize.

During those days, they became, in a certain sense, friends. Miral would never be able to share her political passion with Lisa or speak to her of the pain that all Palestinians suffered because of the Israeli army's raids. For her part, Lisa felt a deep fondness for this girl who was so different from herself, but she thought that she could never confide to Miral the doubts that assailed her at night, a mixture of the fear caused by the terrorist attacks that were striking various cities and her sense of uneasiness whenever her father returned home. Their conversations were limited to their expectations in life, their favorite pastimes, their dreams for the future, pop music, Ping-Pong, and boyfriends.

The stories Lisa told also led Miral to think for the first time about sex. Every time the subject came up, it violated Miral's taboos, embarrassed her thoroughly, and caused violent blushing—as well as a great deal of nervous laughter. She had never discussed such things with anyone. Lisa, obviously more experienced and much less inhibited, gave her advice about sex, and Miral listened, always half-shocked and half-amused, as there opened up before her a world that religion and the solid walls of Dar El-Tifel had kept hidden from her and whose existence she had only been made aware of during her brief and intense relationship with Hani.

The frivolity of those days seemed to Miral like a gift, an unexpected treasure that would protect her in difficult years to come by reminding her that a different life was possible.

One day Lisa asked her a point-blank question: "Have you ever kissed a girl?"

"Kissed a girl the way you kiss a man?" Miral asked. "No, that's never happened to me," she replied, amused at the thought. "I've kissed my boyfriend, but we're still very shy."

Lisa smiled and explained, "First kisses never amount to much. Once you've learned the technique, things get much better."

"Really?"

"Yes, indeed." Lisa's face suddenly lit up. "Do you want to know how to *really* kiss a man?"

Miral looked at her friend in astonishment, not knowing what to expect from her. Then, in a faltering voice, she replied, "Y . . . yes?"

"You shouldn't answer me with a question, you know. Do you want to know how to do it or not?"

"Yes." Miral felt increasingly embarrassed, but her curiosity was too great.

Without hesitation, Lisa stepped close to her and delicately seized Miral's chin between her thumb and her index finger. Then she looked at Miral with a reassuring smile and said, "Now relax, don't think about anything, and follow me." Lisa pressed her lips to Miral's, and a feeling of warmth flooded through her; when their tongues met Miral spontaneously followed her friend's movements.

Then they both burst out laughing.

"You see? It wasn't so hard after all."

"No, it wasn't," Miral said, laughing, her face all red.

They spent their days together, filling each other in on two different worlds that existed in the same country. Lisa only once crossed the imaginary line they had drawn to safeguard the neutral territory in which they moved, when she mentioned that she would probably be called up to perform her military service the following year. Miral knew that Israeli girls were obligated to serve for two years and boys for three, and she shuddered at the possibility of encountering Lisa in uniform during a demonstration in Ramallah.

What Miral liked most about Lisa was her openness; what Lisa loved in Miral was her nerve.

Without any need to talk about it, however, both of them were perfectly aware that their surreal situation could not last, and that it would be swept away like leaves by the first breezes of fall, when the sea would get choppy and waves would lick the docks of the port.

Miral knew that Jerusalem wasn't Haifa, and that back in Jerusalem she would find the intifada, protesters fleeing from soldiers, and refugee children doomed to grow up inside a few square meters on the margin of everything.

One afternoon, while Miral and Lisa were strolling around from shop to shop, they ran into Lisa's father. Miral was taken by surprise; she had never considered the possibility of such a meeting, and the last thing she wanted to do was to stand face-to-face with this man, whose existence she had so far succeeded in not thinking about. She was repulsed by the idea of introducing herself and shaking his hand.

Lisa's father was a very tall man, with an oval face, regular features, and a lean body that he trained every day. Miral would never be able to define his expression; while he surely didn't smile—in fact, he looked as if he had never done so—he didn't seem to her like a bad person. He appeared normal, the kind of person whose profession you would never have been able to guess, were it not for his clothes.

Fortunately, Lisa—perhaps sensing her friend's discomfort—stepped out smartly to meet her father and left Miral behind. As a matter of fact, it was fortunate for everyone, for if Samer's family was unhappy about his relationship with Lisa, hers was openly hostile to it. Lisa didn't know exactly how her father had found out about the relationship, but one evening he had come home, called her into his study, and asked her to explain certain rumors he'd heard regarding her.

Lisa denied nothing, and when her father gave her a lecture on consistency and on the type of behavior he considered the duty of every member of his family, she limited herself to lowering her eyes without replying.

A few days later, when it became clear that his daughter had not broken off the relationship, he went so far as to threaten to kick her out of the house in the event that she and Samer were seen together again. Lisa spoke about this with no one, not even Samer, who in his ignorance continued to labor under the illusion that the only problem lay in trying to avoid places frequented by her relatives.

Before Miral's time in Haifa was over, the girls promised each other that they would remain friends, whether Lisa was still with Samer or not.

When the date of Miral's final exams was approaching, she received a telephone call from her father asking her to come back home. A few days after her return to Jerusalem, Miral learned that Samer had been arrested on a false charge and held in an interrogation center for three days. He and Lisa were forced to face the real facts of their situation and, shortly afterward, they decided to break up.

13

Miral and Lisa, on the other hand, remained in touch, as if their friendship represented a challenge primarily to themselves and only secondarily to other people. A few weeks after her return to school, Miral had already taken her last exam when she received a telephone call from her friend. Lisa had some errands to run in Jerusalem the following day, and she asked Miral if she'd like to get together. It would be their first meeting outside the sphere of protection that Haifa had—up to a certain point—guaranteed them, and Miral felt a bit uneasy at the idea that someone might see her with her Jewish friend.

Miral appeared at the designated place and time, wearing a pair of close-fitting jeans, a blue T-shirt, and a white cotton sweatshirt. Lisa was lovelier than usual: her yellow dress was cut low enough to reveal the perfect shape of her breasts, and her hair fell loose on her shoulders, except for the two tresses that framed her face. Miral hadn't imagined that she would be so happy to see Lisa again; she led her to a quiet restaurant, where they had lunch and exchanged news.

As they were chatting, Lisa casually communicated her most important piece of information. "It turns out that I'm exempt from military service because of my asthma. I won't have to join up. I'm really happy about it," she said, keeping her voice low. Miral began to cough, stopped, and started again. Her second outburst attracted the attention of the owner, who started to approach their table, only to be stopped by a gesture from Miral, who indicated that everything was all right. Not even noticing this, Lisa went on: "You know, I've thought a lot about what you told me when you were in Haifa, about the Occupied Territories."

When the coffee came, Miral wanted to read the grounds in her friend's cup and tell her fortune. She told Lisa to drain the cup in one swallow, took it from her, and quickly inverted it on a saucer. Then, turning the cup upright, she began to scrutinize its contents carefully. "Something is going to change your life," she announced, interpreting a thick trace of sediment left by the cardamom coffee. She upended the cup again and rolled it, gently pressing its rim against the saucer. Then she inspected the coffee dregs once more, smiled, and said, "Before the end of next year, you're going to fall in love with an older man. And this time it will be true love." Samer immediately crossed Lisa's mind, and with him their romance, which had been wrecked for absurd, unacceptable reasons. "Come on, don't think about that," Miral said, guessing her friend's thoughts and smiling. "You two weren't meant for each other anyway. He's a great guy, but he's also a narcissist and a little immature. You need to be with someone sensitive and sweet. . . ." Lisa laughed; here was more proof that their friendship was leaving behind the sources from which it had sprung and becoming something exclusively between the two of them. They were two friends, simply two friends.

After paying the check, they decided to take a walk through the Old City. The air was pleasantly cool. "I'd like to see the place you feel most attached to," Lisa suddenly declared, interrupting the thread of their conversation. Miral wavered for an instant, fixing her eyes on her friend, and then hailed a passing taxi.

"Ramallah please."

When Lisa heard Miral tell the cab driver their destination, her first instinct was to get out of the car. She opened the door when the cab was already in motion, but Miral held her back with a gesture both delicate and forceful; her eyes, and an almost imperceptible movement of her head, let Lisa know that it was all right.

Meanwhile, the brown Mercedes was traveling on Saleh el-Din Street, crowded with shoppers carrying their purchases. Lisa looked at the shops, which extended out to the edge of the street, and the merchandise, which was displayed from floor to ceiling. The asphalt surface was riddled with potholes, and the taxi bounced along, leaving the last houses of Jerusalem behind. Neither of the girls uttered a word.

They were barely out of the cab when Lisa cried, "Why have you taken me here? Is this some kind of test?"

"I only want you to see that there's another world just a few kilometers from yours. A forgotten world, but it exists," Miral replied, walking a few meters ahead of Lisa and trying to avoid the puddles that the preceding days' rains had left everywhere.

"Has it occurred to you that I can get hurt here? Israelis aren't allowed!" Lisa said, crying out again and doing her best to keep up with Miral's rapid pace.

"Come on, Lisa, you know I'd never make you run unnecessary risks. Stay close to me, don't open your mouth, and if you really must talk, speak English, never Hebrew. I'll say you work for a European nongovernmental organization. You won't be in any danger."

Lisa noticed some kids playing soccer with an improbable ball that seemed to be made of rags. As soon as the children spotted the girls, they abandoned the makeshift playing field and ran toward them. As she watched the group of dirty, shouting little boys coming closer, Lisa thought that they were surely carrying rocks in their pockets, and once again her instinct was to run away, retrace her steps, return to the Ramallah road, and wait for a taxi to pass. But seeing Miral walk calmly toward the children, Lisa only slowed her pace. She saw the children surround her friend, who started distributing candy among them, stroking their heads, and affectionately patting their backs or behinds.

"A warm hand clutches mine," Lisa wrote in her diary that evening.

> I was expecting hostility, and instead I find myself
> surrounded by smiling faces. They take me by the hand
> and give me a tour of the camp. The children are poorly
> dressed, with patched pants and holes in their faded
> T-shirts. They show me their small, dark houses, where
> their mothers are cooking, bent over makeshift fires, or
> sitting before the doors and sewing. The kids speak to
> me in Arabic—except for the older ones, who use broken
> English—but I don't even need words to understand
> what they want me to know; they communicate with
> their eyes. There was just one boy who made me feel a
> little uneasy. He observed me from a distance. His black
> hair fell in a clump over his forehead, he had an
> extinguished cigarette stuck in the corner of his mouth,
> and he looked at me as though he knew I was Jewish. I
> saw Miral talking to him. They seemed serious, but she

didn't introduce me. For the first time I saw what
segregation is. Be that as it may, the fact remains that
this is a world we can't even imagine. These are
supposed to be our enemies?

Miral had her eyes on Lisa. The kids were holding her hands and leading her from one shack to another. They wanted to show her photographs of their dead brothers or fathers, or the few books they possessed, which they displayed as though they were precious heirlooms. Lisa was able to perceive in their eyes suppressed but intense emotion. She reciprocated the children's smiles and let herself be pulled along. In a few minutes, the kids were able to erase everything she'd ever heard about the refugee camps.

Miral went up to Khaldun's friend Said. He gave her a half smile and then handed her a package that he drew out from under his T-shirt. While Miral was hiding it in her backpack, Said lit a cigarette.

"So you're smoking now, too? When did you get this package?" she demanded, snatching the cigarette out of his mouth, throwing it to the ground, and stamping it out with the toe of her boot. Her brusque gesture took Said by surprise, and he remained immobile for a few seconds, a questioning expression on his face and smoke slowly issuing from his nostrils.

"A relative who came here through Jordan brought it about a week ago. There was a letter for me, too. Sounds like he's doing fine."

Miral put a hand on his shoulder. "Promise me you'll stop smoking?"

Said replied, "Is it going to kill me? I wake up every morning, and I know my chances of sleeping in my bed again that night are about the same as my chances of getting picked off by an Israeli sniper or crushed by a tank and winding up in a coffin." Then, without pausing, he added, "Tell me, how much is the life of a boy in a refugee camp worth?"

Miral didn't answer.

"I'll tell you how much, Miral. It's not worth anything, because we don't exist—we're outside the world. Cigarettes aren't as bad for you as growing up here." He kicked a can lying on the ground near his feet.

"What right do I have," Miral wondered, biting her tongue, "to come here all full of my Dar El-Tifel healthy-living theories and talk this way to a boy I hardly know, a boy who lives in these desperate conditions?"

Lisa's arrival rescued Miral from her embarrassment, and she walked away from Said to meet her friend. After a few steps, Miral turned around to wave to Said, but he had already disappeared.

During the trip back, Miral saw that Lisa was still shaken, as though ghosts that up until a few hours before had existed only in a few newspaper articles or television reports had suddenly become corporeal and taken on well-defined names and faces. "From now on," Miral thought, "she'll have those kids' faces burned into her brain. She'll feel their hands squeezing hers, and she'll see their eyes looking at her without pleading, showing her their living conditions with dignity, when nothing they have is dignified."

As the taxi negotiated the curves along the road on its way back to Jerusalem, Lisa clasped her friend's hand. She was unable to speak but felt as though she must make Miral understand that their visit to the camp had meant a great deal to her. That day she had seen that the ugliest place in the world, where the sewers are open to the sky, where the houses are made of mud and straw or corrugated metal, could be a place where solidarity, the sharing of the same condition, could lead to very solid relationships. Anyone who entered that place unarmed won everyone's heart immediately, by the mere fact of having come there. Lisa was shocked to discover that her country contained such dark corners. She repeated to herself over and over, "How can places like this exist? This can't be my country."

14

Once she was back at school and had reached her room, Miral closed and locked the door, sat on the bed, and opened the package. The first thing she saw was a photograph of Khaldun with some of his comrades, all of them dressed in black, with black-and-white kaffiyehs around their necks. Khaldun was smiling; a cigarette protruded from his mouth. On the back of the photograph he'd written, "As you can see, I haven't quit smoking, but in every other way I've changed a lot."

He did seem different. Now he was a man; she couldn't say he was handsome, but charm and confidence emanated from him. Miral was amazed to see his softened expression, so much less angry than when he was just a kid. The package also contained a letter, which she ripped open impatiently. Khaldun's handwriting, too, was more relaxed, more mature than it used to be.

Dear Miral,

I hope this package reaches you. I know you're still in Dar El-Tifel, but it's not easy for my friends to get to Jerusalem. Here's a picture of me. How do I look? I feel different already! I'm also sending you a book I wrote—

life is full of surprises. Sometimes when I look at the manuscript, I can't even believe it's there! It took me a year to write it, and I'm more interested in hearing your thoughts on it than anyone else's.

After my training was completed, I tried my hand at being a bodyguard for one of the leaders of the Popular Front, a serious intellectual and a writer. He's given me many books to read, he encourages me to write, like you, he tells me I'm too intelligent to be carrying a rifle. And so he gave me an old typewriter and obliged me to write down my story, all the things I've lived through, how I grew up in a refugee camp and how I found a way out of that inferno. I feel as though I've had to live several lives at once, but maybe I've come through all right, after all. You're in the third chapter. You had to be; I couldn't leave you out. I've understood many things in the past couple of years, Miral, and above all I've realized you were right when you said that a pen was often a more effective weapon for our cause than a rifle. Unfortunately, there are fewer and fewer of us who think so; difficult years are ahead of us, and the echo of explosions is going to drown out the sounds of words. I'm afraid that demagoguery will have a powerful impact on the masses. But more than anything else, I fear the impact of the religious fanatics. Where have these lunatics come from? We've always been a secular people. I've seen enough of them here in Lebanon to understand that the danger isn't in the holy books; it's in the heads of those who interpret them. You can't reason with them. They believe they're soldiers of God.

*I sound like a pessimist, right? Believe me, I'm not—
I'm just well informed. Please watch what you do. We
need people like you, who are interested in telling the
truth, without frills and without ideological censorship.
Meanwhile, will you write to me? I'm curious to know
how you are and what you've been doing all this time!*

*A month from now, at the same time, the boy who
gave you this package today will have another one for
you. If you want to send me a letter, the best thing to do
is to hand it to Said or my mother.*

*I'm sure that one day—before too long, I hope—we'll
be able to meet again. Maybe in some Arab country.*

> *Love & Kisses,*
> *Khaldun*

Miral wept for joy. Not only was Khaldun alive, he was even safe. She immediately went to Hind's residence and entered her office. Hind was examining some documents with three of the women who worked with her. "Mama Hind, I need to talk to you," Miral said, holding out the letter. The two of them stepped out onto the balcony. "I'd like to read you a fabulous letter," Miral said, visibly excited.

"But can't you wait a few minutes? I have to finish my work here. The documents can't wait."

"No, I can't either. It's really urgent. I need to know what you think about this."

Surrendering to Miral's insistence, Hind sat on a stool and prepared to listen to the contents of Khaldun's letter. When the reading was over, she smiled in simultaneous amusement and admiration.

"What profound, beautiful words. This boy is a poet. And God knows we need romanticism, we need to dream. Miral, do you realize that a life has been saved? Now, I've got great expectations for this boy's future. He makes some very intelligent observations. I think I must compliment you on that score, Miral."

Miral hugged her, gave her a quick kiss on the cheek, and hastened away with the letter.

Despite the fear she felt after her arrest, Miral continued to be politically engaged but in a different way. Jamal had noticed that when she was home during the weekends, some young men would come to visit Miral, among them the leaders of the resistance in the neighborhood. They met to discuss secret peace negotiations, the eventual makeup and development of the future state.

Jamal felt weak and incapable of protecting his daughter. One night, at two o'clock, there was a violent knocking at the door. Jamal got up, but before opening the door, he looked into the girls' bedroom. Miral, still awake, was holding a stack of about ten books. "I'll hide them. You go and open the door," he told Miral, his face white with fear. Miral got dressed while her father went out the back way and into the courtyard. With great effort and the aid of a stout pole, he opened a drain cover and dropped the books inside. The soldiers looked everywhere but found nothing.

The moment they left, Jamal collapsed into the armchair, his forehead dripping with sweat. The next day, when he retrieved the books from the drain, he saw a few sheets of paper sticking out of one of them and recognized Miral's handwriting.

The intifada broke out on a calm, sunny morning in
December 1987, after an Israeli truck ran into a car full

*of commuting Palestinian workers, killing four of them,
and then kept on going without stopping to help. Ever
since that day, there has been no indication that the
riots and demonstrations are going to die down. In the
beginning, the popular uprising spread like wildfire
throughout the Occupied Territories, Jerusalem, Nablus,
Jenin, Hebron, Gaza, Ramallah, all places where people
spontaneously gathered in the streets to protest. This
was the last straw, the drop that made the glass
overflow. Initially, the demonstrations were peaceful
and the protesters' faces were uncovered, but eventually
boys started throwing rocks at the tanks, which were a
symbol of the occupation and of our dashed hopes. The
Israeli suppression was massive and ferocious. They
hoped to put down the revolt in short order, but the
phenomenon forced the Israelis to change their tactics.
That was when the infiltrators and the rooftop snipers
appeared, the prisons filled up, and the soldiers began
to break the arms and legs of kids in the Occupied
Territories who were captured during clashes. At the
risk of dying, boys who are sometimes not much more
than children defy the Israeli tanks, launching stones at
them with slingshots or their bare hands. When their
uncovered faces emerge from the clouds of tear gas,
they look desperate, their eyes seething with adrenaline
and hatred. The soldiers on the other side, children of
survivors of the Shoah, are almost embarrassed, fighting
an invisible enemy from behind the protection of a thick
layer of steel. The Arabs have lost three wars, and it is
clear that Israel has military superiority. But protests in*

Palestine have made headlines all over the world. This isn't a war between two regular armies or even between poorly trained and badly equipped fedayeen and the most powerful army in the region; it's rather an instinctive, basic, desperate form of protest, which, in one of history's most grotesque paradoxes, resembles the Jewish uprising in the Warsaw ghetto. The intifada, the war of the rocks, an improbable and impossible revolt, a distorted, upside-down representation of David and Goliath, will strike the imagination of the West so forcefully that it will be awakened from its ten-year slumber regarding the situation in the Middle East. The rocks thrown by the young Palestinians have had no military effect whatsoever, but they have probably managed to put a few cracks in the world's conscience.

Jamal was impressed by the authority in Miral's language. She sounded like a reporter. But he was also concerned for his daughter's safety. He called Tamam that same day and asked her to come to Jerusalem and talk to her nieces about the seriousness of his physical condition. The girls' aunt arrived the following day and spoke quite frankly to Miral and Rania. "Your father is worried. You're big girls, and you should understand certain things . . . but there's something more important than anything else right now. Your father has asked me to tell you that he has leukemia—you ought to have been told some time ago—and he's going to have to undergo a serious operation followed by a course of treatments."

The girls were sitting side by side and holding hands, trying to

support each other and to react to the news that had just come
down on them. For some time, Miral had noticed that her father
had lost a good deal of weight, but she had thought he was suffering
from a psychological indisposition as a result of his concern for his
daughters. "He's very sick," Tamam went on. "You must stay close
to him, and most of all you must avoid doing anything to worry
him; you're going to have to stop your political activities. The idea
of soldiers in the house again greatly upsets him."

Rania suddenly began to cry, clutching her aunt, while Miral
remained in petrified silence. Their father had always been their
foundation in difficult moments, the one who had helped them
through the hardships of life, both small and great. Miral ran into
the bathroom and saw her frozen face disappear in the mirror in the
blur of her tears. The thought of losing her father had made her
invisible.

In the course of the following days, Rania decided not to sleep
on the school campus anymore but to live at home with Jamal.
Miral knew that this decision would have a bad effect on her sister's
studies, but since she perfectly understood Rania's reasons, she let
her do as she wished. Before long, as Miral had envisioned, Rania
stopped studying. She spent her days at her father's bedside, together with the woman who came every day to assist him. Every
now and then during the night, Rania would get up and go to his
room. She would observe him as he slept, and she could see that he
was getting thinner with each passing day. She wanted to tell him
not to go away, not to leave them on their own, to say that they
would never make it without him.

Miral came to see him every afternoon, but she didn't stop
participating in the authorized demonstrations, although she went

with less frequency. During that time, she became even more prudent; she would never want to be the cause of her father's final grief. Meanwhile, Jamal was sinking fast, but his mind remained clear, and he never complained about the spasms of pain caused by his disease. He loved to know that his daughters were nearby, and he was fond of showering them with advice and direction. Every time they entered his bedroom together, he would say that the sun had lit up his day. They would lie beside him on the bed and hug him for hours. Again and again, Rania would kiss her papa's cheeks, hollow though they were; his skin seemed extremely soft and transparent. Jamal continually implored his daughters to remain close and to take care of each other, no matter what directions their lives should take. He realized that Rania was neglecting her schoolwork, but he'd been unable to persuade her to apply herself more. In the end, Rania abandoned her studies altogether. Miral tried to dissuade her, but Rania was inflexible: "I'm not like you, Miral. Politics don't interest me, I don't like to study, and I don't have many friends here in Jerusalem. Next year I want to go and live in Haifa with Aunt Tamam."

This seemed like a long-prepared speech, and there wasn't much that Miral could add. While searching for convincing words, she started to say, "Rania, listen—" but her sister interrupted her at once. "Forget it, Miral. I've already made up my mind, and there's nothing you can say to make me change it. Really, it's better this way."

At school one afternoon, before she left the campus to visit her father, Miral went to speak to Hind about her sister, but instead she found only Miriam, the vice-principal, who was busy preparing some documents that needed Hind's signature. "She went out about half an hour ago. I don't know where she was headed," Miriam told Miral. "Do you want to leave a message for her?"

"No, thanks. I'll see her another day."

As she set out for home, Miral felt a little disappointed. Hind had to know that Rania had withdrawn from school, and yet she had done nothing to stop her. When she reached the house, Miral found Hind sitting at her father's bedside. Rania was in the kitchen, preparing some sage tea. Upon seeing Miral enter, the others stopped talking.

"How are you, Miral? Everything all right?" Hind asked, smiling good-naturedly. "I came here to speak with your father about Rania's situation, and we've agreed to let her do what she considers most appropriate."

"What do you mean?" Miral couldn't believe that this combative woman, who wouldn't let her go to demonstrations, was now surrendering so easily to her sister!

"Miral." Her father's voice was little more than a whisper. "For now, it's better this way." His hand, scrawny as it was, could still exert a powerful grip.

Rania came in with the tea.

"If you want, Miral, I'd very much like to have a private talk with you, just the two of us. How do you feel about coming to see me tomorrow afternoon?" Hind asked. Her look did not betray the least concern. Miral nodded. "Good," Hind said. "Then it's agreed. I'll expect you in my office tomorrow afternoon after classes."

"All right," Miral replied mournfully. Rania, by contrast, looked serene; as though liberated from a heavy burden, she moved swiftly and surely around the room, occasionally adjusting her father's bedclothes or the pillows supporting his back.

Hind left after tea, and the other three fell to chattering as they had always done. Somehow, Hind's serenity had infected them. They even joked about Rania's new shoes, whose color was so garish that it went with none of her dresses.

The following day, as agreed, Miral went to Hind's office. "You see, Miral," the headmistress began at once, barely giving the student time to sit down, "contrary to what you think, Rania's not just indulging some whim."

Miral looked at Hind questioningly. The girl was hoping, in fact, to change her sister's mind, precisely because she, Miral, was convinced that Rania's plan was a passing fancy, a bizarre idea that had come to her one day and that she had decided to act upon only because she didn't like studying.

"Rania has a psychological block that's very common in certain cases," Hind went on. "If we try to remove it by force, the result will be a definitive break. Right now nothing exists for her except helping your father. If she didn't do that, if she didn't dedicate all her time to it, she would feel that she hadn't done enough, and ultimately she would always feel guilty about your father's death."

At the word "death," Miral gave a start, and the tears that had been welling up in her eyes without her realizing it slowly began to fall. Before she could stop herself, her weeping became disconsolate. Hind let it go on for a few moments, then rose and went to her. She put her arms around Miral, and the two of them stayed that way a long time, until at last Miral stopped sobbing. Only with Hind could she let herself go to such an extent, and she was not ashamed of having dropped the mask of the self-assured young woman that she had felt obliged to wear in front of her father during the past few months. "I'm not saying it's easy," Hind added, holding Miral by the shoulders and looking her in the eyes. "But if we insist that Rania change her mind, there's not only the risk that she'll never go back to school; there's also a good chance that she'll consider us, and you in particular, enemies who want to prevent her from helping your father."

15

Toward the end of May, Miral, too, decided to sleep at home with her father and sister, but Jamal's condition worsened, and he was taken to a hospital. Despite his disease, he continued to give advice to his daughters and hold long conversations with them. He would try to recall as many episodes as possible from their childhood and the time when their mother was alive. He wanted to transmit his memory to them. He pressed Miral to continue her studies—he wanted her to become a university professor—and at the same time he insisted that she should apply herself to becoming less impulsive.

Jamal's serenity of mind in those days contrasted with the suffering in his limbs. The doctors said the only possibility of saving him was a bone marrow transplant. The two sisters, who were considered the most desirable donors, discussed the possibility with their father. But Jamal became worried and refused to undergo the operation. "At least let us get tested first, to see if we're compatible," Miral said.

"No no, really. It will be as God wills," he replied. He was smiling even as he gave that response, which was like a death warrant without possibility of appeal, but Miral could see that he was anxious. She didn't understand why such a reasonable man as her father would suddenly become so obstinate.

"Look, it's not even a very difficult operation, and it works. The doctor showed us its success rates. They're excellent," Jamal's daughters insisted.

"Yes, girls, I know; he showed them to me, too. But it's too late for that now. I want to spend my remaining time like this, with you near me, and not in some operating room."

Not at all convinced, Miral and Rania went to be tested the following day. A few days later, the two sisters went to see the doctor again. He smiled pleasantly and showed them into his office. Sitting behind his desk, he briefly scrutinized some papers; the girls watched his face darken. He addressed Rania first, telling her that she had a degree of compatibility with her father, and that in the event he should consent to the operation, the chances of success were remote. Then he cleared his throat and gently asked her to have a seat in the waiting room, because he wanted to have a word with her sister. He and Rania would discuss details later.

"But why does she have to leave?" Miral asked in surprise.

"Well, because I want to talk to you in private first. Then, if you think it appropriate, your sister can come back in."

Miral didn't understand; the doctor seemed positively embarrassed. "I have no secrets from my sister. Tell me what you have to tell me." Her heart was beating fast. She was afraid she had some sort of disease or some other grave condition. Rania took her hand and squeezed it hard.

"In that case, I'll come straight to the point. The tests show that your compatibility with your father is nonexistent."

"So I can't donate the bone marrow? But Rania's compatible, right? Therefore—"

"That's not the only issue here. The DNA examination shows that Jamal is not your biological father."

The blow made her lose consciousness. When she opened her eyes again, she saw Rania weeping and the doctor offering each of them a glass of water. The two sisters embraced in tears, unable to comprehend how such a thing was possible. Neither of them believed it, but all attempts to request another analysis were in vain. "Miral, this is a very precise test, and we did all the appropriate verifications. Believe me, there's no possibility of an error," the doctor answered, visibly mortified. "I'm sorry."

Rania hugged Miral as the girls left the doctor's office. "What should we do?" Miral asked her sister.

"I don't think we can tell Papa."

"But that would mean—"

"Yes, Miral, I know. It means he won't have the operation. But what do you think would happen if he found out that we know the truth?"

"It would break his heart," Miral said with a sigh.

"Right."

When they were near the exit, Miral asked Rania to leave her alone for a while and advised her to go home and try to rest.

"And what are you going to do?"

"I don't know—I need to think. Don't worry about me."

Many questions came crowding into the two sisters' minds. Who was Miral's real father? Did Jamal know? How could it have happened? And why hadn't anyone ever told them anything? Before they separated, they embraced again, promising to see each other later at home.

Miral started walking aimlessly through the streets. She wandered for hours without ever getting to the bottom of the revelation she had just received. She couldn't even weep, although she felt she needed to. Jamal must know; otherwise he wouldn't have been so adamantly opposed to her being tested. But how could she find the courage to ask him for explanations?

In the end, she decided to talk to the only person who could know the truth: Aunt Tamam.

The coffee cup fell to the floor and broke into a thousand pieces. Tamam couldn't believe that Miral had discovered the secret. So many years had passed that Tamam had stopped thinking about it. In her heart, she was truly convinced that Jamal was her niece's only father.

"Aunt Tamam, please, tell me the truth," Miral begged. I need to know."

There was no longer any reason for Tamam to keep the secret; Miral had found it out, and she had a right to know her mother's story. The whole story, uncensored.

And so Tamam told it from the beginning. She recounted the abuse she and her sister had suffered at the hands of their stepfather; Nadia's flight; her dissolute life, first in Jaffa and later in Tel Aviv; her time in prison with Aunt Fatima. And then Hilmi, whose sincere love Nadia hadn't trusted because the men before him had let her down. "But believe me, my girl, Jamal has been a real father to you. He knew everything, and still he loves you as though you were his own flesh and blood."

Miral wept; she couldn't believe it was true. She couldn't believe that the mother Jamal had portrayed had never existed, had been but a shred of what Nadia was. For the first time, Miral thought she might understand the origin of the torment she sometimes felt. The pain of living had been what killed her mother.

16

It was a June day, and Rania and Miral were going to the hospital. Along the way, they stopped in the spice souk and bought some of their father's favorite incense. They had decided to make every effort to be cheerful and smiling in his presence that day.

Jamal was lying awake in his room. When he saw his daughters come in, he pronounced that they were really grown up, and that they were both very beautiful. As he watched them moving through the room, the pain racking his weak body seemed to him, for a moment, like nothing but a distant echo. Miral lit the incense, defying the nurses' prohibition. The girls' father followed them with his eyes until the delicate perfume reached his nostrils and he pressed his lids together for an instant. Then, gathering all his strength, he said, smiling as he spoke, "Seeing you two come through that door warms my heart. You've brought joy into my life since the day you were born."

The girls lay down beside Jamal and put their arms around him. Miral could feel how cold his feet were. She tried to massage warmth into them, but it was useless; her father's circulation was shutting down.

. . .

That afternoon Jamal sank into a coma. It was as though he had waited for his daughters to come before he fell into an irreversible sleep. Rania telephoned Miral, who had in the meantime returned home. Sitting in the backseat of a taxi, Miral saw her father slipping away, his eyes closed, his breathing more and more labored, his hands colder and colder. When she got to the hospital, she found Rania weeping desperately in the arms of their aunt. Miral wanted to cry, too, but she held herself back. She knew that she couldn't collapse in front of her sister. However, she was very much afraid of being left alone, and the desire to give her feelings some release got the better of her. She ran to the bathroom, locked the door, and surrendered to a long, liberating fit of weeping, which went on until a nurse came to fetch her.

In a voice breaking a little with emotion, the nurse whispered that the moment had come for Miral to go to her father and say good-bye for the last time. Miral plucked up her courage, raised herself from the hospital's aqua green tiles, got to her feet, and glanced at the mirror; it required all her strength. But how much strength would she need from now on, she wondered, to survive her father's absence?

She squeezed Jamal's hand and fought back her tears. "We'll make it, Papa, don't worry," she assured him. "You've given us a lot. You'll see. We'll be fine. I'll take care of Rania, and she'll take care of me." About an hour later, Jamal breathed his last.

Miral felt profound grief. That night she and her sister and her aunt all slept nestled together in Jamal's bed; they wanted to preserve his smell and his love in their memories. Only when they awakened the next morning did they realize that he wasn't there anymore.

That same morning, Hind read in the daily *Al-Quds* the news of Jamal's death. Not long afterward, Miral arrived. They embraced for a long time, and then the girl begged Hind to help her persuade Rania not to go to Haifa. With all the delicacy at her command, Hind replied, "Miral, I understand your grief, but there's nothing unusual in your sister's behavior. She's crying out for help. It's understandable. It's human. You're very strong, Miral; you never let your feelings show. That may help you defend yourself, but at the same time it will condemn you to a lifetime of solitude. You mustn't be too hard on yourself."

Before the funeral, the girls paid their last respects to Jamal. Rania stayed back, but Miral approached the coffin and kissed his cold forehead and his hollow cheeks. Miral pressed her father's hand, which in life had always been warm and soft, and felt its cold stiffness. His skin was pale, its color almost surreal, but his features were placid and relaxed; he had finally left earthly suffering behind.

When their cousins lifted the coffin, the girls uttered cries of grief. All the tension accumulated during those last, tragic hours seemed to be channeled into their lamentation.

Almost a thousand people attended Jamal's funeral. Only then did Miral realize how beloved her father was. After the services were over, a man came up to her and handed her a white envelope. "This is money your father loaned me," the stranger said. "He was a good and honest man. I didn't repay him in time, but I felt it my duty to give what I owed him to his daughters. If there's anything I can do for you, you need only ask." The envelope contained twelve hundred dollars.

Through this incident and other, similar stories, Miral discovered that her father had silently assisted almost everybody in his neighborhood. His generosity was like his character, humble and discreet.

In the days immediately following her father's death, Miral often lingered for a while in his favorite places, sitting on the stone bench that offered a view of the Dome of the Rock or on the wooden bench under the pomegranate tree in front of their house, where Jamal would read the Koran or watch the neighborhood kids playing soccer.

Now a neighbor was coming every day to water the plants. The jasmine had perfumed summer nights with its intense fragrance, and in the autumn the pomegranate provided the fruit with which Jamal had prepared the delicious tarts he distributed to the neighborhood children. Miral recalled a gentle afternoon when her father had told her that the jasmine was like her: beautiful, fragrant, and dignified, capable of adapting to circumstances and of overcoming the difficulties of life by climbing over everything to find new light. The pomegranate, on the other hand, was like her sister, Rania: more practical, more solidly rooted in the earth, repaying the care of tending it with its sweet fruit. Now they were two grown plants, Miral thought, frozen in a sea of cement.

It took Miral a long time before she could gather the courage to visit her father's grave. He lay in the Muslim cemetery on the slope of the Mount of Olives, which overlooked the Old City. The Jewish cemetery, with its white tombs reflecting the sunlight, was located a little farther down the slope. Paradoxically, Miral thought, Jews and Arabs, who in life had kept themselves as far away from each other as possible, in death found themselves just a few meters apart, separated only by a low wall.

Although her father's death had opened a void in her soul that nothing could fill, Rania managed to find a balance in Haifa that she had never been able to reach in her school. Soon after going back there to live, she became engaged to a neighbor. She was very young, but she felt a desperate need to build the family that she had lost early.

By contrast, Miral threw herself headlong into politics again. During those terrible days after the death of their father, the two sisters saw their lives inevitably taking two distinct paths, even though the affection that had always united them would never waver.

For Miral, her final high school examinations in May had meant the end not only of the scholastic cycle but also of her life at Dar El-Tifel. And although she continued to live on campus, leaving was only a matter of time. She would have to make a quick decision regarding her future, but she couldn't think of anything but Hani. Rania's hastily arranged wedding plans had caught her off guard. Miral had hoped that her sister would complete her studies before taking such an important step. They even had a sharp argument on the subject, but then Miral remembered Hind's words, her repeated admonitions to the effect that one could not force a person to do something she did not wish to do. Rania had suffered so much, first because of her mother's death and then because of her father's; surely she could not be blamed if her sole desire was to start a family of her own.

In the meantime, Hind was hoping Miral would be one of the

recipients of a scholarship for study in Europe. Many of her class-mates would go to the university in Ramallah, while others were set to begin working. For the first time in her life, Miral wallowed in uncertainty; finally nothing stood in the way of her deciding for herself what path she should take. She went out into the Old City to do some shopping in preparation for going to Haifa to visit Rania in her new home.

17

Miral bought a copy of the daily *Al-Quds* and sat in a café near the Damascus Gate. Over the past few years, the number of Orthodox Jews walking through the covered lanes of the souk had steadily grown. Many houses in the Old City had been bought or seized from their Arab owners and quickly decorated with Israeli flags and seven-branched candelabra. The counterpart of the bloody war in the Occupied Territories was, in Jerusalem, a submerged struggle for the possession of the Old City, where every square meter and every stone took on a symbolic value.

After scanning the front-page news she turned to the inside pages, where she lingered over a report about collaborators killed by al-Fatah militants in Gaza and a car bomb that had caused the death of a militant from the Popular Front for the Liberation of Palestine in Lebanon the previous day. The victim was described as having been only eighteen, and Miral speculated that there must have been some error. Then she thought about Hani and Khaldun, fearing for their safety. The victim was with one of the organization's leaders, for whom he had worked as a bodyguard until a few weeks before, and who was said to be the attack's real target. The article did not, however, exclude the hypothesis that the perpetrators had in fact targeted the young militant, the author of a book—published in Lebanon as well as some European countries, among them Germany and France—in which he recounted his adolescence first in the Kalandia camp and then in the Sabra and Shatila camps in southern Beirut. His spare, forceful prose had led some literary critics to acclaim the young Palestinian writer as a new Ghassan Kanafani. Unfortunately this comparison must not have escaped the youth's murderers. The writer was Khaldun. And he suffered the same brutal fate as the author of *Men in the Sun* and *Return to Haifa*, who met a premature end when, on July 8, 1972, a bomb placed in his car by the Mossad in Beirut killed both him and his sixteen-year-old niece.

A silent scream of intense pain paralyzed her body. She couldn't think, she couldn't move. She felt the despair of being aware and at the same time powerless. She had thought Khaldun was safe because he was far away, but no one is safe; your destiny follows wherever you go.

Drops of tears were blurring the print on the newspaper in front of her. And at that moment, the warmth of Jerusalem's sun went cold.

The next day, Miral went to the same coffee shop hoping that Jasmine would pass by and give her news of Hani. The café had become a regular meeting place for Miral and her girlfriends. The proprietor was a middle-aged man, bald and robust, who hummed songs as he prepared cold drinks for his young customers. He would always welcome Miral with a broad, affectionate smile and offer her the best table.

It had been too long since she'd received any news of Hani, and Miral had grown increasingly worried. His friends in the neighborhood replied to her questions with vague answers, and his former comrades in the Popular Front were reluctant to give out any information about him whatsoever. Nobody knew where he might be; perhaps he had left the country. Miral knew that if he was still in Jerusalem, he was most probably living as a fugitive. She imagined hopefully that after the signing of the peace accords there would be a general amnesty and that Hani would benefit from it, but how much longer would it be before that happened? It could take years.

Miral decided to leave a message with Hani's mother. In her note, Miral planned to tell Hani about the discovery of her real father, Hilmi, whom she had finally been able to trace. He lived in Europe, where he was a university professor of literature. He'd sent Miral a letter that touched her deeply, a letter in which he told her that they must meet and talk about everything. He wrote of his love for her mother, Nadia, and of his respect for Jamal, and invited Miral to come visit him, declaring that she could count on him at any time and in any circumstance. Enclosed with the letter was an airline ticket to Berlin. Miral had thought long about meeting him there, but then decided she wasn't ready.

As she sat there, absorbed in her thoughts, a young man wearing a pair of black sunglasses approached and asked if her name was Miral. Surprised, she answered that it was. The stranger looked about him nervously for several seconds, then reached into his pocket, drew out an envelope, and placed it on Miral's table, saying, "This is for you. It's from a friend." He turned around and swiftly melted into the crowd in the market, vanishing as though he had never existed. Miral didn't even have time to thank him. She pulled the envelope closer and saw that it bore the words "For Miral."

Tears welled up in her eyes, and she felt a searing heat similar to what she experienced when she ran from the soldiers during demonstrations. She opened the envelope, which contained a note from Hani and, to confirm its authenticity, a photograph of him, sitting on a patch of green grass framed by yellow flowers. Hani had an unkempt beard, and he was wearing a red and white kaffiyeh around his neck. In the note, he asked Miral to meet him that afternoon at four o'clock inside the Russian Orthodox Church of Maria Magdalene, on the Mount of Olives. Miral's heart beat wildly; she leapt to her feet and left the café without saying goodbye to the owner. She even forgot to pay her check.

Despite the difficulties she met along the way, Miral reached the appointed place with some time to spare. Her pace had been slowed by the many Orthodox pilgrims who were filling the streets and obstructing all the exit points in the Old City. Crossing the Via Dolorosa had been a particularly complicated undertaking because of all the faithful who were making their way toward what Christians consider the most sacred of stones, the sepulchre. Miral felt frustrated and anxious because she couldn't run, but once she arrived at her destination, she found a deep fascination in observing how religious faith continued to draw people into the city from all over the world. It was hard not to let yourself surrender to the meditative atmosphere that pervaded the place, to its antique severity. At the entrance to the imposing basilica, the sunlight reflected by the gilded onion domes prevented Miral from seeing the interior. Once inside she was enveloped in the cold mystery conjured up by the darkness and the powerful smell of incense, which managed to cover even the scent of Middle Eastern spices. Guided by the uncertain light of the candles in the chapels, she found herself overwhelmed by a sense of genuine mysticism.

As she watched the pilgrims moving past her in silent file, Miral failed to notice Hani, who stood in a dark alcove a few paces away, quietly gazing at her. When she saw him, she threw her arms around his neck and held on while emotion surged through her and tears filled her eyes. Their faces were close together; she could feel his breath and read all the nuances of his expressions. Hani stroked her face and hair. "God, how I've missed you," he said.

After a long moment, they released each other, and only then did Miral see that he'd lost a great deal of weight since their last meeting. He hadn't shaved for days, and his beard gave him an appearance both rugged and tragic.

"I can't believe you're here in front of me!" Miral exclaimed. "I thought you had left the country, and I'd given up all hope of seeing you."

"I'm a fright—please don't look at me," Hani said hoarsely, covering his face with his hands.

"Don't be ridiculous," Miral replied. "I haven't done anything but think about you, day and night. I love you, Hani. I don't care if you're a little damaged. As a matter of fact, I think you've acquired a mysterious charm." Her eyes betrayed both her ardor and the grief of the past weeks.

He hugged her and said, "My darling, I love you, too."

"Tell me how you're getting along and what you're planning to do now," Miral said.

"Life as a fugitive isn't so bad," Hani replied in a reassuring tone. "I change houses every day and sleep in different places, because I've got many friends in the refugee camps and in our villages. I try to avoid the city as much as possible. People seem more paranoid and suspicious in metropolitan areas, and it's more likely that I'll be captured in Jerusalem than anywhere else. But I wanted to see you—I heard about your father. I'm so sorry, Miral. The people who harbor me are poor, and I share the little food they have. But by now, I'm used to everything, and nothing frightens me anymore. You sée, Miral, there's no turning back. We have such a thirst to live in freedom in our own state that we can bear anything, any sacrifice." Hani took her hand. "But let's talk about you, Miral, *habibti*. How did you do on your final exams? Are you ready for what comes next? I hope you get a very high grade so you can be admitted to a good university—but I have no doubt you'll make me proud of you."

"I think my exams went very well, Hani. I studied so much. Still, all my friends have already decided what they're going to do, and I don't know yet. I've applied for a scholarship to study abroad, but I'm not sure I really want to go. I'd like to study political science."

Hani kissed her hand and replied, "You just have to be tough, Miral. I know you've got it in you. Besides, it seems to me that you've already made up your mind. You must get a university degree, and I think political science is a very fitting choice for you. And whether you study here or abroad, I'll come and find you."

They talked at length, forgetful of the time and the dampness of the church. Hani had grown nervous. "It's better that nobody sees us together," he said. "Unfortunately, the investigations that led to a hundred arrests several months ago are still open."

Miral kept holding his hand tightly in hers.

Hani gazed at her tenderly. "Now that you've graduated, where are you living?"

"I'm still living on campus—Mama Hind thinks that's best for me right now. The school is basically my home. Among other things, I often go to the American Colony Hotel to follow the course of the negotiations."

"What are the chances that you'll get the scholarship?" he asked.

"Oh God, five of us have applied, and I'm not the best student in the group," she said, lowering her eyes. "We'll see."

Hani smiled for a moment, but then his face took on a look of great passion. "I think we're close to peace this time, Miral. Everyone's making a serious effort—us, the Israelis, and the Americans, too. For the first time, they believe it's possible."

"What will happen to the PFLP? What reaction can we expect from them?" she asked, surprised by his optimism.

"They're probably splitting up as we speak, and this time the decision is going to be between real, concrete choices and the unattainable goals of blind ideology. The people have already made their choice—now the parties can adapt, or they can disappear." Hani's voice deepened. "Many people disagree with me. They've accused me of being a collaborator, but when peace comes, you'll see. None of that will matter anymore. They're meeting every day, both here and in Oslo, talking about partition. I really believe this time it can work."

"How can you say that?"

"Miral, this road is too bloody, it has no exit. We'll accept twenty-two percent of the land—it's more than we have now. We can't go on fighting forever."

"Twenty-two percent? Why can't it be one country for everybody, where we all have the same rights? Real democracy like in New York City?"

Hani looked at her lovingly.

"It is too soon for that. We should have two states—an Israeli state and a Palestinian one. The truth is that the Arab regimes and the United Nations are not our real allies. It's the Israelis themselves. Miral, we have to remember that in 1982, when Israel invaded Lebanon, four hundred thousand Israelis went in the streets and protested and that led to the fall of the right-wing government and the withdrawal from Lebanon. They are the ones we need to reach. They're not going anywhere and neither are we. One state, two states—I don't care. I want to live. I want a future for our children."

Miral stopped and stared at him with frightened eyes. "Have they threatened you? What exactly have you been accused of?"

"Don't worry. The problem exists because, unfortunately, several comrades have been sold to the Shin Bet recently, but the accusations against me are only rumors. I still have many friends in the movement, many people who think highly of me and will never abandon me. Naturally, my positions concerning the peace accords make everyone a bit nervous."

At that point, the tone of Hani's voice left no room for discussion; the subject was closed. By now they were in the midst of the religious procession that was taking place on the Via Dolorosa. The air was fresher there, permeated with the smells of pine and olive trees, free from tear gas. Miral couldn't help crying as all the tension and drama of the past weeks, as well as her fear of abandonment and solitude, overflowed into a tender kiss.

Hani interpreted her weeping as tears of relief, and he held her close without speaking.

"*Habibti*, on Friday there's going to be a big peace demonstration around the walls of Jerusalem, and we're all going to be there this time: Arabs, Israeli pacifists, and supporters of the peace accords from Europe, America, and the rest of the world. It's the first time the Israeli government has authorized this type of demonstration. I'd like you to participate if you can."

"Will you be there, too?" she asked hopefully.

"It may be risky for me, but I'll try my best to come, I promise. Now, however, I have to go. I've got to get back to the camp before the curfew begins."

"Wait here a second," Miral said. She turned onto a side street and returned after a few minutes with two sandwiches—falafel and kebab—and a container of fruit juice. As she handed him the food, she said, "Eat them both—you're too skinny. Do you need money?"

"No, I don't need money, I just needed to see you. I'll have you contacted again by the same boy who delivered my note. If you want to reach me for any reason at all, leave a message with my mother, and she'll pass it on to me."

They said good-bye a few minutes later. It was the last time she would see him.

18

That evening, Miral decided to ask Hind for permission to attend a peace rally. As she knocked on Hind's door, Miral worried about what she would do should Hind's response be negative.

Hind watched as Miral entered, and felt proud of the way she had grown up while in her school. Hind had noticed a great change in Miral since her return from Haifa. The dissidence and rage she used to read in Miral's eyes had been transformed into melancholy and introspection. What Miral told her only confirmed her impression that the girl had reached a new level of maturity.

"I'd like to ask your permission to leave the campus next Friday. There's going to be an important march for peace, the first ever organized by Arabs and Israeli Jews together. I really want to go, but if you tell me not to, I won't."

Hind waited to smile until Miral had finished. "Of course you can go. You've graduated from school and passed your eighteenth birthday besides. I'm no longer making decisions for you. And to tell you the truth, I think the demonstration is a good idea this time; however, I would ask you to be careful. Have you thought about taking someone else along? I'm sure Aziza would like to go."

Their eyes met, and they stood there looking at each other, smiling, for several seconds. Miral said only, "Thank you," and left the office. Hind trusted her. Something really had changed.

On the following Friday, as on every other day, Christian pilgrims, Muslim faithful, and Jews from Israel and elsewhere reached the Damascus Gate. Normally, after passing through it and walking half the length of Via Dolorosa, they would come to an intersection; there the Christians would continue along Via Dolorosa, while the Arabs and Jews would take El Wad Street, which would bring them to their holy places. But that day, a crowd gathered right on the steps descending to the gate. It wasn't a gathering so much as an enormous human cordon that surrounded the gleaming white walls of the Old City, holding hands for peace.

All the demonstrators were young, euphoric, filled with hope, united by dreams of living in freedom and peace. Having finally compelled the politicians to listen to them, they felt invincible. The authorities were surprised at the number of demonstrators, enough to bring the city to a halt with their songs and high spirits.

They were finally speaking the same language; they were different people with a common objective, looking in the same direction for the first time. And there was nothing sweeter than the language of peace, without tear gas and Molotov cocktails. This time, the antiriot troops, bewildered and embarrassed when the young people gave them olive branches, stood by and watched with their helmets in their hands. Miral and Aziza joined the huge circle of people. From the windows of the houses, men and women were hanging flags: the multicolored flag of peace or the flags of Palestine and Israel, side by side. Others were applauding the demonstrators as they passed. The city was invaded and conquered by a feeling of brotherly love.

That demonstration sent an important signal: humanity had prevailed. It was a clear and evident message directed at both Palestinian and Israeli politicians. The extraordinary level of participation in the event confirmed the polls, according to which crushing majorities of both peoples were in favor of peace. And later that week, Prime Minister Rabin delivered a speech to the Israeli legislature in which he advocated increased openness to dialogue. He said that progress in the peace negotiations must continue as if there were no violence, and that efforts to combat violence and disorder must continue as if there were no negotiations. Now it was no longer the generals and colonels who were dictating the political agenda but the will of the people, which was shouting at the top of its voice: "Enough violence! More diplomacy!"

Miral was in the midst of that crowd, which was peacefully laying siege to the ramparts of the city, when she heard a female voice call her name. "Miral, Miral! Here I am!"

"Lisa! My God, you're here, too?" She said, surprised to see her.

"I wouldn't miss this for the world."

The girls embraced like old friends. Suddenly Miral felt self-conscious. It was so different to encounter Lisa in Jerusalem, in the city where there was such a clear-cut separation between Israelis and Palestinians. "Who did you come with?" Miral asked.

"Some socialist friends from Haifa. Five buses of us," Lisa said. "You want to join our group? You can bring your friend."

Miral cast an uncomfortable glance in Aziza's direction and

said in a low voice, "Oh, no. Maybe we'll see each other tomorrow. I'll call you." She gave Lisa a kiss on the cheek and hurried off. Lisa tried to stop her, but Miral was already too far away.

With Aziza at her side, Miral made a complete tour of the demonstration, looking for Hani the whole time. She was surprised to see some of his ex-comrades from the PFLP. Miral and Aziza stayed until the end of the march. It was the most joyous and impressive rally in many years. The echoes of the songs and slogans invoking peace carried all the way to the Israeli parliament building, the Knesset. The legislature suspended its session, and an extraordinary meeting of the government was convened to listen to the popular will.

Toward evening Aziza suggested that they return to school. She and Miral were still full of enthusiasm, skipping as they walked through the streets and sometimes even breaking into a run. Even though she hadn't seen Hani, Miral was happy.

He probably stayed away out of caution, she thought. The police had blocked off the city.

"Hani was right not to come," Aziza said, trying to reassure her. "Don't worry about him. He must not have wanted to get arrested right at the most delicate moment of our lives." The two friends hurried back to school. They hadn't realized it was already dinnertime. With an automatic gesture, Aziza picked up a flyer from the street, a communiqué issued by the Popular Front for the Liberation of Palestine. Seeing that Hani's name was written on it in thick letters, Aziza read the first line, and suddenly her expression changed. She awkwardly slipped the flyer into her pocket.

"Why did you hide that piece of paper like that? What does it say?" Miral asked.

"Nothing. Let's go, Miral. It's late, and Mama Hind will be worried." Aziza began to run.

Miral caught up with her. "Please let me see it," Miral said. "What's the matter?"

"I'll give it to you after we get back to school," Aziza said.

"Please no. I want to see it now."

Aziza remained silent for a while and then suggested they go to a café.

She didn't want to give her friend the flyer, but she knew she had to. "I'm sorry, Miral. This is going to hurt you a lot," Aziza said, handing her the folded piece of paper.

Miral read the few lines in silence.

> *Several collaborators were executed yesterday morning by order of the PFLP, among them Hani Bishara, the ex-secretary of Jerusalem. According to overwhelming evidence and eyewitness testimony, he was an informant for the Israeli secret service inside our party and betrayed the cell that operated in Jerusalem under his command.*
>
> *In the struggle to attain the liberation of our land, there is no room for compromise or for traitors. We must be united as a people, particularly in our most difficult decisions. . . .*

Miral made a fist with her right hand and pressed it to her mouth. She tried desperately to hold herself back, to keep from screaming. She couldn't speak; she couldn't move. The grief she felt added itself to that of the many tragedies her family and her people had suffered for years, and it was so intense that she could hardly breathe.

Night fell all at once; the sun, as it does in Middle Eastern countries, glowed with an intense red and then suddenly disappeared below the horizon. Overcome by nausea, Miral felt that all was lost; she crumpled up the flyer and dropped it on the ground. Everything had been useless. She walked along in shock amid the jubilant throng. Her struggle had no more meaning; her peace was lost. Aziza caught up with her at a corner and embraced her. Miral tried and failed to keep from vomiting. "My God, what are we doing to ourselves?" Miral whispered.

Darkness surrounded the walls of the Old City. Miral could not get over how suspicion could lead to indiscriminate murder, how hatred overwhelms and destroys everything, even the most righteous causes. Her barely newborn hope was swept away as soon as it appeared.

⌐

19

That summer night in August Miral waited for the lights to go out, and then slowly opened the door of her room. The corridor was empty, its darkness barely relieved by the dim moonlight. She tiptoed down the stairs swiftly, careful not to trip over any of the flowerpots, and gently half-closed the door behind her. Walking through the garden, she inhaled the evening dampness. She quickly ran to the lowest point of the wall that bordered the parking lot of the American Colony Hotel. In the garden, absolute silence reigned, broken only by the rustle of leaves and her own heartbeat. She looked around one last time, to make sure no one had seen her, and jumped over the wall.

Emotion and haste had taken her breath away, and now she could feel her legs trembling. She was violating the rules of the school and feared more than anything that she would be discovered by Hind herself, who had welcomed her to stay and live at the school after her graduation. But she had not been able to resist. She had impatiently paced up and down her room the entire day, not speaking to her friends and not going down into the schoolyard. That evening she hadn't even touched her food, so great was her excitement about what was happening nearby at the American Colony Hotel, adjacent to the school.

She crossed the parking lot and found herself in front of the entrance. Making believe they didn't exist, she walked past a group of soldiers who were chatting beside the sliding door. One of them, a man with a thick mustache, noticed her and asked her who she was. After a moment of surprise, her temples pounding, Miral replied in English, saying the first thing that came into her head: "I'm an interpreter."

The soldier took a puff on his cigarette, threw it on the ground, and crushed it out with the heel of his boot. He came close to Miral and stared into her eyes for a long time. "You don't have a pass, and I don't remember seeing you here before."

Miral held her ground and did not turn away from the soldier.

At that moment, a riot came to her mind in vivid detail: the bitter odor of tear gas, the crush of the crowd, her sister's voice getting farther and farther away, the dull thud of gas canisters, and then bullets; a green stain in the middle of the smoke, a soldier running toward it, rifle in hand, the visor of his helmet raised, his mustache lending him a threatening aspect as Miral covered her face with her hands.

"Come on through, miss, but next time don't forget your pass."

Miral snapped back from her memory. She smiled and made her way into the hotel lobby, pretending to know perfectly well where she was going.

She found herself at the white marble counter of the reception desk, where she recognized her friend Sara. According to Sara, rumor had it that an accord between the Israeli delegation and the representatives of the Palestine Liberation Organization was imminent. They were discussing the birth of the Palestinian state.

Miral felt her heart beating faster; to her ears nothing sounded better than the word "accord." It was a word abstract enough to leave ample space for the workings of the imagination, and it contained all the hopes she had nourished over the years. Too excited to talk calmly, Miral took a few steps in the direction of a small sofa on the opposite side of the lobby, facing the reception desk.

"Could you bring me a cup of coffee, please?" A voice abruptly yanked Miral out of her daydreams of peace. She turned and saw a middle-aged woman, dressed in Western clothes and looking at her with a questioning expression on her face.

"I'm sorry, but I don't work here."

"Oh, I beg your pardon. I saw you talking to the girl at the reception desk, and I drew the wrong conclusion. You're so young. . . . Are you a journalist, too?" The woman smiled at Miral, revealing two large, parallel rows of exceedingly white teeth.

Miral realized that the woman's mouth, which was really big, reminded her of some singer, but she couldn't think of her name.

"Not really," Miral replied, a little embarrassed. "I'd like to be."

"Well, then, I could tell you a few things—after we order two coffees. It gets boring, talking only to colleagues all the time. Besides, they're mostly men, and therefore all the more boring." With this declaration, she burst into loud laughter.

"I'll be glad to listen. I'm Miral," she said, extending her hand.

"And I'm Samar Hilal. I write for *Al-Quds*."

The woman made a sign to a waiter who was passing through the lobby carrying a tray laden with drinks. With a gesture, the waiter acknowledged her request and continued on his way. "That tray's on its way to room sixteen. The delegations have been holed up in there for hours, debating," Samar informed Miral.

Miral's new acquaintance told her that she had been a journal-

ist for almost thirty years, and that she'd worked for the same newspaper for the last twenty. "This will be my fifth coffee today, but I
have a feeling that we're going to have to stay awake all night long. It
will be several more hours before they deign to tell us anything, but
this time I think it will be worth the trouble."

Miral liked her right away, and the feeling was mutual; Samar
wasn't in the habit of giving away secrets to strangers. She had
penetrating eyes, a thin face, and slender hands with tapering fingers that she waved about as she spoke. Miral admired Samar's
style. She had on a pair of light-colored linen trousers and a blue
blouse, and around her neck she wore a beautiful necklace of silver
filigree, one of those worked by the knowing hands of women from
the nomad tribes of the Yemeni desert. It was difficult to pinpoint
Samar's age, but considering her long experience, Miral thought
that she must be at least fifty.

"By now we've become so accustomed to death," Samar continued after a long swallow of coffee, "that sometimes it seems as if
it's become just another ordinary, daily occurrence."

Samar took a long sip of coffee and paused for a moment, gazing at an indefinable spot behind Miral. Then, as if waking up, she
blinked rapidly a few times and gazed again at the girl beside her,
who couldn't have been more than twenty. She must have a great
deal of nerve to dare come anywhere near the American Colony on
an evening like this.

"Imagine," Samar continued, "when the war in Lebanon started
I was working in our Damascus office. A colleague from the *Herald
Tribune* and I hired a taxi to take us to Beirut. During the trip we
noticed that the whole flow of vehicles was in the opposite direction. We saw burned cars and bodies lying alongside the road, and
then I said to my friend, 'Look what we do for our job. When every-

one else is running away, we journalists head for the scene of the disaster, just like soldiers.' At a certain point, our Syrian driver refused to go any farther. He was terrified and wouldn't accept the additional money we offered him. Eventually, he unloaded us in Sidon and headed back to Damascus." Samar saw Miral turn her head away for a moment. "Excuse me, I'm boring you," Samar added. "Once I get started, it's hard to stop me."

"No no, you're not boring me at all. On the contrary—but I just saw a waiter come back and whisper something to my girlfriend at the desk. I'm sorry—I was hoping there might be some news."

"I believe it's still too early for that," Samar said with a smile. "You'll see. When there's news, we won't be able to avoid hearing it." She signaled to the waiter again and asked him to bring her another coffee.

Miral stared at her new friend's broad smile, wondering how her teeth could remain so white with all the coffee she drank, but then berated herself for thinking of such a thing on such a night.

"Please go on," Miral said.

"As I was saying, we had to stop in Sidon. We could hear mortar fire quite distinctly, and Israeli planes were flying above our heads. Then and only then did I realize that I was in the middle of a battle. I was a frontline journalist, as they say. But it's one thing to read about that in textbooks and quite another to wind up there for real. So we both panicked, until I saw the flag of Qatar flying from the balcony of a consulate building and ran toward it with my press card and my life in my hand. Through a window, I caught a glimpse of a man wearing a long white galabia with a kaffiyeh on his head. I waved and screamed at him, 'Journalists! We're journalists! Let us in!' The people from the consulate opened the door and we took refuge inside. At one moment, I could see the building across from us, where there was a Lebanese antiaircraft position. Then it was gone."

Samar paused, gazing for a moment at the black liquid in the bottom of her cup, and then resumed. "After about two hours, things calmed down. The Qataris in the consulate loaned us a car, a little red Fiat, and that's how we got to Beirut. People there were sitting in the cafés along the seafront, drinking coffee and aperitifs. They would point out the airplanes flying overhead and say, 'That one's going to bomb Shatila.' 'That other one's heading for Tripoli, where the Syrian positions are.' And then they'd calmly sip their drinks, as if life and death lived together in perfect order as far as they were concerned. You could hear the muffled sound of explosions not many kilometers away, and you could see the smoke from the fires. I don't want to sound too melodramatic, but it seemed to me that I could smell the persistent odor of death. No one else seemed to be paying any attention to it. Well, all right. By now you can tell me that I'm indeed boring you."

"You're doing the opposite of boring me," Miral promptly replied. "I agree with you—the boundary between life and death seems different here from what it is elsewhere. Sometimes I go to one of the refugee camps and teach the children English. It's hard to tell there if life is a gift or a curse."

"I know what you mean. The refugee camps are absolutely the most unnatural places on the face of the earth, or at least on this part of its face. There, the concept of time doesn't exist, and there's not enough living space to do anything but wait. It's an impossibility, living on edge, outside of everything. They don't want a handout; they deserve the tools they need to recover normalcy, their dignity."

Samar picked up her giant purse. She rummaged through it

before finding a pack of American cigarettes. She held one out to Miral, who shook her head. Samar lifted the cigarette to her lips and lit it with a slow, almost weary gesture. As she inhaled deeply, a cold silence settled over the two of them. Both the woman and the girl were thinking that a new chapter in the life of their people was beginning, and each considered herself in some way both an extra and a protagonist in the drama that was unfolding. Their eyes met, and Miral felt that her activities so far—the classes in the refugee camp, the demonstrations, the flights from school and from the police—had not been undertaken in vain, or at least had not been completely useless.

At that moment, Samar's mind was assailed by a legion of doubts about what she had written previously and what she would write the following day. She wasn't fond of sentimental prose, and she was frightened of losing her objectivity.

Thus it was that Miral came to know—before her schoolmates, before the citizens of Jerusalem, even before the journalists had time to communicate the news to the whole world—that the negotiations had reached a positive conclusion, and that an accord between Palestinians and Israelis, at least in draft form, had been reached. The meetings between the leader of the Israeli delegation, Yossi Beilin, and Hind's cousin Faisal Husseini, the head of the Palestinian negotiating team, would ultimately lead to the famous handshake between Rabin and Arafat in the White House Rose Garden.

That night Miral's eyes were full of hope and clouded with emotion as she hurried through the garden of Dar El-Tifel, light-heartedly whistling the Beatles' song "Here Comes the Sun." Before slipping back inside the dormitory building, she turned toward the city, which seemed to be lying under a light mist. Al-Aqsa

Mosque, the Dome of the Rock, the Wailing Wall, the Church of the Holy Sepulchre—they were all enclosed within the same walls, so near to one another and yet still so disparate.

Upon reaching her room, she opened the door without hesitating, confident that she had made it back undetected. Great was her surprise when she sensed in the darkness the presence of another person; greater still, when she discovered that the other person was Hind. Miral's astonishment only intensified when the strict headmistress, instead of scolding her, immediately asked her to sit down and tell her the news of the negotiations.

After giving Hind a detailed account, including her meeting with Samar—whom the headmistress admired as a journalist—Miral accompanied Hind back to her room.

When she returned to her own room, Miral stretched out on the bed without undressing and lay there staring at the ceiling. Unable to fall asleep, she tried to imagine how happy her mother would have been to learn the joyful news, which was running through the presses at that very moment and would soon spread throughout the country.

While the whole world joined Palestinians and Israelis in watching, on live television, the historical handshake between Arafat and Rabin, which put an end to decades of violence and distrust, Miral was discussing her future with Hind. The results of Miral's graduation exams had come in, and Miral had passed them all with excellent scores. Hind was beaming with pride over her performance and had summoned Miral to her office. As soon as she stepped inside, Hind embraced her, saying, "My dear daughter, congratulations!" Miral would never forget the elderly headmistress's parting words to her that night: "Today has been a great day for our people, a new beginning, but let us not delude ourselves; there's still a long way to go. I had lost any hope of living to see even this historical moment, but you, you're young, and you'll have the good fortune to witness the birth of a democratic Palestinian state. There will be a need for all of us but especially for you and other educated young people. I called you here to tell you that you've won the scholarship. You will go abroad to study, my dear, and the time has come for you to dig down deep and give it all you've got. I know you've been going through a difficult period, but of all the girls who applied for the grant, I thought you were the one who most deserved it. Go and study and come back. Make us all proud of you once again. I love you very much, you know—you're like a daughter to me. You'll study in one of the best universities in Europe. Believe me, Miral, sometimes you can serve your country much better from a distance."

Emotion overcame her and she started to cry: for the passing of her father, and for Hani's sudden, violent death. Hind was right, Miral thought: for a time she must get away from Jerusalem and from mourning. She would have liked to talk to Hind at length, to confess everything to her, to tell her the *whole* truth, that she had fallen in love with Hani, that she had taken part in all the demonstrations, including the violent ones, throwing stones and Molotov cocktails against Israeli tanks, that she had been a militant member of the PFLP. But Hind looked at her with eyes full of comprehension, and there was no need to talk further; Hind had understood everything from the first time Miral had opened up to her about her political involvement. Hind hugged her. No words could have said more than that.

20

Miral was scheduled to leave the following morning. She had already said good-bye to Rania and her aunt Tamam in Haifa and was now gathering everything as she prepared to leave her life in Jerusalem.

On her way back from Haifa, a trip she had made many times, she tried to memorize the places that were most dear to her: the Mount of Olives, which seemed to wear a coat made of eucalyptus, pine, and especially olive trees covering the entire hill right down to the foot of Jerusalem's ancient walls; and the golden dome, which emanated warmth to the entire city. Nor did she want to forget the strong odors of the market.

She would never be able to forget her bright, fierce city. She didn't know what was waiting for her in Europe, but she did know this was her only choice for a future. It would be easier than continuing to live in her own country, where every place reminded her of all that she had loved and lost. As she was packing her suitcase, assisted by Aziza, she placed in it all her music CDs, her photographs, and the few articles of clothing that constituted her whole wardrobe. Hind came to her room and presented her with an overcoat to help protect her from the cold European winter.

Aziza said, "If you have problems, if you can't make it, come back home. Don't be afraid of being judged. We're sisters."

Miral wanted to retain, fixed in her memory, the images of the white walls of Jerusalem, its city gates, Dar El-Tifel school. For forgetting all that—even if remembering should prove painful—would mean that one day, however far off, she would plunge back into remorse. She would not let time erode the voices and echoes of her past, and even the silences, the many leaden silences of her life. She wanted to remember everything.

The room, the window, and even the bed that had seen her grow up and mature; that pillow, on which she had laid her head, had absorbed her tears of grief over the deaths of her loved ones: Nadia, Jamal, Khaldun, Hani.

Tomorrow she would weep elsewhere, on a different pillow, far from everything, and perhaps she would laugh as well, for her life would change radically once she got far away from Jerusalem. Miral was afraid of losing her identity, even though she knew that remaining in Jerusalem would mean losing herself.

Before she fell asleep, an image came into her mind, as clear as a crisp photograph. She was on the stretch of level ground that led to the Kalandia refugee camp. A path of intense yellow flowers with red centers, nourished by rains, had grown up amid the rubble and the scrap metal. She hurried down that path, as though it would lead her to a happy future. But the road of flowers was a mirage, a dream: all that remained for the people in the refugee camps. When Miral opened her eyes, she realized that the dream was both an illusion and a prediction.

The dream was a representation, a symbol, of her name, which is Arabic for a beautiful yellow tulip, one of those that can be seen sometimes, when they manage to bloom, after an extremely rare rain in the Sinai or the Negev. Miral is the attachment of roots to the earth; let the walls of Jerusalem and all the holy places and museums and state buildings come tumbling down, and the flowers, which are the land's true children, continue to spring up. They would never disappear.

Jerusalem was still given over to celebrations on the day that Miral left. Convoys of cars flying Palestinian and Israeli flags were everywhere. It was the first time since the accord had been signed that people were celebrating in both the eastern and western parts of the city at the same time. Late that afternoon, Miral waited for her taxi outside the school, looking expressionless in the midst of her friends, who were all gathered around her. She had tried her best not to cry, but now, as she watched Hind hang the Palestinian flag from her balcony to join the celebration, Miral could not hold back her tears. Hind came down and embraced her. "Miral, continue to make me proud." Before Miral climbed into the cab, Hind paused and touched her arm. "My dear girl, you are leaving nothing behind. Everything you need is already inside of you. You will never forget who you are and where you come from. The things you've lived through here will help you to be successful anywhere, whatever you decide to do. Nothing is decided, Miral, but nothing happens by chance either. You're the master of your own fate."

While the taxi was driving off, Miral glanced back for one final look, in time to catch a blurred glimpse of Aziza and the other girls, running after the cab, and her old headmistress, standing by the gate, waving. Miral had no idea that it would be the last time she would ever see Hind.

"Where to?" The taxi driver's voice interrupted her thoughts.

"Ben Gurion Airport."

"Where are you traveling to, miss?"

"Europe," Miral replied, as she passed the Dome of the Rock, which was gleaming in the sunlight. On their way through the Orthodox Jewish neighborhood, she saw religious settlers holding weapons and protesting the imminent signing of the peace accords. Some of them were carrying banners with an image of Israeli prime minister Yitzhak Rabin and underneath it the words "Traitor, you have betrayed us." Her city, Jerusalem, was once again hovering between peace and war.